This modern fable, told as an adventure story, treats with humour and irony some of the harsher absurdities and realities of our time, the rule of tyrants, the power of the mad dressed up as military generals, political corruption and legalized violence.

When John-Paul, the young protagonist, sets off in pursuit of Klaus Krenk, an international arms dealer selling weapons on the basis of "no questions asked", he has to travel from New York to South America, from Africa to Asia, before the chase ends and he can confront his enemy.

States of Excitement has many of the qualities of great satirical novels, concerning itself with universal issues and extending the action across the whole world.

Of Charles Humana's earlier novels, critics have written:

"Something of D.H. Lawrence's skill in suggesting depths of feeling that are never expressed openly"

Times Literary Supplement

"To read his book is to have one's basic faith in humanity renewed" *Daily Telegraph*

"This novel should make a very definite place for its author in contemporary English fiction" *British Book News (R. Greacen)*

"A storyteller who never bores. . . He has the novelist's precious gift of being able to fix a reader with his eye"

Sunday Times

"One of the most delightful books I have ever read"

Evening Despatch

STATES OF
EXCITEMENT

Charles Humana

STATES OF EXCITEMENT

a novel

BREESE
BOOKS
LONDON

First published in Great Britain by
Breese Books (A division of Martin Breese International)
164 Kensington Park Road, London W11 2ER, England

© Charles Humana 1991

ISBN: 0 947 533 18 4

Typeset in 10½/12½pt Bembo by
Ann Buchan (Typesetters), Middlesex
Printed and bound in Great Britain by
Biddles Ltd, Guildford and King's Lynn

To
W H G 'Tim' Armytage

Greatness and generosity
unrecognized by himself

CHAPTER ONE

As the dead were being carried away on stretchers from the smoking hijacked aircraft, immigration officials directed the surviving passengers towards the terminal. Above the low, neglected building was the crudely erected name CUCUTA. It meant, realized John-Paul Bonuomo, that they had landed in Colombia; and this was confirmed by an address system which welcomed the rescued passengers to the country. And invited them to make use of the bar, where all foreign currencies would be accepted.

Not all of the arrivals, however, were allowed to enjoy the comforts of the bar, and a number of them were led to an outer part of the building resembling a military barracks. One of the first to be interrogated was the young man, John-Paul. He was pushed rather than led into a small office cooled by a weary fan on the ceiling and with an armed guard half asleep on a crude chair just inside the door. A surly immigration officer behind a trestle table contemplated him with hostility, as if the triumphant soldiers had brought in a prisoner of war.

"Passport," he demanded.

The Community of Mankind document was handed to him. Its unfamiliarity caused it to be scrutinized suspiciously, Cucuta obviously not the chosen point of entry for visiting diplomats.

"That's the world organization," said John-Paul, deciding that the man had not even heard of COM. "I enjoy diplomatic immunity."

The helpful information provoked a challenging stare.

"Who said? You're in Colombia now. What's in your briefcase?"

"I repeat — I'm covered by diplomatic immunity." The conversation was in Spanish, which was no problem for the polyglot John-Paul. "You need special authority to search and interrogate a representative of the Community of Mankind."

The response of the official was to stand up, walk round the table and punch the young man in the stomach. As John-Paul gasped, the sleepy soldier roused himself to point the rifle at him. The official returned to his seat, placed the briefcase on the table and unfastened the two locks. The first object he produced was a pistol. Its discovery brought a smile of pleasure to the scowling face.

"Shoot him if he breathes," he shouted at the guard. "The man's dangerous."

"Dangerous! Can't you read — I have diplomatic immunity!" protested John-Paul. "That weapon is for my own protection. Don't forget the aircraft's destination was Cuba. It's not my fault we landed in Colombia."

There had been three objects on the table, a bottle of red wine, almost empty, a pornographic magazine and an army field telephone. The immigration officer asked for a number.

"Colonel," he said, a moment later, "I've caught another of the hijackers." A pause. "How did I know? I suspected him as soon as I set eyes on him."

When the call ended, the immigration officer came round the table and slid his hands over the suspect's clothing, removing John-Paul's diary, wallet and bulky sunglasses.

"I expect my belongings to be returned," protested the young man, angry rather than frightened, aware that if these lunatics were to release him without his notes and the considerable sum of money in his wallet, it would be pointless to continue his mission. "I come under international law. Your government will have to answer for this."

"Shut up with your jokes," the officer said warningly. "This is Colombia."

A military truck and a staff car arrived noisily and dustily outside the open door. Hasty footsteps announced the approach of an officer in a uniform featuring much gold braid, his entrance bringing the sleepy guard to his feet.

"Yes," confirmed the colonel, the moment he saw the suspect. "He's one of them all right. You can't mistake the type. Well done, Martinez."

Two of the accompanying soldiers were ordered to march John-Paul to the truck. It was a long journey through the crumbling suburbs of the neighbouring town and ended in the courtyard of a fortress-like stone building. He decided, as it seemed the dominant structure in the whole area, that it served as the local police headquarters, the court house, the town hall, the prison and probably the fire station.

The grim interior of the building into which he was marched did not, however, intimidate John-Paul. This was simply an example, he concluded, of bureaucratic stupidity that would be corrected the moment he was given the chance to protest to a higher authority. But the opportunity did not come immediately. Once away from the public entrance hall, he was pushed by the escorting soldiers along a corridor of bare stone, the building becoming more menacing, until they arrived at a high iron gate. Here they were met by guards wearing a different uniform which John-Paul recognized as that of prison warders. He was handed over to them.

"Jump to it, you bastard," shouted one of them.

A thump in the back impelled him in the direction indicated, faces along a corridor of iron bars peering at the new arrival. There was a stench of prisoners' slops and a century's decay, and the unmistakable sound of a madman raging against imagined enemies. Only when he was thrust into semi-darkness and the ultimate door clashed behind him did John-Paul finally accept that not all the laws and treaties of the high institutions of the outside world could protect him from the idiocies of bullying local officials.

"Welcome, fellow prisoner," a voice called out. "Come in. Make yourself at home."

Incapable of responding immediately, the young man needed a few moments to become familiar with his surroundings. As the semi-darkness lessened, he saw that the cell was hardly more than a cubicle, that the concrete floor showed the wear of long prison sentences, that the stone walls were brown, as if painted with nicotine spittle, and that the small window was striped by three iron bars. To one side were two bunks, one above the other, and on the lower sat a white-haired, white-bearded shrunken individual.

"My name's Anselmo," said the ghostly prisoner. "It's nice to have some company. You're welcome to stay as long as you like."

The man did not speak jokingly.

And John-Paul did not feel like joking in return. As the Pan-Caribbean airliner had lifted above New York a few hours earlier, there had been a sense of chains dropping from his limbs, fears from his mind and doubts from his purpose; yet now, so soon after departure, here he was behind iron bars. Even more bewildering, it was not the country of his intended destination, his COM passport had failed to protect him at its first test, and in fact he was one of the victims rather than one of the hijackers.

Ignoring the company of the white-haired individual, John-Paul marched the three steps to the iron door and shook the bars. As thousands before him had done. But a prison was a prison and neither indignation at the injustice nor the urgency of his mission could change the situation. Across the corridor, behind identical bars, a negro prisoner stared back at him, at the welcome sight of a new face, but the man was invisible because John-Paul, having accepted that there was to be no easy escape, had returned to the events of the last few weeks. And which had concluded with the sober resolution to murder Klaus Krenk.

By nature, the young man was a casual and tolerant individual, unlikely to be moved to violence by the usual conflicts and irritations of life; but Grace's decision to become the personal secretary to Klaus Krenk, a notorious international arms dealer, had affected him so deeply that an emotion close to a primitive need for survival had overwhelmed him. Throughout history, young men had chosen to kill for their country, for their religion, for numerous higher causes; what cause could be higher than being similarly motivated for the sake of saving the woman he loved?

Grace was a young woman of the same gentle disposition as his own, and when his fiancée had happily and innocently announced that Krenk's offer was an opportunity 'too good to miss', he had instantly recognised a crisis. For her, and for her father, who had arranged the introduction, Krenk was a man of international distinction, deserving his title of merchant statesman, but for John-Paul he was simply an arms dealer, a merchant of death. And, if press comments and social gossip were to be believed, a man with a reputation as a philanderer so colourful that even the most trusting of partners and lovers would have been alarmed.

Briefly unaware of the prison surroundings, John-Paul continued to ignore the persistent Anselmo trying to force him into conversation and recalled how he had met Grace. It had been at a Greek diplomatic function to which his mother, as deputy-director of the Community of Mankind, had been invited and at which, in place of a husband who had divorced her and then disappeared, he had acted as her escort. And had expected, on that particular evening, the usual obligations of boring formalities, politeness and stiff smiles.

But the expected, as ever, had led to the unexpected. In the great salon, John-Paul had stood with a small group sipping cocktails when a deep-voiced, middle-aged Greek, deciding he had a captive audience, began to address them on subjects inappropriate to the occasion. The dogmatic monologue went on from contentious politics to the world's indebtedness to Ancient Greece, then to the virtues of old-fashioned family life, with the father the undisputed authority, and finally on to religion. At this point, when even the circle of polite and patient listeners were beginning to shuffle restlessly, the Greek suffered what seemed to be an unfamiliar experience. He was interrupted. And not only that; the source of the interruption appeared to add to his surprise.

"There are a few things I don't agree with, father," said the only young woman in the group, her voice contrastingly pleasant and who, again contrastingly, was shy and modest. "First, what you said about the differences between New York and Athens isn't really true because . . ." And, growing in confidence, she had proceeded to put forward some very sensible arguments until, having been permitted to speak for some minutes, she had concluded with a hint of humour by saying: "Anyway, it would be a dull world, wouldn't it, if we all thought the same."

To this winning humility, however, her father had responded with furious anger. And in Greek. As no one else understood, except his daughter, the others had listened with polite smiles and expressions that reflected their embarrassment. They were suddenly intruders at a family quarrel, or rather witnessing a daughter being reprimanded by a severe father . . . Until, on impulse, the young woman had dismissed him with a shrug, turned away hastily and had crossed to a distant corner of the salon. Soon after, John-Paul had followed her. He had fallen in love.

And he had remained in love for the following year, hardly a moment between them that had not been exciting and affectionate and trusting. Every meeting had been a celebration, the celebration of discovering what, unrealised by themselves, they had both been seeking until . . . Until Grace's remarkable announcement about Krenk. That normally prudent girl had been tempted, induced, persuaded to take up his offer.

"I'm sorry, I won't let you," John-Paul had said, a shocked response to her disclosure. "Don't mention it again."

"Don't speak to me in that dictatorial manner," Grace had replied. "I'm not your property."

"Yes, you are," he had exclaimed, a response of such firmness and intolerance that he hardly recognised his own voice. "You know his reputation. You know very well that your duties won't stop at being his secretary, being company on his travels . . ."

"First of all," Grace had interrupted, her sharpness as uncharacteristic as his own, "let me remind you that I'm not yet your wife. Secondly, what is even more insulting is to imagine I can't take care of myself. And, thirdly, the worst insult of all, that I'd ever allow myself to be touched by an ugly old man."

"You fool. You innocent, gullible . . ."

John-Paul had failed to dissuade her. And, gripping the iron bars of a Colombian prison cell, the sense of failure struck him more despairingly than ever. What else could he do except try to save her! A demented lover's choice of action ranged between doing nothing, meekly accepting her decision, or going to the other extreme. Of direct action. Of direct violent action.

And, still reliving the recent past, John-Paul recalled their last conversation. It had been on the telephone, a surprise call from Cuba, Krenk's first destination with his new secretary,

Grace sounding cheerful and reassuring.

"Where are you?" the young man had demanded, as much an accusation as a question. "Where the hell are you!"

It had required some persistence to break into the excited flow of words but at last she had relented.

"You know it's against my orders to tell anyone. But I know you'll keep it to yourself, darling. We're in Havana. Yes, staying at the president's palace. Remember, it's a secret."

At that point the line had gone disturbingly silent, possibly because of the obsolete equipment of the country or because the unsuspecting Grace was under surveillance. But the call had not reassured him. It was only a matter of time before the inevitable happened. And, as well as the horror of thinking of the deed itself, in John-Paul's mind was a vivid picture of Grace being drawn into a new life style. Of luxury, of excitement, of that great world outside and beyond what he himself could offer.

But before he could inflict further despair on himself, and how that call from Cuba had forced him to consider murdering Krenk, he was aware of someone standing at his side. Was it possible, so real had been his recollections, that Grace had materialized, that the dear, beautiful young woman was there to prove it was all a terrible dream?

Instead, a white-haired, white-bearded head pressed against the next few bars and a croaking voice that was hardly Grace's said: "The sooner you accept your fate, friend, the better for you. Otherwise, you'll go out of your mind."

Anselmo spoke as though they already knew each other well and, suggesting he was a shrewd student of human nature, took John-Paul's elbow and drew him from the door.

"You're right, old man, I've got to stay sane," he admitted.

"Yes, that's the best we can hope for. Staying sane."

The only furniture in the cell was the two-tiered bunk, the slops bucket and a small wooden box; and John-Paul chose to seat himself on the words: *Handle with care.* As a student of law about to begin his final year, his studies would never include the first-hand experience of prison, the most universal feature of systems of justice, or a physical discomfort at the other extreme of his normally agreeable life; but he was not in the mood to appreciate such extensions of his knowledge. If he could not protest to the authorities, well, he could inflict his indignation on Anselmo.

"They're going to suffer," he exclaimed. "I carried a diplomatic passport but it wasn't recognised. I told them that Colombia wasn't my destination but it made no difference. I told them that the pistol I was carrying was for my own protection in Cuba but they still concluded I was one of the hijackers . . ."

He was interrupted by Anselmo.

"You mean you were a diplomat? Well . . . Which country?"

"Never mind which country, old man," went on John-Paul. "First a mob of drug-crazed soldiers storm the aircraft, shooting at us as if we were there for target practice, women and children killed, then they massacre the hijackers as they surrender and celebrate as though they'd defeated a Prussian army corps. After that, a few unfortunate passengers like myself were selected . . ."

The young man was about to elaborate on the iniquities of the authorities when Anselmo tapped his knee.

"Listen, you're not a genuine diplomat — what have you been up to? In any case, you look too young to be one."

The direct question reminded John-Paul that the newly-arrested were frequently placed with informers and, suddenly cautious, he regarded his companion with suspicion.

"I've told you why they've put me here — now, what about you?" he demanded. "Since this is Colombia, you must have been involved in the drugs business."

Anselmo ignored the question, his persistence that of an interrogator.

"How old are you? You look like a boy to me."

"I'm no boy," replied the indignant young man. "I'm in my middle twenties."

"Middle twenties? What sort of an age is that?"

"All right, I'm twenty-two. And you?"

The question brought pleasure to the withered face.

"Guess."

"Sixty," said John-Paul, taking twenty off his guess.

"I'm thirty-eight." Anselmo, seated on the lower bunk, stretched out his arms as if putting his miserable condition on display. "And in a few years' time, since they're bound to keep you here, you'll look like this."

"Keep me here!" exclaimed the young man with disbelief. "Well, that won't happen to me. I'll be out in days."

Anselmo smiled. John-Paul was clearly offering a rare form of entertainment. And from across the courtyard came a series of screams, as if to the regular rhythm of flogging.

"Hear that? We call these cells our shelters. Because once they take us out, we're really in trouble. But listen . . ." The face that was a complexity of wrinkles and deeper folds suddenly displayed concern. "If you trusted me and told me what you'd been up to, I might be able to help you."

"You can't possibly help me," John-Paul said with conviction. "And I've no intention of telling you about myself."

But, ten minutes later, as if in that short time a comradeship had formed, the young man found himself without doubts, confiding his purpose, speaking almost apologetically because, yes, he had started out to murder a man and, yes again, once he was released, he would still try to do just that. Kill Krenk. And he went on to describe Grace, her folly and her predicament, and how there was only one way to rescue her. Then there was that scoundrel, her father, a banker and business colleague to Krenk, who had encouraged his daughter to accept the offer. What could be worse than a father who traded his daughter as part of a business deal!

Until, almost in tears, John-Paul asked: "So what could I do except set out to rescue my girl?"

"By killing?"

"By killing. I bought two pistols. One went into my briefcase, which they found. The other's in the suitcase which went into the hold. When they let me out, if they haven't already found it . . ."

"Forget it, you young fool. You'll never have the opportunity." And Anselmo displayed yet another of his rare smiles. "But how can I be so sure? Well, let me tell you." He proceeded to make the surprising disclosure that he had been one of the country's judges, one of the youngest, in fact, and that he spoke with all the authority of someone who had been both the representative and the victim of the system. "To conclude, forget the chivalry. Don Quixote lived five hundred years ago. Get back to your own country and accept that evil is all around us and that the best we can do is to stay clean and survive. If your girl has chosen to go off with a rich man, well, that's obviously what she wanted."

"What she wanted!" The cynical remark instantly destroyed the illusion of a growing comradeship and, angrily, John-Paul exclaimed, "Let me tell you, Anselmo, that Grace's motives were above question. She took the job to travel round the world, to put money aside for later, perhaps for when we get married . . ." And the anger forced him to go further. To cruelty. "In your present state, a bitter wreck of a man, how can you be on the side of love! The world's divided into the few who would agree with what I must do and the many who'd say I was a dangerous fool, a murderer."

"I'm sorry," said Anselmo, "but in this case the majority would be right. The sooner you learn the lesson that I refused to learn, the better for you. And probably for Grace. Simply put, evil always triumphs over good, wickedness over virtue, bad intentions over principles and meanness over generosity."

This time John-Paul's protest was even more vehement. In that case, if evil nearly always triumphed, why was there so much goodness and beauty and decency in the world, why wasn't society infinitely worse than a pessimist like himself saw it, he demanded; and if evil was man's natural state, why were we all born innocent?

"Come on, Anselmo, answer that! No, we move from innocence to a little more maturity, then finally to being a responsible adult," exclaimed John-Paul.

The argument had introduced a little passion into a prison cell grim with despair and stained with one wretched lifetime after another. Both men, the young and the seemingly old, had briefly escaped from their surroundings, a triumph for their conversation; and there was an inevitability to the way in which Anselmo went on to recount his own story.

"You've got to expect me to speak harshly and bitterly," he began. "And if you think I've been tough on you, it's because I was once an innocent myself. Believing we could change things for the better. But first let me tell you something about the country we're in, just in case you still have any illusions."

His country, it seemed, had a number of armed factions fighting among themselves, though most of the victims, as everywhere, were ordinary people. The trigger-happy men formed the private armies of the drug barons, the regiments of the national army, left-wing terrorist bands and right-wing para-military gangs, but they all had one common purpose. To settle matters by violence.

"Which brings me to my first and only appointment at a senior level. It was in Bucaramanga, where I volunteered to replace the good Judge Hernandez. Ah, Eustacio . . . Poor fellow. He had bravely defied the drug cartels by sentencing men who had killed dozens of peaceful citizens, and pronounced his judgement with brave sincerity. But not for long. When he persisted in ignoring the warnings of the drug barons, he was seized and taken to the local flying club. They pushed him into a private helicopter and when it was over the town centre, they lowered the judge out of the door and had him swinging on the end of a rope. The helicopter flew round and round the great plaza filled by crowds, the judge screaming his lungs out, a few warning shots fired from balconies. The rope was released exactly over the fountain."

Then John-Paul heard how Anselmo's career began.

"No judge is appointed unless those who decide these things are absolutely sure that he'll obey the bosses, and I still can't think why they thought I'd be that sort. But they did. For a short time I enjoyed a popularity I'd never known before. And couldn't understand. Then things changed, the moment it was apparent I was following the example of the good Judge Hernandez. Very briefly, I presided over my court as if it was in Sweden or Switzerland, one of those countries that seem on another planet. Murder was murder, extortion was extortion and drug operations were drug operations."

But Anselmo's logic had not been shared by others.

"They gave me perhaps three months, then the threats started to roll in. Did I love my wife and family? Did I wish to enjoy an honourable retirement? How would I enjoy life without my balls? When they realised that the threats were having no effect, the local police chief visited me. Why couldn't I realize that everyone who mattered in the town was enjoying a good standard of living thanks to the generosity of the cartels? Why wouldn't I cooperate? If even the government ministers in Bogota went along with the system — the 'honourable tradition' — why couldn't I? Who did I think I was — opposing the system!"

But Anselmo had continued to oppose it. Instead of being richer by half a million dollars, he had preferred to fulfil his task as an honest and fair-minded judge. It did not matter that all the criminals he sentenced, by one method or another, had escaped or been released from prison within a month, or that the barons flourished more prosperously than ever, at least he, Anselmo, had done his duty.

"Then, one day, I was visited by the police chief. He was with two other officers. I waited for whatever story he had to tell me then he simply said that I was under arrest. I thought he was joking, even when I was put into handcuffs. But he wasn't."

Meanwhile, although John-Paul was absorbed by what he was hearing, it was adding to the sense of alarm he had felt earlier. Were there reputedly civilized countries where the law of the land was not respected, where courts represented not justice but the interests of the criminals and where the police, from top to bottom, were totally corrupt? What an innocent I must be, he thought, as he continued to listen to Anselmo. And this country was one of the members of COM. Did his mother know — was she aware?

"What had happened was this," continued Anselmo. "The local barons had decided that I was an even greater threat than the good Judge Hernandez, which in a way was the highest compliment they could have paid me, and that death or the murder of my wife or the kidnapping of my children was too good for me and that I should suffer an even worse fate. Which, as you see, I have."

The charges against Anselmo had been the misappropriation of huge sums of government money and receiving bribes from those wishing to influence his verdicts. In response to his scornful dismissal of such preposterous accusations, the police lawyers had produced sworn testimonies, certified bank accounts in Anselmo's name crediting him with unexplained cash payments, and copies of incriminating correspondence apparently signed by himself. There were enough falsified documents to fill an office.

"There was no trial in court, my dear young man," Anselmo went on. "It was done discreetly, the way they work. In the office of the police chief, the evidence was laid in front of me. You're a judge, they said. Go through these papers and tell us what you think. I told them, in reply, to stuff their papers up their arses but that made no difference. Oh, and I've forgotten to explain that Judge Jose Mendoza from a neighbouring district, and the government prosecutor, were present. They gave their concerted opinion that if the evidence in front of me was not the clearest proof of my crimes, then I was unfit to pass judgement on anything."

That had been three years earlier. From that gathering of high officials, Anselmo had been brought straight to prison, to this very cell, he explained, where he was held as an exhibit. They kept animals in zoos, and people paid to see them. Also with fish in the aquarium and glass cases of butterflies in the museum; and the exhibit Anselmo Benitez in his cell.

"So that has been my fate," he concluded. "People are brought to me as a warning, to gape through the bars. If they had killed me, that would have been that. As an exhibit, I shall be of use to them for the rest of my life." A sigh of exhaustion came from the dry, crusted lips of the white-haired but not old prisoner. His hand again reached for John-Paul's knee. "So if you have any mistaken notions that evil does not triumph, forget them. Evil is encouraged by goodness, cruelty by kindness and a repetition of crimes by indulgent forgiveness."

"But you've said nothing about the trial," said John-Paul, interrupting for the first time. "If you've been here three years, there must have been a proper trial."

"Oh, such innocence," murmured Anselmo.

He was probably about to expand further on the theme of the triumph of evil when a shadow appeared at the door and a key was inserted from the outside.

"You," said one of the two warders, pointing at the new prisoner. "Come out of there."

"Ah, and about time," exclaimed John-Paul. "They've come to their senses and they're going to release me, Anselmo. So let me wish you goodbye."

But before he could reach out and shake his companion's hand, he was dragged from the cell.

It had been one of the most traumatic confrontations of Signora Carla Modeste's life. Why had she, the respected deputy-director of the Community of Mankind, succumbed to the folly and weakness of agreeing to her son's request? A week earlier she had handed him a COM passport, a document that allowed the holder the privileges of diplomats all over the world. In this case a son who had seemed demented. Again, why?

The deputy-director's offices were situated on one of the top floors of the Manhattan skyscraper that served as the COM headquarters, the centre of the international body created after the second world war to bring peace, friendship and prosperity to the affairs of its one hundred and sixty member-states. If there was a single building with an importance that exceeded those of the holy places of Christianity, Islam and any of the other religions, and which enjoyed more real power than the mightiest armies in existence, it was this one. And yet its Number Two, when it came to this particular personal crisis, had ultimately behaved like the over-indulgent and loving mammas of her native Italy.

Again and again, why?

Signora Modeste was well-qualified for her high office. She had become, from long practice and from principle, the friend, counsellor and representative of Asians and Africans, Europeans and South Americans, in fact of every one of the delegations filling the building. And she was helped in her role by certain unique virtues. She had a range of instincts that served her better than any kind of training and she had a warmth of manner that prevailed where even her seniority failed; and she believed in listening. She was, therefore, a popular figure with the bureaucrats, ex-politicians, ex-ministers and ex-military officers of the delegations. And they called her La Mamma, a nickname, an appellation that was meant both respectfully and affectionately.

The crisis had begun when John-Paul, inheritor of his father's handsome looks though not that long departed gentleman's dubious character, had marched into her thirtieth-floor offices to announce that he intended to kill Klaus Krenk. Her first response had been her professional one; to nod and wait. When the waiting had brought no further explanation, she had calmly suggested that there might be something to talk over.

With uncharacteristic rudeness, the young man had dismissed the suggestion.

"There's nothing to talk over, mother. I'm going to end the bastard's life. The sooner he's out of the way, the better."

On that point, Signora Modeste had been in silent agreement. As the king of arms dealers, a close friend and partner of the murderous leaders of countries nevertheless declaring themselves loyal members of COM, Krenk's demise would be a cause for celebration rather than mourning. But such thoughts had been kept to herself.

"This can only have something to do with Grace," she had eventually concluded. Aloud. "She means more to you than anything in the world, so it's not difficult to guess. But how is she involved with Krenk?"

With the same unfamiliar belligerence, he had replied: "I've no intention of giving you explanations. And I haven't just come here to tell you . . . To come to the point, I want a COM passport."

The middle-aged woman filling the executive chair behind the vast desk had studied the set face of her son for further indications of his purpose; and his state of mind. As she might have stared at a Zairean tribal leader or a Nepalese delegate, someone whose thought processes were quite beyond her comprehension.

"I see," she had murmured, defeated.

"But I'll promise one thing, mother," he had said more calmly. "I won't kill him in New York. I promise that."

She had frowned with disbelief; at such an absurd assurance. A mother brought up a child thinking she knew his character, and suddenly one was confronted with a stranger. Intent on murder.

"I can't listen to any more, *figlio mio*. Please don't go on."

Her plea had been ignored. Her disbelief had intensified.

He had said: "Without your help, I'm forced to buy a forged one. I want to come back alive. Don't you want to see me again?"

Signora Modeste lived and worked in an environment of bluffs, threats and dishonesty but, facing her son, she had known that this time she was not involved in the devious game of diplomacy.

"Your problems are mine," she had replied, her manner still one of professional calmness. "Let's talk things through. Just relax. Please. And face the reality that I simply haven't the authority to issue COM passports. Do you want to involve me in murder?"

"I'm not asking you to pull a trigger," her unrecognizable son had replied. "In any case you've told me often enough that this building is the biggest crime centre in the world, with half the delegates as corrupt as *mafiosi*. Okay, you'll follow the fashion."

That day, a week earlier, she had listened with remarkable patience. Her distinguished career had been devoted to bringing decency and compassion to governments that killed their own citizens at will, that practised limitless atrocities, murderers enjoying the title of king or president, yet now, in her presence, her son was proposing to become one of them.

"You can't expect me," she had said, "in my position, to be bullied into this, to making me a party to murder." She had suppressed a sob, her first for years. "And apart from that, don't imagine that the deputy-director is above being disgraced, dismissed or even prosecuted." She had leaned forward, pleading. "Now, sensibly, to your mother, let me have the whole story."

A little of the reasonable and relaxed young man had briefly appeared, confiding more calmly the extent of Grace's folly, her choosing to work for Krenk, the young woman's excitement at the prospect of travelling round the world. And what her eventual fate must be. Which he need not put into words. Then, the picture in his mind driving away his more normal manner, he had gone on to remind his mother that the prize of a COM diplomatic passport, forged or genuine, could always be bought. Wasn't it true that the delegates of poorer countries formed part of a network called *Favours for Sale*? With pass-ports costing a thousand dollars?

John-Paul had then stood up, his intending departure an ultimatum.

"Where are you going?" she had demanded.

"You're not going to help me, mother," he had replied. "So what's the point of discussing it further?"

"Wait," she had called out as her son had reached the door. "Why don't we talk over your problem away from this place? It wasn't fair of you to march in here without warning. What about tonight?"

And so, that evening, the skilled diplomat of the Commu-nity of Mankind had settled down with her son to try to reach an agreement. As she might have done with one of the delegations. Her carefully chosen approach had been to show sympathy and patience, though not at the cost of hard-headed good sense, and, as always, to work cleverly towards a compromise. In reply, her son had shown that he was not without some effective arguments of his own. There were, he had reminded her again, other ways to acquire a passport; then there was the money his absconding father had placed in a trust, which would give him the means to follow Krenk round the world. And, lastly, a frightening argument, a declaration that he was prepared to die for Grace.

An overwhelming helplessness had settled over Signora Modeste. A son, one's own offspring, stood apart from all the rules and principles by which she conducted her professional life. With a son in this demented state, what was the most she could achieve? The word compromise came to mind; and, once fixed in her head, it seemed to offer the only solution. With the knowledge of her ultimate helplessness, she sug-gested he was motivated by two contradictory purposes. One was that of love, to save Grace, the second that of hate, to commit a murder. If he could succeed with the first, surely that was the really important part?

She had then announced a concession. If he needed to travel with a minimum of restrictions, of being spared the wait for visas, of being in a better position to help Grace, once he had found her, well, it was just possible . . .

"But I would never get such a passport to turn my son into a murderer, John-Paul," she had said, with all the authority her despair permitted. "All you have to do is promise, promise not to kill. Please. For my sake. Certainly for Grace's sake . . ."

The son transformed into a menacing stranger had bowed his head but she thought she had detected a frown of doubt. A silence had followed, a silence she had interpreted in her own way. No, her son could not be a murderer. She must have a mother's faith. Besides, what was the alternative?

"I trust you," she had murmured eventually. "I trust you not to murder."

Afterwards, she had sustained herself with the thought of the number of compromises she had made in her long career. Sometimes they succeeded, sometimes they failed.

If John-Paul, when brought before the prison commander, Colonel Perez, had known anything about the man who was about to interrogate him, he would have discovered that he was called The Absolute. This title had nothing to do with absolution, or the granting of it, in fact the very opposite, but because the colonel's standards of rigidity, severity and discipline, were totally alien to a part of the world that was relaxed and lazy by nature. However, the man was as he was, and running a prison was one of the few positions in the country that would have tolerated such a grim tyrant.

The prison was called Golden Way, after a nearby valley, but for most of the thousand inmates there was hardly a glimmer of light in the lives of men who had once known the loving affection of mothers or the caresses of wives and mistresses. All the same, for the colonel, this was where they all deserved to be because, in his eyes, every prisoner sent to Golden Way Prison was guilty. It was a conviction that banished all doubts.

The prison had been built a hundred years earlier and anyone returning to it after that period of time would have been immediately familiar with it. Nothing had changed. The stone cells, those for prisoners condemned to "solitary", the

Opera House where they were tortured, the exercise yard where legs were permitted a little activity, the high surrounding wall and the dungeons below ground, a relic of even older days, were exactly as they had been.

"Do you speak Spanish?" were Colonel Perez's first words to the young man escorted into his presence.

"Yes," said John-Paul, firmly. "And I'm glad you do, too, because there's plenty I've got to say."

He was aware, though not directly because his anger seemed to eliminate his surroundings, of five men in various uniforms sitting at or near a large desk, grand enough to have been seized from a palace, of faded portraits of uniformed leaders on the walls and of a flag erected in the manner of a coat-stand in a corner.

"Well, you've picked the right person to hear your complaints," the colonel replied with a mildness that contrasted with his heavily moustached face. And, with a similar mildness, quickly added: "I'm glad you've decided to make a full confession. That'll make it easier."

The threat went unrecognized.

"Since you've clearly made a mistake in throwing a representative of COM into one of your filthy cells," John-Paul said with hardly controlled anger, "I expect not only my instant release, I insist you put me on the next plane to Cuba, which was my destination."

With escape from the grey cell, he felt he could speak out without fear of the consequences. Within every society there was a line that divided those who could make themselves heard and those who were condemned to remain unheard. But his last remark had caused Colonel Perez to frown.

"I'm the only one round here who will be doing the insisting," he said, a manner different from his mild greeting. "Let's get down to business. First of all, this COM nonsense of yours . . . Even if that passport isn't faked, so far as we at the Golden Way Prison are concerned, that bunch of do-gooders have nothing to do with us."

"Let me remind you that your country has its obligations," John-Paul replied, in what he thought to be appropriate to his COM status. "So be careful what you say."

The colonel's response was to place his boots on the desk and light a large cigar; and to nod his head at a private conclusion.

"Right, I'll tell you what we've found out. You were the leader of the hijackers, the one who stayed incognito in his seat. Correct — so why deny it?"

"Of course I deny it!" The colonel's accusation was so preposterous that John-Paul's anger faltered. "Look, stop jumping to conclusions just because you found I was carrying a gun."

"No one risks concealing a gun unless he's got a crime in mind."

"I carried it for protection."

"You certainly did. Against the security forces. Now, listen . . ." Colonel Perez's voice was rising in volume as he spoke, as though the force of logic went with loudness. "We've already got the facts from one of your comrades. When you arrived at the airport, you were to be met by a band of your left-wing cut-throats who were going to kick off the passengers, commandeer the aircraft and fly off to Suriname. Once there, you were going to help some of the local revolutionaries to seize power." His shouting was accompanied by nods of agreement from the others in uniform. "Unfortunately for them, and for you, we were able to round up your waiting comrades." The colonel laughed. "They put up a bit of a fight. Well, for as long as it took us to slaughter them. Which was about five minutes."

More laughter from the assembled officers. But the colonel's speech had been protracted enough for John-Paul to adjust to the astonishing situation and to the absurd charges. Anger again triumphed over fear.

"This isn't a court of law," he protested. "You're just a prison commander. If I have to be interrogated, I expect it to be done properly, by someone legally appointed to question me." He was encouraged by a hint of hesitation on the colonel's face. "Now get me on the next plane to Havana and stop behaving in this way."

It was not, considered John-Paul, a bad effort for a young man in his early twenties. In fact, when it was behind him, at some time in the future when he had qualified as a lawyer, he would regard it as a most useful experience. But the colonel's next words ended the brief euphoria.

"Well, I'm not the sort to waste words," he said, though no longer shouting. "I've got a reputation to keep. I get results and I get them quickly. Now, you two, take him to the Opera House. I'll be following in a few moments."

As John-Paul's arms were seized by the two warders, he had a passing sensation that he had only to keep asserting his legal rights and to remind them that they were civilized human beings to shame them into some kind of decency. Not shame, however, but the colonel's shouting, prevailed.

"Stop!" The warders obeyed his order. "And before you start singing, let me tell you why that COM passport was a mistake. COM isn't a country. It has no reality except a voice." The colonel smiled, but with self-satisfaction. "You didn't expect a security policeman like myself to be able to speak about such things, did you? I happen, however, to be well read, well informed and, unfortunately for you, able to distinguish between real power and the illusion of it. Your passport is issued by a great debating chamber. It might have its representatives all round the world but in itself it's a lot of fine resolutions, clouds of hot air, an army of delegates instead of soldiers and, if you try to equate it with a country, a population of well-paid functionaries who put their jobs first." He waved to the warders to take John-Paul away, then shouted after them: "You would have been better off with a passport from a meaningless country like Belize or Haiti."

Confused, helpless, frightened and courageous in turn, John-Paul could only shout: "You wait until I get out of here!"

A concert of laughter answered his defiance and the warders gave his arms a warning twist, to remind him that struggle would be useless. They descended from the ground floor into a large basement room. John-Paul's first impression was that he had entered a gymnasium. A number of ropes hung from the ceiling, some with iron rings, three bare couches — for massages? — were arranged in the centre, two large dials with electric wires — for measuring the pulse rate after exercises? — were attached to a wall, and a set of clubs and sticks — for games? — were prominent in one corner.

But John-Paul's first impression lasted only a moment. This

quiet room, resembling a gym before the crowd had arrived, was the most frightening sight that had ever confronted him. How long, he wondered, before he cried out? And, even worse, what could he say that would satisfy the brutes?

There were three men in green combat uniforms, as though the difference between those upstairs and in the Opera House was that of the headquarter staff and soldiers in the front line. There were no windows in the room and it was very hot and no one spoke. To John-Paul's puzzlement padding was placed round his wrists but the reason for this was made clear when they pushed him towards the hanging ropes and tied his hands above his head. Two more men in combat dress came into the room.

Then John-Paul was prevented from following the ominous happenings because a thick cloth was placed round his eyes and tied behind his head. Almost simultaneously, he felt his arms being stretched. Behind him, passing through pulleys, the ropes were drawn up by the men so that he was swinging in the air. At this point, he felt the first physical discomfort, that of his arms being stretched. And two more men in combat uniform came into the room.

John-Paul's next sensation was of his shoes being removed then, curiosity giving way to an acute embarrassment, that his trousers and underpants were being pulled off. And still no sound from the men, not a word, until pain struck with such force that consciousness of everything else disappeared. The soles of his feet were being struck forcefully and with an even regularity with wooden bats shaped like paddles. John-Paul's first screams were those of outrage, that this could be happening to him, then those of acute pain.

"That's it, boys. Soften him up."

The voice was that of Colonel Perez, who had just arrived, and his shouted remark was loud enough to penetrate the pain of the man hanging from the ropes.

"You bloody bastard!" screamed John-Paul. And added every abusive word in the Spanish language. Then some from the English, French and Italian languages. "I've nothing to say! I'm not a hijacker, you idiot gorilla . . ."

The striking of the soles of his feet stopped. They seemed on fire, making John-Paul wonder if he would ever walk again. And, having stopped screaming and swearing, he heard, and not from the colonel:

"He's one of the educated ones, isn't he? The trouble with them is that they break too quickly. With the *campesinos*, those tough little bastards can take almost anything."

"Well," said Colonel Perez, as though what had just been said had given him an idea, "if he's so educated, let's give him a choice. That's what democracy is all about, isn't it? Free choice?"

As he heard this remark, John-Paul felt a strong hand grip his member and give it a painful tug. Then two more.

"Stop that!" he cried, but more with indignation than from the pain. "I've nothing to say, so let me down."

"Well, if you've nothing to say, that's your decision," said Colonel Perez. "And we'll continue in this democratic way by asking you to choose whether you want the electrodes on what I've just pulled, having your head immersed in the piss bucket until you're on the point of drowning or whether you'd like the hot rods treatment up your arse." The prison commander paused to laugh, then added: "You can't say we're not democratic here. You claim to be a good member of that COM outfit, so you should appreciate that."

The warder who, from long experience as a torturer had observed that intellectuals, men from good backgrounds, artists and idealists, usually broke before his team had completed the whole programme, proved to be absolutely correct. Within half an hour John-Paul was unconscious. The electrodes had driven him to the point of madness rather than unconsciousness, the clubs on his back and thighs and buttocks to no longer being able to utter a cry, but it was when his dripping head was pulled out of the piss bucket that his torturers accepted that further treatment would be pointless. The soft product of New York city life simply could not take it.

Consciousness returned to John-Paul about an hour later. It was not the kind of consciousness that brought awareness of himself or even of the pains hitting him from every part of his body. It was the sensation of light, dim though it was, as his eyelids parted. After a moment, he realized he was staring at a white-bearded face bending over him. So God really existed, he thought, as consciousness made a little more progress. Fancy — so I was wrong all along. Then, moments later, he was able to give a name to the face.

"Anselmo . . ."

"They've brought you back."

"That was nasty. I'm hurting all over."

Later, when he had drunk the water offered him by Anselmo and submitted to being washed and cleaned, he had to repay the man's kindness by listening patiently to more of his philosophy. It was another triumph of evil over good. Why did so many people refuse to face reality? Why were so many concerned with concepts of right and wrong, trying to defeat forces infinitely too powerful and refusing to face the truth that the individual was helpless?

"Well, you do agree now, don't you?" Anselmo demanded, having spoken long enough for the young man to recover a little more.

"No," said John-Paul.

CHAPTER TWO

The moment Signora Modeste heard that an aircraft bound for Cuba had been hijacked, she was certain it would be carrying her son. Like John-Paul, though not from information received from Grace but from her own sources, she knew the whereabouts of Klaus Krenk and could presume the sequence of events. It was therefore a relief that her son's name was not on the list of those killed or that the Colombian authorities had made no special mention of him.

She did not expect John-Paul to reassure her with a telephone call or to choose to return to New York, but the anxiety built up as she allowed herself to assume he could be on the flight. Quite apart from the madness of his expedition, there was the troubling matter of the misuse of a COM passport. If the boy, in some way, had chosen to challenge the hijackers and become headline news, his assumed identity would have come under the closest scrutiny.

The following day, after an anxious night, the deputy-director of COM arrived at her office to find a report that brought the event even closer. An armed man had been discovered among the passengers and was suspected of being one of the terrorists. He was carrying a Community passport and his name was John-Paul Bonuomo. The Colombian authorities would be detaining him until they had obtained further information on the man.

Her first reaction was that of a weak mother who had allowed herself to agree to a son's dangerous request. She had cursed herself, she had almost wept from frustration, she had even wondered whether, having disgraced her position of trust, she should resign her senior post. But the clear-headed administrator inside her calmed the motherly side and turned to the task of retrieving the situation. To begin with, the passport had not used the family name, a point on which

John-Paul had sensibly insisted, and, secondly, she could always clear herself by affirming that the document had been stolen.

But that would mean certain imprisonment for her son and probably confirm Colombian suspicions that he was one of the gang of hijackers. She therefore chose a solution in the highest traditions of diplomacy and international protocol. A discreet and civilized arrangement was the answer. Between the head of the Colombian delegation to COM and herself. She directed her secretary to invite him for cocktails that evening, an invitation that was immediately accepted, which suggested to the experienced deputy-director that she might not be alone in seeking a favour.

The years had taught La Mamma, to use her appropriate sobriquet, that running a world of nations was like managing a large family of diverse, wilful, and wayward children. Between those children and herself, however, were the nannies, the nursemaids, who made up the delegations to the Community of Mankind. The public, or otherwise the children, had to be treated considerately though, for their own good, kept in ignorance of what was really happening.

This pragmatic attitude towards the billions of adult children they represented was one shared by all the delegations, including the veteran Colombian diplomat, Senor Rafael Kessler. When, that evening, the South American arrived at her suite, she welcomed him with a blend of effusiveness and formality, a technique that suited and flattered Asians and Africans, Nordics and Latin Americans. In fact, everyone.

"Madame," Señor Kessler said courteously, when they were settled in the luxurious annexe to her office, "you have been promising to visit Bogota for the last year. When are we going to have the pleasure?"

"Very soon, I hope," replied Signora Modeste, with equally correct hypocrisy. "There's nothing I would like more."

The friendly but slightly formal exchanges and the obligatory sipping of drinks continued for many minutes, the elderly Colombian diplomat a man of impressive presence, his blue silk suit and diamond tiepin correctly suggesting great personal wealth. Then Signora Modeste mentioned the curious, 'curious', she stressed, matter at the Cucuta airport. She knew nothing about this reported COM passport holder. Perhaps he was better informed?

"Ah . . ." murmured Señor Kessler, as though he found the episode equally puzzling. "Well, like you, I've heard only what's been on the radio. The passengers are of course being allowed to continue their journey."

"But not this young man with one of our passports. Apparently . . ." Signora Modeste hesitated, deciding how best to handle the matter without indicating that her interest might be personal. "Part of my job, I suppose, is to make sure our passports aren't being misused or forged."

"Of course, madame."

"The young man has been detained. I'm sure you'll keep me informed of any developments."

"Naturally. It's to all our advantage to keep COM above suspicion."

There was a pause while Signora Modeste carefully chose her words, she and the diplomat involved in a familiar but circumspect contest.

"We can assure you that the young man with one of our passports is not one of the hijackers," she said. "As a favour, and with no intention of interfering in the affairs of a member-state, we would welcome the release of the young man."

The silences of diplomats and high officials, like language, were rich in meanings. In fact, since Señor Kessler was not deaf, his variation of silence could be taken as a willingness to consider the request. She added to the martini in his half-empty glass, then went on to discuss the scandals of the moment, child slavery in India, sex diseases in New York and the extent of Japanese government corruption that would have settled half the debt problems of South American countries. At seven o'clock her visitor departed. She spent the evening troubled by the thought of her son in the hands of a Latin American security force.

During the course of the following day, her invitation was returned. Would she care, if she were free, to call on Señor Kessler that evening? For drinks. She was free, she assured his secretary, then proceeded to cancel a lecture on the need for a higher morality in public service.

At the appointed hour, Signora Modeste returned the

Colombian's visit. She was not surprised as the polite conversation moved through a number of predictable courtesies to the real business. It was part of the training of delegates to the Community of Mankind. First there was the greeting, polite or amiable, depending on how well the parties knew each other, then there was an exchange of flattering respectfulness followed by generalities on the affairs of the day or the state of the world; lastly, to the point of the meeting.

Señor Kessler said: "My government appreciates your wish to avoid bad publicity for COM but there's a little matter that's causing great resentment throughout my country."

"A little matter?" inquired Signora Modeste. "Resentment?"

Her expression suggested that she was about to hear something astonishing.

"It's not helping my efforts. You see, administratively speaking . . ."

He paused deliberately, a diplomat's artifice for gaining an advantage.

"Ah," murmured Signora Modeste, resorting to her own way of prevaricating. "You mean you need larger offices in this building? In fact I'd already given some thought to it."

"I am referring to negotiations with the Bank of Mankind."

"With BOM?" Her exclamation suggested that something completely unrelated had been introduced into the conversation. "You can't be suggesting . . ."

But he was. Her unfinished protest that COM and BOM could never be seen as the same organization, and that she could have any influence with the bank, was politely ignored.

"You are respected everywhere," went on the polished diplomat. "You are able to make requests, have off-the-record meetings, and never, not in any way, have your motives questioned."

For almost the first time in her long and admirable career, Signora Modeste knew she was defeated and would have to compromise. And compromise her principles.

"How much?" asked the deputy-director, as briefly as she could.

"Really, signora," protested Señor Kessler. "You make it sound as though I'd asked for a ransom. However, you may not be familiar with the crisis between my country and BOM but it concerns a promised loan for the construction of the new dam on the Caqueta river. BOM insists on linking the loan with our undertaking to make a number of changes in our economy. These are so severe that we fear, if implemented, they will lead to a left-wing revolution." A moment of undiplomatic honesty caused Señor Kessler to tremble at the prospect. The weakness passing, he continued with: "The bank's directors are equally divided, madame, on the loan. It only requires a little push from a top figure here at COM, perhaps pointing out the social consequences if it's turned down, to get their agreement."

"I'm sure you're being optimistic," observed Signora Modeste, though the tone of her voice already indicated her readiness to cooperate. "Highly optimistic."

All the same, John-Paul remained in a Colombian prison. She stood up and walked to the window. The traffic of the Manhattan avenue moved like a crawling monster, the end of office hours crowding the sidewalks with the tired, the impatient and the hurrying, the area a weaving of tensions and purpose. Like all those problems coming towards one from the future, problems colliding with one in the present but then, somehow, disappearing as they were resolved.

"Give me a few more details, Señor Kessler," she said. "Is it a loan being considered by one of Penney-Brown's committees?"

The following day was a busy one. After decades of experience, Signora Modeste was inured against hindrances and hitches and prevarications. A series of confidential meetings gained the agreement of three of the dissenting BOM directors. In the case of one, she accepted that an enquiry into torture in his country should be deferred, with another she agreed to recommend a statement clearing his country of religious intolerance. The request of the third director was the easiest of all. He simply wanted his brother to be promoted within the organization.

In this manner, Signora Modeste completed yet another 'arrangement' in her distinguished career, a compromise that meant this for that, that for the other, in the time-honoured tradition of international organizations; and with everyone relieved or pleased — or richer — at the outcome.

When John-Paul Bonuomo, erstwhile Modeste, entered the airport building at Havana, he had the impression that it was a national occasion. The crowd of Cubans could not possibly be passengers or those waiting to meet them, and since their baggage was entirely made up of banners proclaiming the achievements of their country, national flags being vigorously waved, and large portraits of their long-bearded leader, his first thought was confirmed. There was also some singing of political songs to the accompaniment of guitars and rumba music, and an excited atmosphere.

"What's happening?" asked John-Paul.

"He's coming at any moment," said a stout man, pushing against him.

They were not, guessed John-Paul, referring to God or Christ or the Pope but to their own revolutionary leader. His only wish, however, as he was crushed by the crowd, was to find a hotel and spend a comfortable night recovering from his painful experiences in a Colombian prison. The next step, of rescuing Grace, was not something to be undertaken in a state of exhaustion. And if there was one factor that could be regarded as encouraging, it was the way in which the COM passport had been respected on his arrival in Havana. Viva Cuba!

The crowds and the banners and the cries filled a baggage hall that was modern yet already decaying, evidence of fine ideals that had run short of money. Unable to escape, John-Paul noticed a remarkable number of uniforms but he was unsure which of them signified soldiers, the police, customs officers, porters, sweepers or canteen workers. It was not the kind of society, he guessed, where he could complain to the authorities about delays or obstruction.

His helplessness was further indicated by the crowd's excited rush towards the windows. Someone important had clearly appeared on the tarmac below. By good fortune, or otherwise, John-Paul was forced against a window directly above what was happening outside. Looking down, he had an excellent view of steel barriers and armed soldiers holding back a crowd even larger and noisier than that now surrounding him and that, moving towards an aircraft bearing the markings of Air Nigeria, was the group that was causing all the excitement.

Near the aircraft steps John-Paul observed that the group divided into three men and a woman, those clearly about to depart, and the local dignitaries who were wishing them farewell. Most distinctive was the bearded leader of the country, dressed in a green combat uniform as if the enemy was at the gates of the city. Halfway up the steps into the aircraft, the departing group divided. Two massive men, obviously bodyguards, disappeared into the aircraft, leaving a distinguished white-haired individual to exchange exaggerated waves of farewell with those standing below.

Only then did John-Paul turn his attention to the young woman standing subserviently behind the important visitor. As she allowed him to pass in front, before following him into the aircraft herself, a cry escaped from John-Paul's throat.

"Grace!" he cried. "Grace!"

Unmistakably, in a familiar light linen suit, and from her elegant bearing, the distant figure could only have been his affianced. As he pressed against the window of the air terminal, the door of the Air Nigeria aircraft was closed and the steps dragged away. The group of local dignitaries, from a safe distance, gave their final salutes.

"Who's he seeing off?" John-Paul demanded of the nearest face.

"What! You don't know!" exclaimed an unshaven comrade worker. "The old fellow is one of our best friends. He's helping to supply our great armed forces. Cuban soldiers are the best in the world but we can't defeat the Yankees without the right weapons."

But the young man's attention was on the departing aircraft rather than on the future defeat of the Yankee army. If he had actually recognized Grace, and he was convinced he had, then his plans must be instantly changed. His sight followed the aircraft as it rose into the sky. The most obvious destination, surely, must be Lagos. And with an airport gathering like this, Krenk's movements were hardly being kept secret.

"What country is this?" demanded the proprietor of the

Ernesto Hemingway Hotel when John-Paul, an hour later, presented the man with an unfamiliar passport.

John-Paul explained as patiently as he could. Besides, there was the *Entrada* stamp and that day's date. Hadn't the man heard of the Community of Mankind? At this, John-Paul was warned not to talk politics in Cuba. But if he wanted to change dollars, the hotel offered the best black market rate.

"What I need is today's newspapers. Where do I find them?" asked the young man.

"Give me a couple of dollars and I'll have them sent up to your room."

The single newspaper that the hotel boy eventually delivered to the top floor room was a week old and had pages missing. But the front page was intact. Across three columns was a report on the arrival of that great friend of all progressive countries, Klaus Krenk. There was also a photograph of the merchant statesman being greeted with a hug from the country's leader. In the background was a woman's indistinct face, too blurred to resemble Grace except . . . But who else could it be? John-Paul asked himself.

The information he wanted was contained in the last paragraph of the report. After Cuba, Krenk would be flying to Lagos. The newspaper's readers were then referred to page three, to an article that dealt with the need for all African countries to be armed to the teeth so that they could resist the old colonial powers seeking to exploit their wealth. Hesitating no longer, John-Paul left the Hemingway in search of a travel agency.

It was late afternoon and the people were out in crowds. The streets and squares were lined with shops but it was John-Paul's first experience of a society that described itself as progressive and fulfilling the needs of the people yet which had very few goods in the shop windows. Except posters extolling the country and pictures of the leader. When he stopped to ask for travel agencies, he gradually learned that with travel abroad almost forbidden, no foreign currency available, the risk of being politically suspect at wishing to leave the country, only foreign tourists would need such agencies. And, for them, there was a government agency.

Two attractive young women were, however, more helpful. Large silver earrings contrasted with the light brown skin
revealed by their low blouses, and they invited him to follow
them because they were passing near the agency. In the
company of the laughing ladies only a little older than himself
but displaying a bright intelligence and talkativeness, John-
Paul felt a little cheered.

"I want to get on a flight to Nigeria," he explained, grateful
for their help. "But you're going to too much trouble for me."

"Nothing is too much trouble," the ladies assured him
simultaneously.

They had soon left the shopping area and begun to walk
along a narrow road of old Spanish-style houses, people sitting
around the front doors, children playing noisily and Cuban
music in the background. A short cut, thought John-Paul, but
halfway along the street the two young women stopped by a
doorway displaying a sign that read Gomez Voyages and
determinedly took his arms.

"Special travel," said the smaller woman reassuringly, her
lips very painted but toning with her complexion. "Don't look
so worried."

"I'm not worried," John-Paul replied bravely, thoroughly
alarmed and ready to retreat down the flight of stairs up which
he was being pushed. "But this can't be for international
flights . . ."

"It's for everything," said the taller of the women, who told
him that her name was Marta. "Anything you want."

On the landing there was no evidence of Gomez Voyages.
And certainly not in the large room into which he was led and
which was dominated not by evidence of travel but by a large
brass-railed bed that looked as old as the house. As the door
was closed behind John-Paul, Marta gave him a determined
kiss.

"Now, ladies, please . . ." he protested. A perverse male
pride prevented him from forcing an escape but he managed to
release himself from their grasping hands. "I'm really grateful
to you but I must stay faithful to my fianceé," he pleaded. "I
love her very much."

It took the women a few moments to comprehend such

noble sentiments. Then they laughed with a delight approaching hysteria. The young man's honesty and innocence seemed to add to his attractiveness.

"Come on," said Graciela, the more vivacious of the two. "Five dollars. Let's get out of our clothes. Come on."

But John-Paul was not to be tempted or persuaded or forced. He pulled some loose dollar bills from his shirt pocket.

"Five dollars for you and five for you. It's not a gift, however," he explained, his manner remaining friendly though his face had reddened with embarrassment. "I must get a ticket to Lagos. It's urgent." He remembered that the concept of urgency was alien to this part of the world. "Or do you know anyone with influence? I'll pay the extra."

"You mean you don't want love-love?" Graciela asked disbelievingly.

"He's staying true," said her friend. "I've known one or two strange ones like that."

The two bewildered women sat on the edge of the old bed, the springs clanging as they did so, and held a whispered conversation. In the middle of the private exchanges, Marta looked up and asked the young man if he was sure, really, really, that before they helped him . . . Again John-Paul assured them that he intended to remain faithful, and with such firmness that the girls at last committed themselves to helping him.

"Okay. But you'll never get on the next flight unless you have a fixer," Graciela said. "You must believe us." The frivolous manner of the two sympathetic ladies had disappeared. They looked, and obviously were, concerned and trustworthy. "We meet tourists all the time. The travel agency will delay your flight so you can spend more money in the country."

"You could be here a month," agreed Marta.

"A month!" cried the alarmed John-Paul. Then, following his instincts, said: "You must help me. What do we do?"

In Colombia his prison cell had been four metres by four. Now, a whole country seemed hardly any bigger. He was still a prisoner. But the two young women, products of their society, proved to be remarkably adept at overcoming problems. Even that of helping stranded tourists to escape.

"You stay here," ordered Graciela. "Don't move. We might even be an hour."

"I'll be here," promised John-Paul.

The women left him on his own. How unbelievable, he reflected, that trust should so quickly have been established between himself and these two prostitutes. Then, suddenly realizing how exhausted he was, he crossed to the great brass bed, lay down and fell asleep. Or, rather, fitfully asleep because his mind was soon troubled by thoughts of Grace. In how many ways was she suffering? What treatment was the monster Krenk inflicting on her? And yet, as she had followed her employer into the aircraft, her demeanour had shown nothing except that of a proficient secretary doing her job.

John-Paul preferred, however, to torture himself. Had Krenk used force to take her or had she been cleverly and willingly seduced? Innocent he might be, he admitted of himself, but he knew that the constant presence of an exceedingly attractive woman must always excite a man's desire. And, most painful of all, remembering his own limited experience with women, if Grace was conquered by an expert philanderer and became a willing slave, how could their previous loving relationship be restored?

But the return of the two women rescued him from such despairing thoughts. They were accompanied by a very fat man with the face of a bully and the bearing of someone very important.

"This is Comrade Virgilio," said Marta, introducing the man. "He's head of our neighbourhood committee. He can help you."

The man's deep voice matched his appearance.

"I don't like helping capitalist enemies of our system but if you've got the money, we can fix things."

"I've got the money," John-Paul assured him.

"Virgilio's very important in the Party," said Graciela. "He knows everybody."

"How soon can you get me on a plane to Lagos?" demanded John-Paul.

"First, how will you pay the money?"

"With dollars."

"Travellers' cheques or cash?"

"Cash."

The mention of cash brought a softer look to the menacing face of the people's representative, as if the word was the name of a father's favourite son or daughter.

"It's because of you capitalists that the world's in such a mess. You realize that," said Virgilio. He did not expect to be contradicted. "All you think about are profits and exploiting the workers."

The two young women agreed dutifully.

"If I can't go direct, maybe I could be routed through Madrid or even Caracas?" suggested John-Paul impatiently.

"Leave the route to me. I know everything," Virgilio said threateningly, as if insulted that his capabilities could be doubted. "You might not be travelling on one of the regular airlines."

"What do you mean by that?" asked John-Paul, suspiciously.

"Well, between Cuba and Africa we've established our own routes, private planes and things like that. Even military planes."

"I simply want to get to Lagos in the shortest time possible," the young man persisted, at this point so frustrated that he was prepared to agree to anything.

"I can get you away the day after tomorrow. It'll be two thousand dollars. Cash. If you agree, we can walk across to my friend at the central travel agency," said Virgilio. "Without my friend, you may be here for weeks."

The two young women were smiling appreciatively, as if they were the ones receiving Virgilio's favours. Then they nodded encouragingly at John-Paul.

"Agreed," said the young man.

"Okay. Now there's the little matter of my commission," said Virgilio. "If I'm drawn into a bit of dirty capitalist business then I must behave as they do. Two hundred dollars for my services."

"Trust him," Marta said. "He's high up in the Party."

"Really high up," added Graciela, as if that put him above corruption.

John-Paul handed Virgilio two hundred in ten-dollar bills. The man counted them carefully, then extracted two of them.

"Change these. They're worn," he said.

The man received a clean twenty for them and then, pleased with the little transaction, stood up and patted John-Paul's shoulder. It was a comradely gesture, meant to seal a deal. On the landing outside the room, the young man received further encouragement from the two attractive women. They refused to say a final farewell. Since he would be passing that night in Havana, they promised to make it a memorable one. He replied that they were very kind; and that he would think about it.

CHAPTER THREE

After a lunch that deserved to be described as a banquet, everyone was happy. Although Nigeria's neighbours were pygmies by comparison, the country's air force would be expanded, infantry battalions equipped with even deadlier weapons, the tank brigades made even more invincible and the arsenal of chemical weapons augmented by the latest advances in the paralysing, burning, choking and infecting of the young warriors of any adversary. Yes, there was much for the negotiators to celebrate.

The guest of honour was Klaus Krenk and as he stood in the tropical heat on the front steps of the Ministry of Defence, his hosts indulged in an exaggerated ritual of farewell. There were boisterous compliments, proclamations of eternal friendship, painfully strong handshakes and a degree of backslapping that seemed customary to less sophisticated societies but which Krenk endured for the sake of enormous commissions. As he endured air travel, which he hated, exotic food which was poisonous, local drinks proudly offered to him, and an obligation to show respect for the leaders and customs of countries which no civilized man could take seriously.

"You will, of course, be staying for the Independence Day celebrations tomorrow," exclaimed General Oliver Cromwell Oluwole, head of the Nigerian delegation. "You must have timed your visit to coincide with the greatest day of the year."

Until that moment, Krenk had cheered himself with the thought that he would soon be putting Africa behind him, which he considered to be a mess from "top to bottom", as he put it, but the general's remark was received like a blow.

"Ah . . ." said Krenk. But he was used to recovering quickly. "Nothing would please me more but my schedule . . . Well, to be precise, I'll be leaving for Indonesia tomorrow."

Krenk's hand was taken and shaken by one many times larger and stronger than his own.

"Airport's closed for the celebration," the general replied, with lying cheerfulness. "No hope of getting away. Now you'll be able to join the President's party for the parade."

"But what do I say to the Indonesians?" the arms dealer persisted. "It happens to be their own Freedom Day and I'm one of their guests of honour."

"Independence Day comes before Freedom Day," the general half shouted in the way of someone ready to fight over the matter. "You tell that lot out there that our airport's closed. And if it's not, I'll make sure it is."

Krenk suffered the rare embarrassment of having to acknowledge defeat, in this case to an African, but at least he was released from the iron handshake. He was also free to descend the steps to the air-conditioned limousine placed at his disposal by the government, give a farewell wave to the delegation assembled above him and, at last, enjoy being alone and sinking into a soft seat. And the limousine had hardly passed the armed soldiers at the gates before the excesses of wine and food consumed over a full two hours dragged him from consciousness.

With sleep, an expression of unguarded innocence settled on a face normally engaged in a battle with a challenging world, with hostile parties and formidable opponents. Asleep or awake, however, the shape of the man was the same. At sixty-three, Klaus Krenk had moved from being physically heavy to being corpulent and was probably on his way to being grossly fat. His face, too, had passed through similar stages, the pink complexion, though natural, suggesting a constant state of anger, and his slightly misshapen features seeming to have been left unfinished by their creator. His bald head was trimmed by a crown of fluffy white hair.

With the formidable Klaus Krenk safely asleep, and only in that unconscious state, would it have been possible for a sorcerous intruder to have invaded his mind and to uncover something of the real individual. And the first discovery of that prying spirit into the man's secrets would have been the extent of his total obsession with money and power. Money was power. Money was success. Money always prevailed.

And if that intruder into his mind had persisted in trying to measure Krenk's wealth, it would have discovered that the sleeping arms dealer could comfortably have kept company with the Rockefellers, the Rothschilds, the Krupps and the Nobels at the peak of their riches and power.

The phantom invader of Krenk's secrets would than have been further astonished; the man had a notion that he might live forever. Certainly he wanted to reach two hundred. But the intruder would soon have discovered the reason for this secret obsession. Death was something to defy. That could be defied. If Krenk carried a particular grievance, it was that he was described as a merchant of death. Deals were conducted in the staid offices of ministries, in discreet bars and restaurants and in the suites of luxury hotels — what could be more remote from the actual battlefields and the carnage of war? But no matter how he tried to distance himself from the ultimate consequences of his trade or put together arguments to prove that a high level of military preparedness was more likely to deter than to lead to war, the result remained the same. Secretly, Klaus Krenk was obsessed by death.

His belief, however, that the way to conquer this obsession was to be determined to live for hundreds of years would not have been shared by the sorcerous invader in his mind. There was a simpler explanation for Krenk's desperately serious game of make-believe. There had been a number of attempts on his life. His body had escaped with little more than minor injuries and a tendency to jump at sudden noises, but the deeper wound lay in his mind. To survive, he was prepared to do anything.

The self-deception by which Krenk eliminated his enemies yet spared himself the guilt of feeling himself responsible for murder was an extension of the technique, perfected over his lifetime, of keeping his hands clean, of always needing to appear blameless. Over the years, close friendships had been established with the leaders of certain international networks of criminals and assassins. Under the code known as "no questions asked", Krenk had been a willing supplier of their needs while they, in turn, ensured that enemies were murdered or disappeared or chose to retire from the trade. But Krenk, he was happy to claim, had never made a direct request. A hint, a casual admission that a certain party was proving troublesome, was always enough.

The sorcerous intruder into the man's mind would then have made another remarkable discovery, that Krenk singly conducted an international operation that would normally have required a headquarters building and a staff of a hundred. With a small team of two bodyguards, a secretary and a phenomenal memory, though having to transport portable filing cabinets with his baggage, Krenk was convinced that not only had he discovered the secret of efficiency, he was also protected by being constantly on the move. And when his own experts needed to be assembled, lawyers, agents, scientists, bankers and accountants, they were summoned like servants. Their job done, these experts were promptly paid off and sent back to their own countries.

Such, then, was the man who was being pursued by John-Paul, who employed the young man's fiancée and who would be travelling on to Indonesia once his enforced attendance at the Independence Day celebrations was over. And, as the limousine reached the government villa for important guests, two things happened. The Hausa soldiers at the gates slapped their rifles in salute, the noise rousing Krenk from sleep and, his face again alert and forbidding, the sorcerous intruder in his mind was driven from existence.

Early that same evening, released from four days of intense negotiating, Klaus Krenk sat on a verandah extending the length of the villa and remembered the first of his Ten Commandments. Everything comes to those who want it enough. And, briefly in harmony with the world, he reflected on what he now wanted.

It was that moment in humid tropical countries when the heat became less oppressive, when the spirit could respond to the beauty of distant hills and plantations of palm trees, and when that lethargy suffered by overweight Europeans relented a little. Life, yes, had a good side to it.

"Manoel!"

One of his two bodyguards sat at the far end of the verandah.

"Sir!"

"Go and invite Grace to come and sit with me. I don't know why she keeps herself hidden away."

With the man's departure, Krenk considered an intention that had been teasing him for weeks. It was time to make a little progress towards the seduction of his attractive and desirable secretary. On an earlier visit to Japan he had been told that one of the great ironies of life was the fact that men emerged from that place to which they were forever trying to return. A very true observation, Krenk now conceded. But in his case there was never very much trying. For a man as rich and powerful as himself, the prizes were not there to be won — they were there to be taken.

"You called, Mr Krenk?"

A thick, grey-lipped smile welcomed the attractive young woman from another world, a contrasting, cooler presence in this sweatier part of Africa.

"Sit down, Grace," he said, his voice and manner different from the preoccupied and frowning employer who had kept her so busy as his secretary. "Time to relax. I'm very satisfied with you. Sit down."

The fair face and bright eyes seemed to consider the invitation for motives, as if already, in his employ for only a short term, she realized the calculated nature of everything he said or did. Then, but hesitantly, she sat down.

"Good," said Klaus Krenk. "Africa is the best place in the world. I love it. The people, the climate, everything." He beckoned to his bodyguard. "Here, Manoel. Grace, what will you drink?"

"Nothing alcoholic, if you don't mind."

"Ah, an old-fashioned girl. Manoel, bring Grace one of those long and fresh drinks of guavas and pineapple."

His quiet secretary murmured her appreciation and with a determined effort he fixed a smile on his face and prepared to be charming. And that was the worst part of all the seductions in which he had been involved, having to be charming. A man, reflected Krenk, particularly one whose life was conducted at the highest level and where everything had a meaningful importance, had suddenly to prostitute himself by becoming charming. The idea pleased him. Not women but those who needed them were the prostitutes because it was the men who paid the higher price. With their loss of self-respect, the humiliation of submission to an inescapable weakness.

And with this determination to be charming, Krenk said, "You know, Grace, a lot of people regard me as a tyrant. But you've seen how I work. I have a job to do. Supplying what the customer needs."

"Of course, sir."

"Good." But the attempt to be charming faltered. With every seduction the gap between himself and a woman narrowed. Lovers became equals. "You like your work?" Her ready reply established that she was still his secretary. "I'm pleased. I like my staff to be happy in their work."

"This is such an adventure, Mr Krenk," confessed the young woman, carefully sipping the concoction in the long glass. "It's my first time in Africa." She smiled a little nervously. "Do you travel very often to these parts?"

The need to be charming restrained Krenk from replying with the anger he would normally have shown at such an improper question. A secretary to ask about his movements! Except that, for the moment, the secretary had disappeared and a desirable, attractive female had taken her place. And Krenk recalled another of his Ten Commandments, not from any Holy Bible but from the Book of Life. Never rush things. Do it step by step. Business, politics, a seduction that would require all his practised skill — one applied the same technique.

Charmingly, he said: "As you'll discover, if we can work together, I'm travelling all the time. In the course of a year, you'll see perhaps twenty countries. Doesn't that excite you?"

"Oh, yes. Very much," she replied, and again smiling with a certain nervousness, as if life had become a succession of new and unfamiliar experiences but about which she was still wary. "Here it's all so quiet yet it seems more exciting than New York."

Krenk gave an approving nod. The girl might seem quiet and restrained but already there were hints . . . And he was reminded of a French saying: *Un petit morceau pour le gourmet.*

"I seem to recall your father telling me you were engaged to be married," he said. "Won't that mean you have other plans for the future?"

"The future is a long time, Mr Krenk. We have plans but they're not for next month or perhaps not even for next year."

A promising topic of conversation, Krenk realised, had presented itself. Life was a series of designs and tides, ebbs and flows, light and shade . . . Recognise them, follow them or retreat with them, and the advantage had been seized.

"Well, I'm sure you know what you're doing. I also remember something else your father told me — that the young man was a promising young law student. That means he can go far."

And then the confidences began to come. Create trust, thought Krenk. After all, wasn't that what charm was all about?

"I'm sure he will, Mr Krenk. The only thing that troubles me is that he's idealistic."

"Idealistic?"

"Well, in a quiet way. He's not really interested in money. And he's so easy-going." Grace had begun to relax as if the glass of guava and pineapple juice was as intoxicating as palm wine. "Except about coming away with you. He's worried about my safety."

"Your safety!" exclaimed Krenk, manufacturing a little indignation. "But with me, you couldn't be better protected." Then he decided that he could safely be a little more direct. "I take it you two live together? How very romantic. But it was different when I was young. It was all kept for marriage, if you get my meaning."

She got his meaning; and cheerfully, as if what he was inferring was a familiar subject with her friends.

"When John-Paul qualifies in law, Mr Krenk, we'll get married," Grace replied, appearing unaware of his undisguised curiosity. "In a little over a year. That'll be the right time to start a home."

It seemed, listening to her and enjoying the sight of her presence, which hardly belonged to the surroundings, that this short period together had added immensely to her desirability. And this reminded him that as well as charm, he might profitably introduce that special attraction of the wealthy seducer. To all women. A temptation they hardly ever resisted.

"Allow this elderly gentleman to pass on some of his wisdom," he confided pleasantly. "Marriage is when couples realize the value of money, Grace. Marriage without money hasn't really a chance."

"But if you love each other enough . . ."

His laugh stopped her predictable reply. The future, a rather distant future, seemed suddenly to enclose her, to descend over her thoughts, and Krenk said: "Don't look so troubled. It'll work out."

"Oh, it must, it must!" she exclaimed.

Step by step, he resolved; and listened patiently while she confided her ideas about bringing up a family, where they might live and what her father thought of John-Paul. Until, in the middle of what he considered her absurd chatter, a remarkable idea entered his head. Was it possible that Grace was still a virgin?

In his life Krenk had pursued, bought and enjoyed women in about fifty countries, enough experience to place them in a number of specific categories. But the most exciting of all, a real prize, was that most rare female of all, a lovely adult woman still a virgin. *Un morceau pour le gourmet.*

"It would seem, Grace," he said, in a lightly teasing way, "that you belong to an almost extinct species, a modern young woman who has vowed to stay a virgin until she's married."

To his surprise, she replied without embarrassment and apparently with conviction. It was all a matter of choice, wasn't it? She didn't regard herself as old-fashioned. Besides, it was something that she and John-Paul had decided together.

"And so on and so on," Krenk murmured at last.

"Oh, I think you're being sarcastic," Grace said; but laughingly.

"Well, if I am, it's with admiration." And, aware that they were staring directly at each other, and that the conversation had reached a degree of intimacy, he said: "Let me pass on a bit more of my wisdom. Everything in this world, Grace, has a price. And when a lovely young woman discovers that she has a unique value, well, she can make the most of it."

It was the most serene moment of a tropical evening, the sun slipping behind a horizon of hills and clumps of palm trees of a darker shade. On the young woman's face, however, was the first hint of an unease. Of an awareness of a possible disaster not before considered. She placed her empty glass on the table and stood up.

"I'd like to go back to my room, Mr Krenk," she said, a defiance in her tone, on her face, scarring the loveliness. "If you don't mind . . ."

"But I do mind, Grace. You can go in a moment." His patience faltered. How did one remain charming and yet the assertive master at the same time? "We were just talking, weren't we? Are you so childish you can't bear to hear one of the facts of life? Now sit down and stop taking offence. Of course I didn't mean you to take it personally."

She sat down; but watchfully. As if suddenly surrounded by threats. Could she ask a question? Certainly, agreed Krenk. Anything.

"When I started, we didn't discuss what would happen if I gave up the job. How I would get home, for instance?"

To one side of the house, the noise of a car approached along the drive. Sensible girl, thought Krenk. Now you're learning.

"There are no quick resignations or escapes in the arms business," he replied, not charm but menace in his expression. "We are all playing for high stakes. It's the same for me as for you. Our obligations are to governments, not companies. Wherever we go, if the authorities decide, we can be seized and held on a number of pretexts. Oh no, you can't fool around with a country's military, at least not the countries we visit." Then, more directly, he posed a question: "Why, do you want to leave?"

For the second time in a few minutes, he had confused Grace. Her continued silence seemed an opportunity to set out her situation, her vulnerability. And to speed the flow of the tide.

"I have a great responsibility to my clients, Grace, and I must take precautions against being let down or betrayed." He hesitated before explaining further but instinct told him that it was time for a threat. And to create fear. "Consider your position. Your passport is in my possession and will remain so until we agree that your job is over. Remitting your salary to your New York bank is in my hands, so you have no money, and the countries we visit and the authorities of those countries are my partners. The yelps and protests of a meaningless young woman would be of no more importance than a bar girl marched into the local police station."

Courage seemed to return to the subdued Grace. And speech. She said: "What you've said virtually turns me into a prisoner. Well, that may be, Mr Krenk. But I'd rather be a prisoner in a cell, able to keep to my principles, than be free to have them betrayed."

Sounds within the house suggested the approach not of an individual but of a whole party. But Krenk still had time to say what was in his mind.

Quietly, amiably, reassuringly, he said: "Grace, you can make a lot of money for yourself."

The voice of Manoel, the bodyguard, intruded from the inner step.

"Mr Krenk, General Oluwole's arrived . . ."

The massive Manoel was pushed aside by a figure in uniform of similar stature. Greetings and deep laughs came not only from the general but from three others in uniform. Krenk welcomed them with equal noisiness, indicated to Grace that she should leave, and told his bodyguard to call the servant to bring the drinks trolley. The lines between work and play, between business and pleasure, once one was dealing with Africans, were never very clear, thought Krenk. A quietly pleasant interlude with a naive young woman was ending, a robust meeting with a noisy bunch of killers was about to begin; and so his life as a merchant statesman continued.

"Now, gentlemen, what have we forgotten!" exclaimed Klaus Krenk, instantly adapting to their bonhomie. "Or is this a social call? In which case we have a lot to celebrate."

"Always something to celebrate," agreed General Oluwole, heartily.

It was not difficult for the peregrinating John-Paul to get the information he wanted. He had arrived in a part of the world where the bribe, the tip, the dash and a bit of backsheesh were as much a side of society as self-interest and being cheerful. They were necessary and they were not disputed. In quick succession he was swindled by an airport porter, a taxi driver, policemen at road check points demanding tolls and, finally, by the proprietor of the hotel. But his entry into the life of Lagos also brought the benediction of becoming the target of a barefooted elderly man in a ragged khaki shirt and shorts who declared that John-Paul would need the services of a 'boy' and that he, Gabriel, was ready to work 'all the hours God gave him'.

The elderly 'boy' soon proved that he was indispensable to John-Paul, protecting him from beggars, crooks, touts, guides and the police, as he went on his first reconnaissance of the unfamiliar city. Whether in his native Yoruba language or in English, this faithful servant proved capable of arguing his way into or out of whatever the situation demanded. Soon, John-Paul had decided that Gabriel was someone to be trusted, even if dollar bills seemed to pass regularly from one hand to the other.

It happened on the second day of their association that he decided to confide his purpose to this eager and faithful African.

"Gabriel," confessed John-Paul, "I'm not here as a tourist or on business. I'm here to kill the man who has carried off my fiancée."

To the young man's relief, his servant seemed delighted at the disclosure, and whether it was at the prospect of an even greater flow of dollars or of rectifying an awful crime, it was obvious that he already had Gabriel's loyal support.

"Our first move," said John-Paul, when he had explained his purpose, "is to locate the monster Krenk. His presence here might have been given publicity in the papers, there might even have been an official welcome for him . . ."

"Leave it to me, Mister," interrupted Gabriel, giving John-Paul the title he had used since their first introduction. "But I may have to give a few dollars here and there."

"Of course," agreed John-Paul, parting with another hundred dollars. "I'll stay in the hotel until you get back."

It was the second day of John-Paul's visit to Lagos and a little after midday when the good servant returned with the news that the important Mister Crank was staying at the principal government guest house. They set out at once to make a preliminary reconnaissance, John-Paul carrying his briefcase not because he expected to use the concealed weapon but because even that trusting young man accepted that possessions left in the hotel rooms of Lagos risked swift disappearance.

Across the road from the hotel, an arcade led to a large square surrounded by modern buildings, the dividends of the sudden oil wealth of the country. The square was crowded with cheerful African faces and an unusually large number of police and soldiers.

Gabriel was quick with the explanation: "It's a public shooting."

"Ah, filming," observed John-Paul, with interest.

"No, a man's being shot."

"Being? You mean someone's been murdered? How awful."

"No, it's a murderer being shot. In public. An eye for an eye. Why don't we watch it?"

John-Paul tugged at the ragged khaki sleeve and ordered his "boy" to make a detour of the square. They were not quite out of earshot when the firing squad completed its task. A great cheer rose above the square.

"You feel sorry for murderers, Mister?" asked Gabriel.

After ten minutes of walking, they reached a more open area. John-Paul, in the interests of prudence, had decided against travelling by taxi but the hot and humid air had saturated his clothing. A little further on, needing a cold drink, he indicated that they should rest at a roadside café. Under a canopy of palm leaves, four tables were set out on the verandah and Gabriel, already familiar with his master's requirements, shouted out the order to the empty doorway. A few moments later, a large woman wrapped in colourful cottons emerged with a tray of the local Bomba Cola.

John-Paul had just quenched his thirst when a noisy caval-cade came down the road. It was led by two police outriders sounding their sirens.

"Someone important," observed Gabriel. "Maybe the President."

Following the motor cyclists was a black limousine flying a miniature state flag. It was not carrying the country's president but a white-haired European. The man sat behind the chauffeur, his head high in the manner of the self-important, while, at his side, was the partly obscured profile of a young woman. Obscured or not, however, her identity was familiar to John-Paul.

"It's my girl!" he cried, knocking the table and sending the empty Bomba Cola bottles on to the cement floor. "It's Grace!"

But the limousine had already travelled too far for the occupants to be aware of John-Paul's maniacal reaction; and the first corner was only a little way down the road. The vehicle's disappearance, however, far from making him wonder whether it had all been an illusion, brought back the sense of urgency. Every day that separated Grace from himself widened the distance between them.

"Come on," he shouted at his boy. "That white-haired man was Krenk. At least we know he's out of the way."

"Today is Independence Day. Maybe Mister Crank celebrates with the President," said Gabriel. "Celebrates our freedom."

A free society or not, the government villa still needed the protection of a high wall of concrete blocks capped by sharp iron spikes. Its menacing presence contrasted with the lush vegetation of a hot and wet climate and amiable round-faced Africans walking along the road. At the main entrance, the grim aspect of the place was further manifested by tough Hausa guards.

"Those guys from the North," Gabriel observed. "They real killers."

John-Paul and his boy proceeded to walk along the two hundred metres of the front perimeter, then along the shorter side. There was an unguarded rear entrance but the iron gate was high and secured by a chain as well as locks. In the centre of a cultivated garden was the villa or guest house, a single-storey building surrounded by a verandah and with an extended wing of what was clearly the servants' quarters.

"No problem," said Gabriel, when the reconnaissance had been completed. "I got it all in my head. Now, how would you like to kill Mister Crank?"

The method of assassinating the man had preoccupied

John-Paul for some time. He had eliminated all the complex and unconventional ways and concluded that a bullet in the brain was not only the easiest but also the method likely to be most effective. Not even Krenk's skull could be bullet-proof. It was therefore possible to reply immediately and in detail to Gabriel's question.

"It's got to be done at night, Gabriel, if I need to escape. And of course I want to get back to Grace when it's all over, otherwise what's the point of all that I'm doing?"

"No point," agreed Gabriel. "The dead can't talk — except a tribe up-country where their spirits go and live in the trees and after a hundred years turn into vultures. Maybe this Mister Crank is a Boro-boro?"

"I doubt it," said John-Paul, indulgently. "You see, in a country of black faces, mine stands out like a lantern in the dark. I'd be picked up before I could fly out. So it has to be done at night." He paused to consider the troubling thought that Krenk might not be sleeping alone. And with whom he would be sleeping. Or making love to? The awful picture was suppressed. "You've got to help me to creep to his bedside when he's fast asleep. It'll take me a moment to fire into his ugly head, then I'm through the window and away. Does that sound possible?"

"With money, everything's possible. If you had millions you might even persuade the President to do the job for you."

"Well, Gabriel, I haven't got millions."

"Maybe, with millions of millions, you could become the President of the whole country, Mister. You make everybody rich, and they all agree you President."

They returned to the halfway house of the café that served cold drinks. It seemed the best place, with the fortress up the road just in sight, to make their plans. Or, rather, to listen to Gabriel's more practical suggestions.

"You need an informer," announced the elderly boy, his bloodshot eyes staring cunningly along the road. "You know what I mean?"

"You mean to inform on me?" John-Paul asked naively. "What's the point of that?"

"No, our informer will work in the guest house," Gabriel explained patiently, a couple of flies settling on his greying

African hair. "He tell us when Mister Crank is there, when he's gone to sleep, how to creep in. Maybe, for enough money, he meet us and lead us in."

John-Paul considered the optimistic scenario being laid before him.

"This isn't the time for fantasies, Gabriel," he said severely. "I just don't believe you can go up to complete strangers and ask them to risk their jobs or even their lives for a bit of money."

"You don't know how it is, Mister."

And Gabriel proceeded to explain how it was. His brief speech amounted to an education on the ways of local society, the reality of temptation, the power of money and the corruptibility of everyone up to the President himself. The only person in the whole of Nigeria who was apparently honest and moral, according to Gabriel, was John-Paul's faithful servant.

"How much you want to spend?" he now asked, the nearest he could decently come to discovering the actual wealth of his master.

"You seem to think I'm made of money," said John-Paul, suspecting that even his honest boy could descend to deceiving him. On the other hand, this wasn't a moment to think of money. "Just tell me how much it's going to cost. If I've got it, it's worth it."

More education followed. The art of corruption was to know how far to go, how much to offer, to set limits beforehand, to win an unavoidable battle of wills. When Gabriel had at last extracted a figure, nearly all of John-Paul's money, the young man calculated that he had left himself with just enough to cover his flight out of the country.

"What you carrying in that bag, Mister?" asked Gabriel, who might have been considering that it contained all his master's wealth. "You're holding it as if it's valuable. That's bad."

"One of the pistols," whispered John-Paul. "One of the two I brought with me."

"If we're searched at one of the check points, what then? If a bad guy runs off with it, what then?" Gabriel asked remorselessly. He picked up the briefcase and withdrew a pear-shaped object wrapped in thick brown paper. "I take care of this, Mister."

He returned the weapon to the bag and carried it into the café, really no more than a long wooden hut. When he returned, he asked John-Paul for ten dollars.

"I've told her we'll be back for the parcel in the next two or three days. She's open day and night."

They continued their walk into town. On the edge of the central district, they were suddenly submerged in a crowd apparently retreating from a threat. Gabriel was quick to question one of the less frantic of those pushing past. A large woman in bright cottons, panting from the exertion, explained that there had been a protest demonstration against the rise in food prices. As she ran off, the crowd behind her was being broken up by police swinging long truncheons. Screams and shouts from individual protesters, rather than the sound of a mass commotion, accompanied the rise and fall of the truncheons. Suddenly, John-Paul and his servant, their reluctance to join the others in flight interpreted as resistance to the authorities, were surrounded by uniforms and knocked to the ground.

The disappearing crowd was followed by a line of police vehicles collecting those who had been arrested or were being detained as troublemakers. Despite Gabriel's loud protests in Yoruba, John-Paul and his servant, encouraged by whacks across their backs, were forced on to one of the trucks. When it was full, which only took moments, it was driven off to one of the local prisons. Clinging to the heavy wire of the roof, John-Paul felt there would be no difficulty in explaining that a visitor could hardly have been protesting over the cost of food.

In New York the representative of the other thirty-nine individuals on the truck had just begun his own protest speech to the General Assembly of COM. It was against the inequalities of this world, the expenditure of so much money on armaments when hundreds of millions were starving, the use of excessive violence by the state against civilian populations and the failure of member states to live up to the ideals of the human rights charter. When the representative, a retired general, sat down, he was loudly applauded.

In fact, John-Paul had the greatest difficulty in explaining his
complete innocence because there was no one to listen to him.
At least, no one with authority. On descending from the
truck, he had found himself with hundreds of others in a large
compound, more like a military parade ground than an area of
a civil prison. As the only white face, he provoked amusement
and questions and the joking reassurance that he need no
longer protest about the price of food because it would now
cost nothing. But so long as he was with the cunning Gabriel,
he reflected, he must surely regain his freedom. And sooner
rather than later.

His optimism, however, was misplaced. Towards nightfall
the guards began dividing into groups the hundreds under
arrest, sending them off in truckloads to different and scattered
prisons. His separation from Gabriel brought a first sense of
alarm. Without his boy's reassuring presence, his only friend
and protector in a country where one needed both, he was at
the mercy of brutes and lunatics. Why, he reasoned, he might
even have to face the kind of treatment he had suffered in
Colombia. Torturers, after all, were everywhere.

Half an hour after being driven away from the open parade
ground, he found himself in the skyless enclosure of a prison
cell. Again, memories of his earlier experience returned to
distress him. And this time, for company, instead of the frail
Anselmo, there were six young or youngish Nigerians, tough
and angry men who immediately cursed the authorities,
shouted obscenities at the guards, shook the iron bars and
eventually, though not less bitter, sat or squatted on the mud
floor. As it was a cell without furniture, and only a bucket to
serve nature, John-Paul, too, had to settle himself on the floor.

In this uncomfortable posture, the young man considered
his predicament. He remembered Gabriel's words about the
infinite uses of money, that bribes opened doors, gained
favours, brought protection and even converts to a cause.
Everything. But how did an innocent like himself begin?
Besides, in the company of all these cellmates, there were too
many witnesses. The realization that he would not and could

not emulate Gabriel's skills completed his sense of helplessness.

Outside the cell, dim light bulbs provided a slight glow in
the corridor, the interior courtyard being even gloomier. After
three hours of relative darkness, bowls of a brown-coloured
pap were passed into the cell. His own helping was snatched
away before it had reached his hands. The hostility did not
surprise him. Attempts to converse in English had been met
with sullen stares and mutterings in Yoruba which sounded
unfriendly. With the meal over, his cell companions, after brief
visits to the bucket, seemed to settle down for the night. Only
when most of them were apparently asleep did John-Paul
overcome his embarrassment and stand over the bucket himself.

What the despairing young man did not know, however,
was that he had not been forgotten by Gabriel. The ageing
African in the alien world of progress, Westernization and
modern corruption, had managed to survive by the simple
philosophy of facing each day as it came, of being without
opinions or principles and, being neither cruel nor a bully, had
never made enemies or been downhearted by adversity. From
cultivating his village plot of land, he had seen the world as a
seaman, then come ashore to become a hotel boy, a cook boy,
a laundry boy and a messenger boy. In this last employ, he had
worked for an international news agency, the leading French
one, and had loyally served the director, Mister Dupont, until
modern technology had halved the size of the staff.

In a wing of the prison far from where John-Paul had been
shut away, Gabriel was not similarly inhibited by the presence
of witnesses from bribing one of the guards. The message to
Mister Dupont that accompanied the ten-dollar bill that was
handed to the guard was brief but clear. It stated, simply, that a
representative of the Community of Mankind had happened to
be walking down Victory Way when the food riots were
taking place and had been arrested and was now in Shutaway
Prison. The guard would receive another ten dollars on proof
of delivery.

But for John-Paul, the hours of the night passed without
knowledge of Gabriel's initiative. From time to time, with the
sleeping bodies pressing against each other, a hand would

grope between his legs or even try to pull down his trousers but, miraculously, darkness turned to a pink dawn and the pink dawn to daylight. With waking, came a degree of resolution. He managed to converse with the single friendly individual among his cellmates.

"When are we going on trial?"

"Trial!" exclaimed the young African, his name to John-Paul's ears sounding something like Obobobo. "No trial. We here for one week then they let us out."

"You mean without a trial? We're not charged? And we live like this, like animals in a shed!" exclaimed the disbelieving John-Paul. "But we have rights! They can't do this to us — leave us to rot."

Obobobo shrugged at what he clearly thought to be a protest close to madness.

"We won't rot," he said, with a smile almost of kindness. "It takes longer than a week to rot."

"But what sort of a system have you got!" cried the young foreigner.

"Good system. This way is quick and cheap for the government. No lawyers, no courts, no trials. If it's cheap for the government, it's cheap for the people."

The second day passed. It was longer than the first. It seemed the length of three or four. The major events were the emptying of the bucket, an escorted visit to a wash room, a bowl of food that contained vague evidence of vegetables and grains of maize, and a fist fight between two of the Nigerians in the cell. A second night of sleeping on the mud floor had turned John-Paul's limbs from willing parts of his body to being protesting appendages that inflicted pain with every movement, and his mind was stunned by the single thought that he would have to endure this for a whole week.

★ ★ ★ ★ ★

But he was not to endure it for a whole week. Within hours of Mister Dupont's agency flashing the news round the world, the information was passed on to Signora Modeste. The COM official who was in a Nigerian prison had not been named but since she had quickly learnt of the movements of Klaus Krenk, it was not difficult for her to reach the correct conclusion. Her immediate response was to take advantage of the fact that she was on friendly terms with the country's president. That superficially genial but murderous tyrant had been trying to manipulate COM for the last couple of years to agree to a major aid programme, for which he was still hoping.

There was a good communications system between New York and Lagos, one of the few discernible benefits of the recent oil bonanza, and Signora Modeste was soon speaking directly to the president. His first question was to ask whether she was ringing with good news. She replied that she was doing her best and then enquired whether he knew of the arrest of a COM passport holder. She explained further, adding that the young man was interested in the new swamp drainage scheme near Port Harcourt, which was his only reason for visiting the country. The president assured her that wrongful arrests never occurred in his country, and that there must have been a mistake. Signora Modeste did not believe a word of what the president said and the president did not believe a word of the signora's but he promised that if the unimaginable had actually happened, the young man would be released within the hour.

It was on the third day of John-Paul's detention, after a night in which he had successfully fought off the attempts of two of his cellmates to rip off his trousers, that a small army of officials arrived outside the iron bars of the door. As he was the only foreigner, it was unnecessary to identify him.

"Mister," called out a high-ranking military officer. "Come out of there."

From the apprehensive expressions of his six companions, they were clearly thinking that he was about to be shot. Perhaps to be followed by themselves. But the officer displayed no threat. Instead, he stretched out a hand to be shaken.

As he and John-Paul led the small army past the other cells

and into the administrative part of the prison, it was explained that there had been a dreadful mistake, and so upset was the president of the country that he had asked to apologize personally. This remarkable change in John-Paul's fortunes was followed by a short drive in a large limousine, the aide-de-camp explaining that it was fortunate that the president was staying in his Lagos palace rather than in the new capital upcountry.

John-Paul's bewilderment had been brief. He was not worldly-wise or quick-thinking but he had soon and correctly guessed that a very influential party must have gained his release. One did not receive a presidential apology unless it was to someone's advantage to make it. By the time the limousine was passing through the heavily guarded gateway of the palace he had therefore concluded that his connection with COM, by one fortuity or another, was the obvious explanation. His mood, which had passed in half an hour from despair to disbelief, was now close to elation. The next step would be his release.

"What's your name?" asked the aide-de-camp, before they entered the presidential offices.

John-Paul told him. It was passed on to a secretary in the outer office then spelled out over an internal telephone. When the young man was presented to the president, the impressive figure in a military uniform was able to greet him with:

"Ah, Mister Bob Homo, make yourself comfortable." The president was tall enough to reach over the very large desk and shake John-Paul's hand. "Bad mistake that, I tell you, man. But these things happen. Even in Switzerland."

All that John-Paul desired was his freedom, to get out of the palace and back to his hotel, but clearly he had to adhere to what he imagined to be the protocol of a COM representative. As he sat in a large chair with arms ornately carved by local craftsmen, it seemed obligatory to project the appropriate indignation for someone of his own assumed status.

"Mr President," he said firmly, "I spent three days in a prison that wasn't fit for animals. We slept on the floor, we were not allowed to speak to the authorities let alone consult an outside legal adviser, and we were half starved. And I understand that this category of prisoner, those who are rounded up and spend a week in prison as a lesson, is not even charged with an offence. Think how many international treaties this violates."

The president was a large middle-aged man who had received his officer's training in England. The left side of his uniform was decorated with enough medals to indicate that he had served heroically in every British war from the time of the Crimean campaign. His affected bonhomie clouded at the insolent protest but he managed to suppress his anger.

"Well, I am learning something from this," he said, managing to speak patiently. "The people only placed their trust in me five years ago, after the army were forced to rescue the country from the politicians, so there's still a bit of clearing up to do. However, Mr Homo, please accept my apologies."

"Thank you, Mr President," John-Paul replied. Then he remembered that Gabriel must have been in another part of the prison. Perhaps, in the circumstances, he could ask a favour. "I had a Nigerian with me; he called himself my boy. Could I ask for his release, too?"

At the young man's more respectful tone, the country's leader relaxed in a seat almost the size of a sovereign's throne. He smiled with pleasure, delight at the recognition of his power.

"I am what you call a benign dictator. It's the only system for African countries," said the military leader. On the wall behind him was a framed picture of a pride of lions. "Everything I do is for the benefit of my people. If I have to give my children a little tap . . ." A large, brown hand went through the motions of spanking a child's bottom. "So you want me to release your boy?"

John-Paul had now adapted himself to this unusual situation. If the country's despotic leader was trying to please him, a small favour like this was surely not too much to ask.

"It upsets me, Mr President, to think he's now in prison because he happened to be keeping me company."

"To me the British qualities of fair play and cricket are everything," said the president. "I will now show you what it means to be a dictator who loves his people. All those arrested with you will be released. To the last man jack." He rang a bell concealed under the desk. The female secretary entered and the president said something in the Yoruba language that was clearly a command. "There were six hundred arrested for demonstrating unlawfully," he said, when the woman had gone. "In half an hour, they'll all be released. Doesn't that show love for my people?"

John-Paul agreed that it did. He was now convinced that he was sitting with a madman. Anyone exercising so much power had to be. He recalled that in a neighbouring country, one of the poorest in Africa, its leader had constructed a church to rival Saint Peter's in Rome. In another, a self-appointed emperor had built a bedstead of pure gold, while in a third border country an all-powerful military president of a starving population had the latest *haute couture* gowns flown in weekly from Paris for his twenty wives.

"Well, sir," said John-Paul, deciding that protocol had been fulfilled and that he was free to leave, "I greatly appreciate what you've done . . ."

As he stood up to shake hands across the desk, he was told very firmly to sit down.

"Do you know what I keep in this drawer?" asked the president, reaching to one side of the desk.

"No, sir."

"Diamonds. We have one of the biggest mines in the world and the British company shows its appreciation of my good government by sending me a packet every month." The presidential hand went into the drawer, there was a sound similar to poking into gravel, and a dull stone the size of a cherry was passed to John-Paul. "Take it," said the ruler of the six hundred food protesters. "It's worth a hundred thousand American dollars."

But the generous gesture posed a moral dilemma for the young man. To accept it seemed like taking a bribe, obviously for his goodwill, but to refuse it would give offence, perhaps even a quick cancellation of the presidential amnesty of those in prison. Such were the ways of powerful rulers.

"Thank you, Mr President," said John-Paul, slipping the stone among the coins in his trouser pocket. "It's very generous of you." Again he was prevented from leaving by a commanding gesture. "Is there something else?"

"There is. I understand from the administration of COM

that you are making a private study of our drainage scheme near Port Harcourt," said the president. "It's a priority project and that means that to help your investigations is also a priority. I have made all arrangements for you to spend a couple of days at the scheme."

And so, early that evening, John-Paul was collected from his hotel by a young woman in a uniform similar to an airline stewardess and who was the driver of a large government car. Resigned to the diversion from planning the death of Klaus Krenk, he was driven the four hundred miles to Port Harcourt and there given a luxurious suite in a new government guest house. The attractive, light-skinned young woman was put in the neighbouring room. Before retiring for the night, she informed John-Paul that her orders were to provide him with everything he needed. He looked into the warm eyes of the soft-faced seductress and hesitated. She repeated the word: Everything. But temptation was conquered. He thanked her and closed his door quickly.

His knowledge of swamp drainage was insignificant but since the local experts were intent on impressing the visitor with their achievements, there was little need for John-Paul to offer comments. After two days, the friendly driver returned him to his hotel in Lagos, patted his cheek before departing, as if he defeated her understanding, and he was able to resume his purpose. But not, he soon discovered, immediately. Earlier that day Klaus Krenk and his party had taken the flight to Indonesia.

CHAPTER FOUR

As John-Paul was considering what his next step should be, his mother in New York was deciding on her own first step. The two weeks since her son's departure had been a period of increasing anxiety and guilt. The years as deputy-director of COM had been so totally dedicated to her high office that it seemed they had eroded a mother's care and concern for her child. But now the priorities of life were changing. How could she have been a passive, perhaps active, party to a possible murder by her son? How could she lightly have betrayed her position in COM?

A bacillus had entered existence and was spreading to every area of her life. Her conscience was troubled not only by what she had done but what was now required. There were many courses open to her, starting with the most obvious one of resigning from COM to having her son traced and arrested, so far on the relatively minor charge of possessing a false passport. But her confusion affected her powers of decision. Finally, in despair, she decided to confess everything to the Director himself and leave the question of resignation in his hands.

Count Konrad von Baum was an erect and severe Austrian whose tallness added to the impression of high principles and correctness of demeanour. But Signora Modeste had discovered the slightly haughty gentleman to have those qualities of flexibility and cunning that had enabled the dethroned aristocracies of old Europe to flourish in a brutally egalitarian society. She had also reflected on the incongruity that an international organization so opposed to privilege and caste should have chosen a nobleman as its head.

Incongruity or not, once he had heard her story, the count was soon proving his suitability for the post. And that, at the age of seventy, he was at the peak of his powers.

"Don't distress yourself, Carla. There's a solution to every-thing. But first you must drop this word morality," said her director. "Never did any good."

"But I can't, Konrad," confessed Signora Modeste. "I have a conscience. For me, the Community of Mankind represents the pinnacle of international morality. We must set an exam-ple."

"The example is set by what the world hears and sees. What's out of sight remains out of sight and has not happened. Have you told anyone a word of this?" the count demanded.

"Not a soul."

"Then, unless the boy is caught or exposed, what's there to worry about? If you are considering the importance of COM's reputation in the world, what could be worse than having it splashed across the newspapers that my deputy is so foolish, incompetent and immoral?"

In the director's private office, Signora Modeste relaxed a little. Not that her offences were any less serious but from the fact that her confession had provoked neither condemnation nor fury.

"Here I am, head of COM," went on the count, "but if I were to tell you of all the follies I've committed, you would immediately wonder how I came to be here." His cold, light eyes stared at his deputy with some amusement. Then they began to display warmth and mischief. "Since it is now obviously safe for me to share confidences with you, I can tell you a story or two about myself, Carla. When I entered international service, for example, I did so on completely bogus credentials. I was a scaffolder in a small village near Salzburg. When I was hardly more than sixteen, we were repairing the roof of the church when I slipped and fell twelve metres. I had injuries to the head and when I recovered I went off to Vienna determined never to go back to such dangerous work and to begin a new life."

Signora Modeste was seldom astonished but in this instance she was sincere when she said: "You, Konrad? You? But to me you're an aristocrat to your fingertips!"

"A year later, I was, my dear Carla," confided the count. "In this idiot world of ours, where everyone claims to want equality, people like nothing better than to meet those they consider superior, to rub shoulders with the famous. In Vienna, soon after I arrived there, I was sitting one clear night by the Danube, thinking how I could improve my miserable state. When I stood up and walked away from that moonlit river, I was Count Konrad von Baum, son of Count Heinrich von Baum who had lost all his estates in what is now Slovenia and part of Yugoslavia."

"But you couldn't have got away with it?" gasped Signora Modeste.

"Why not?" asked the count. He seemed genuinely surprised at her doubt. "I used my haughty manner and my imposing height and appearance to the full. When I went for interviews before committees for work in the civil service or on the international circuit of jobs, there was always someone who'd say: 'In your case, Count, you needn't trouble about the references. It's an honour to have you with us.'"

"But I remember when you were appointed by COM, Konrad, you had a most distinguished record. You were sent by the Red Cross to help victims of the war in Ethiopia, by Famine Aid to get food to the starving in the Sudan . . ."

"All of which I did well," von Baum reminded her proudly.

"Wonderfully," agreed his deputy.

"You see, my posts have always been those requiring courage and decisiveness, Carla. They have nothing to do with university degrees or being a clever-clever talker. I developed in the posts I took as a plant set in the right soil. You either grow and flourish or you wilt and wither. But — and I give you this advice . . ." His voice fell to a whisper. "A person must never, never indicate by a word or a doubt that the job is beyond their ability, that they're not absolutely the best qualified for it. And now . . ." A single pause made him more businesslike. "To this mess you're in."

Once again, Signora Modeste was in the presence of her superior, a director distinguished by his logic and objectivity.

"As I've already suggested. No, ordered. You keep quiet."

"This is one occasion, Konrad, when I can't accept your advice. It's squalid."

"And you mean it's less squalid if it's made public?"

Logic, decided Signora Modeste, was not always the answer. If one was fortunate to have a nature that was never troubled by guilt, that simply considered the facts, well, she could have agreed with her superior. But not on this occasion. Not with her own nature.

She said, firmly: "I can't live any longer with the guilt. It's my conscience, not yours, Konrad."

"Indisputably," replied the director coldly. "Because I haven't got one. How would COM be if I had one? We'd never settle a thing." And he stared very severely at his deputy. "Carla, I won't tolerate this loss of nerve. Your own modest misdemeanour, compared with what we ignore every day in our work, is totally insignificant. If we can ignore the behaviour of tyrant rulers, killings and torture by their security forces, and all the other crimes, all in the name of keeping their countries together in the same organization, then we can forget the matter of a trifling COM passport."

The comfortable, motherly figure, greying hair parted in the middle and drawn back, a middle-aged *mamma* from the piazzas and the food markets of Palermo, Naples and Bari, remained troubled.

"I'll feel a cheat for the rest of my life."

"A cheat!" exclaimed the astonished director. "But we're all cheats. Every time we try to create good impressions rather than bad, every time we choose words to win an issue, an argument or a debate, we're cheating. Anything less than total honesty and frankness is cheating." He nodded, as if finding exactly what he wanted to say. "If we cheat for a good reason, if we're not doing it for personal gain, if we're doing it for love of a son, as you've done, it's a desirable form of cheating. God, we don't want a world so rigid that everyone is behaving with total honesty, speaking without ambiguities of any kind, smiling only when they feel like smiling. Come on, Carla, let's be sensible."

And the Director went on to explain the practical consequences of what might happen if everyone was stricken by morality. Did she want to start a war of moralities? Okay, there were issues that brought nations into conflict, ideologies, trade, borders, racial minorities — they were probably unavoidable. But moralities . . .

"And so I say," pronounced Count von Baum, "that your duty to all of us is to keep this affair secret." He relaxed a little, as though a minor problem had now been set aside. "To business. Let us see how we can get the boy back."

He proceeded to cover all the alternatives until he reached what he described as the obvious solution. To undertake a mission to kill the arms dealer, John-Paul must be regarded as mad. Like people everywhere, even employees of COM could suffer nervous breakdowns. COM would proceed with checking the movements of Klaus Krenk. They could then be sure that John-Paul would not be far behind. With his international influence, concluded the Director, he was sure that the authorities of any member state would cooperate in the discreet repatriation of an unfortunate employee.

"My poor boy," Signora Modeste murmured to herself.

Meanwhile, in Jakarta, that sprawling capital of ten thousand islands and a country of nearly two hundred million citizens, Klaus Krenk, like a door-to-door salesman, was continuing with his country-to-country mission of selling as much military equipment as was profitably possible in the cause of world peace and the upholding of law and order. Indonesia was a good customer. Two minor civil wars had been continuing for years in a couple of the remoter islands, the leader of the country, an army general, loved military parades and had ambitions to be the dominant power in the region, and there was always the danger that half the population, being poor and oppressed, might take to the streets. Which would demand an even stronger army.

Just as Africa was the least favoured continent in Krenk's itinerary, because of its backwardness, that area of Asia called the Far East was his most favoured for those virtues which he placed above all others, intelligence, hard work, orderliness and being honest about the absolute priority of self-interest. There was also a less rational reason for his liking of the Far East. Whether he was in Bangkok or Jakarta or Taipeh, a romantic side to his nature seemed to demand a little of the honey of life. Money and ambition, briefly, came second.

Once in those cities, and when he was satisfied that his business programme was on course, Klaus Krenk would spend the evening or part of the night with two of the most beautiful women available. Sometimes they were the most expensive prostitutes in town, at other times women he had met on a previous visit and whose names were worth recording in his address book; but always two in number. A big, heavy man himself, it seemed to need two of these small and neat oriental females to make him feel that the bed was complete.

But not on this visit to Jakarta. Once he had freed himself from the duties of the day, not the local beauties but his secretary, Grace, obsessed him. How could he persuade, manoeuvre or even threaten her, to become his mistress? So far, he now argued with himself, he had been too preoccupied, which he accepted as an excuse, and too considerate, which was an unforgivable weakness. Obsession or not, however, his next attempt to overcome the resistance of the chaste young woman would have to wait for that evening. The second day of any negotiations was always the crucial one, the time when both sides got down to details.

And so, on his second morning in Jakarta, with Grace sitting next to him and his concentration on his affairs rather than on her early seduction, Krenk faced three Indonesian negotiators across the large ministry table. Behind them were impressive portraits of previous national leaders and victorious generals, among whom General Sadikin, head of the negotiating party, would one day feature. His colleagues at the table were called Murdani and Sukarno.

"You will see from the list before you, Mr Krenk, that most of our requirements are for civil unrest," General Sadikin observed, soon after the meeting had begun. "The information that you are the sole agent for a new tear gas that also paralyzes the legs for an hour is a major advance in the battle for law and order."

Krenk agreed that it was. An open file of papers was in front of him and he tapped it as if confirming his claims.

"It also prevents speech," he added with some pride. "And that means no shouts and screams as they are rounded up."

"And therefore no trying to disaffect our soldiers," said Sukarno, removing a military-style Muslim headdress. "No contamination of new ideas."

"New ideas contradict the old," added Murdani. "And then you are offering us an invention that can direct a high-pitched sound at an individual hiding in a building and burst his ear drums. I like that."

Krenk, encouraged, read out the details of this remarkable invention. The great advantage of his reputation was that when manufacturers produced weapons that would be condemned by international treaties or world opinion, they turned to him to market them secretly. The peoples of the world may not approve of them, but the security forces loved them.

"Such advances, of course, have been made at great expense to the manufacturers . . ." went on Krenk.

"R and D — research and development," murmured Sadikin, as if he had just learnt the term in English and rather liked repeating it.

"Which, gentlemen," Krenk continued, "means that they have to be expensive."

"The cost can't be as great as what we spend on eliminating robbers and murderers, communists, atheists and adulterers," said the heavily menacing Murdani.

Krenk's secretary, Grace, sat to the left of her employer. She was taking notes, as she had been instructed, and was operating a small recording machine for which approval had been given. Sitting with the severe and ageing men, she seemed of another species, a creature of beauty and sweetness and radiance. But she might have been invisible. For the negotiators to have acknowledged her presence, even by a smile, would have violated both protocol and the lowly place of women in such company and on such an occasion.

"In our country," declared Sadikin, "we have discovered the perfect system for protecting the good of the people and, of course, the power of the government. Let me explain."

He did, and at length, and although Krenk had heard it all before, he listened with false attentiveness while the twin safeguards to a superior society were explained to him. First, there was religion. Islam demanded and gained obedience to its laws and exalted the spirit of its believers. But, needing to cover the later development of a modern society, with its disrespect for the traditional, a complementary ideology of new principles had been imposed on the people.

"And so, Mr Krenk," went on the distinguished General Sadikin, "between the laws of the mullahs and the more earth-bound ones of our state ideology, we have succeeded in keeping our people contented and law-abiding." He glanced at the file in front of him. "Which brings me back to the battle against lawbreakers. Murdani . . ."

His colleague responded instantly to his superior's command.

He said: "Our intelligence in the United States has picked up information about a new drug that is being delivered to their government. It is put in the water and acts like a tranquillizer . . ."

"Research and development . . ." murmured Sadikin, with admiration.

"It prevents violence at the source of it — in human behaviour. The Americans would never use it against their own people, of course, except perhaps in the water supplies of prisons or lunatic asylums but . . ."

"I know of it," said Krenk, to the surprise and delight of those at the other side of the table. "But it doesn't act immediately. It requires a full month of drinking a normal daily intake of water, in tea, coffee, soda . . . It's all the same. There is, however, one danger."

"What's that?" asked the quiet Sukarno.

"After a year, it can prove fatal. Perhaps in one case in ten," said Krenk.

"Even better," exclaimed Sadikin. "If its existence remains a secret, who will know a year later that we were responsible?"

"And we will have eliminated a tenth of our enemies," added Murdani. "Great. It's just what we need."

"But how do we get it?" asked Murdani.

"You pay for it, gentlemen," Krenk said, with a benign smile. "It's the same with everything in this world. It has its price." He turned towards Grace, with the same smile, and for the first time her presence was acknowledged. "Don't you agree, Grace?"

Grace paused in her scribbling and her fair face went very red. Her expression, from that of being a dutiful secretary, seemed to suffer from a sudden crisis. She made a visible effort to remain controlled but her feelings were too overwhelming.

"What a wicked lot you are," she cried shrilly. "It's as though all these people you plan to eliminate or paralyze or kill are some kind of vermin. But they're not! They may be criminals, they may break the law, but they still have rights!" Whether it was from shock or disdain or helplessness, the leaders of millions of soldiers allowed her to continue a little longer. "People should be tried in courts. Isn't that what the law is for? Instead, it's as if you're at war with your own people. It's awful, awful, awful!"

Her voice rose into the lightest of screams but she managed to suppress her tears. The elderly men at the table, without visible rebuke, paused as if nothing unusual had happened. Krenk followed their example. In this part of the world, he remembered, much that was unwelcome and unpleasant could be closed out by simply not recognizing it. Negotiations were resumed. Grace, after some hesitation, continued taking notes, the retired generals in charge of the defence ministries proceeded to ask about prices, times of delivery, performance data and reliability. At midday, Krenk ordered his secretary to return to the hotel and invited his important customers to accompany him to lunch.

Unlike some countries, particularly effusive African and Central American ones, this part of the world made no great fuss over an arms dealer. Still less would they have indulged in the hypocrisy of seeing him as a merchant statesman. It was a demotion that Krenk accepted philosophically. He was, to their watchful eyes, someone who was prepared to make a profit on anything, many stages above pedlars and hawkers but still in the same vulgar genre known as business. He was therefore not lodged in a splendid government house as an honoured guest but in a hotel suite. It was certainly the best hotel in Jakarta but he was still under the same roof as hundreds of others.

That evening, having refreshed himself after the tiring afternoon of inspecting a missile site, he was ready to confront what in his mind he was calling 'the stupid little bitch' but which another side of him was finding more desirable than ever. To himself, he kept repeating: This one must be tamed.

Grace occupied a modest room on the floor below and took some minutes to arrive after she was called. They had not seen each other since the morning negotiations but the nervousness in her manner and about her eyes indicated that she had spent the afternoon expecting and fearing this confrontation.

She spoke first, as if anxious to learn her fate. And remained standing near the door.

"You called, Mr Krenk."

He kept her standing. Whatever familiarity had been established over the weeks had disappeared.

"Well, that's it, isn't it?" he said with cold deliberation. "What do I do with you now?"

She considered, still standing near the door, his question.

"Does this mean I'm being sent home?"

His first impulse had been to do just that. Among the intentions and the baggage and the personnel of the party which he transported round the world, were a number of strict taboos. They were opinions, indiscretions and, most serious of all, principles. But Krenk's second thoughts had prevailed. This girl must be tamed.

"You'll be sent home, Grace," he now said calmly. "But not yet."

Innocent child, he thought. She thinks I'm giving her a second chance.

"I suppose you think I should apologize," she said, as if hesitating whether to do so.

"Sit down," he ordered, irritation at last expressing itself. "What difference will an apology make? In that silly outburst you showed your feelings, that you can't be trusted at high level negotiations, that you hate what I do, that you hate me . . ."

"I don't hate you, Mr Krenk," Grace said quickly, as if that might be the worst of her offences. "Really, I don't."

Why must I be talking so irresolutely to this creature? Krenk asked himself. I have all this money and the power that goes with such wealth and yet I cannot say what's really in my mind, which is: I'm changing your job. You're no longer my secretary but my mistress. And we make the change now. Right now, young lady.

"You can't leave until I've finished my programme," Krenk said, the voice of a stern judge delivering a verdict. "I can't risk giving you your freedom in the middle of things. You know too much." Somewhere inside his broad chest he was aware of his heart quickening. With pleasure. At beginning the taming. "From here we go to South Korea via Singapore. Then to either Taiwan or Angladesh. There's also a possibility we may be invited to Saudi Arabia. Good payers, big orders."

Across the rug on the marble floor, her feet drew his eyes. One smart sandal moved over the other, one ankle rested on the other, the hem of a light summer dress curved between slightly parted knees, the pale green fabric swathing her body like a sheath round a fruit or a plant ready for picking. A virgin, Krenk reflected. And not after all an extinct species.

"Are you all right, Mr Krenk?"

Her concerned enquiry felt like a slap.

"Of course I am," he said guiltily.

"You went red and began sweating. My father went like that, just before he had a heart attack."

"I won't have a heart attack," he promised her angrily, annoyed at his own discomfort. "These are the changes I'm making."

He announced her new duties. Wherever they went, he would ask for a secretary from the ministry staff of the client country. But only for the official meetings. She, Grace, would transcribe the proceedings later; also what was recorded. Like this, the morning's outburst could never be repeated. There was also the matter of a new project.

He kept her waiting a few moments, then said: "My autobiography. While I still have my memory, I want to write it. It'll shake the world."

But there was no evidence that Grace would also be shaken.

"Is there anything else, Mr Krenk?" she asked, a polite request to escape.

"There is," he said, and momentarily, with this vision of recording his unique life's story for the world, forgot his feelings towards her. "What I have to say will be more devastating than any weapon I've ever sold. My knowledge of what goes on behind the headlines, the secrets of half the leaders of the world, how I've influenced thirty years of history, the importance of the arms dealer, all those things go into my book. And when it comes out, after I've retired, of course, I'll receive that little extra bonus, that dividend of no longer having to hide the fact that I'm among the most important people in the world. You'll be proud, Grace, to have helped me with it."

And he went on to explain that his mind was best at night, just before going to sleep, and that she would have to be prepared to work late because once he was lying comfortably in bed, he would probably dictate until two in the morning. He was sure, he added, that she would quickly adapt to the new routine.

The first thing that John-Paul did when he had safely reached Jakarta and was settled in a hotel was to sell the big diamond given to him by the Nigerian president. Its worth, it seemed, depended on a number of factors: the size when cut, the possible flaws, the shade, and the buyer's opinion of the young man's gullibility. Other considerations also affected the diamond's value. John-Paul learnt that business in the trade was bad, that diamonds were going out of fashion, that foreigners needed official permission before selling anything of value, that the stone might have been stolen and, lastly, that the dealer was running down his stock. Nevertheless, John-Paul received thirty thousand American dollars for a stone worth three times that figure.

The dealer had been right in taking a poor view of John-Paul's business acumen but the young man was not a total innocent. Once comfortably settled in his room, he began telephoning the other hotels. It was possible, he had considered, that Krenk and his party would be in a government guest house, but before he was committed to that conclusion, he would start with the obvious alternative. His call to the third of the international hotels brought the information that, yes, a Mr Krenk was a guest but, no, for security reasons, his suite number could not be disclosed.

This caused John-Paul to note that the arms dealer was occupying a suite rather than a room and, soon after, he rang the same hotel and asked for a Miss Grace Markoullis. When he was told that they were putting him through, he put down the telephone. The realization that Grace was in a hotel in the same city centre affected him profoundly. He even trembled with the intensity of his feelings. Although it was only a few weeks since he had seen her, they had been remarkable ones. And long ones. The travel, the stays in prison, the awful torture, nervousness about his false passport and his unlawful status, had made the period not only seem like months, he had been disturbed by a premonition that he would never see his loved one again.

When he had recovered from the personal crisis, however, he began to make his plans. He had enough money, true, to hire a killer. This was a country, despite the high principles of its religion and national ideology, which had a yearly murder rate in thousands, particularly by assassination squads in the pay of both the government and private parties needing their services. But John-Paul had no intention of employing others. This killing, he resolved, must be done by myself. It is the nearest a modern man can come to a crusade, he resolved. To rescue Grace. And it must be so planned and timed that he could escape on the next aircraft out of the country.

When John-Paul crossed to the Hotel Royal Splendor, he was wearing a white cotton hat and sunglasses, a favoured combination for European men, and his mood was one of intense hatred for Krenk and a little madness. In his hand was a newspaper, the purpose of which was to cover his face should he by accident confront Grace. He would begin by sitting quietly in the hotel foyer and become familiar with the place. A reconnaissance, after all, was the obvious first step. Also, from a good viewpoint in the foyer, he would be able to observe the constant movement of guests.

In earlier times, when the rich and aristocratic lived in castles and manorial homes, and most of the rest of the population were either paupers or peasants, these grand abodes were the glittering heights of society. Similarly, in the centres of cities being developed as suitable capitals for advancing new countries, modern hotels to match those of Paris and New York were suddenly springing out of surroundings that had lain neglected and impoverished for a century.

The name of the Hotel Royal Splendor exactly described its status. For those with wealth, for guests buying self-importance at a daily rate equal to the monthly pay of most of the natives, the hotel offered the kind of luxury and servility of staff enjoyed by the old princes, governors and rich merchants. And for John-Paul, instantly accorded such privileges because of his skin colour and clean dress, he enjoyed, in that marble foyer and under crystal chandeliers that glowed night and day, such favours as having the right to be there and not having his presence questioned.

An hour of uninterrupted watchfulness passed quickly. After nearly two hours, he ordered a tray of coffee from one of the uniformed staff. He had the conviction that he had only to be patient and something would happen. It was an instinct that eventually proved to be correct. As he finished his coffee, the doors of one of the row of four elevators opened and out stepped a large, white-haired man with a pink face and dressed in a beige silk suit. He was followed by Grace and two younger men, obviously his escort.

The party crossed quickly to the entrance, where an official limousine was waiting. With skilled precision the vehicle collected its passengers and drove off; and they were gone before John-Paul could really believe he had seen them. But he had; and the certainty brought an immense relief. He had successfully, across half the world, traced Krenk and his party. And was now sitting comfortably in the building in which they were staying; and where Krenk, that night, would be sleeping.

The sight of the party, and particularly of Grace, whose familiar beauty and poise had been briefly so real, now had a profound effect on the young man. With more confidence, deciding that with their departure he need no longer disguise his presence, he crossed to one of a row of kiosks. Here he bought a book, had it wrapped in expensive paper, then went to the long reception counter behind which were six or seven charming young Indonesian women. With a friendly smile, John-Paul asked if he could deliver personally this package to one of the guests. A Mr Krenk. One of the young women gave him a number for the internal telephone across the foyer. A few moments later he returned and told her that there was no reply, and since the package was urgently wanted by Mr

Krenk, could he ensure that the guest received it by putting his room number on it?

"Put Presidential Suite, sir," the young woman said, with some awe.

A little later, again taking advantage of being a respectable European in a luxury hotel in the Far East, John-Paul walked to the second floor and took the elevator to the sixteenth. At the end of the corridor, a separate and clearly very special lobby had been created. Two French Empire chairs and a sofa had been set out for visitors who might have to wait, and on impressive double doors were the words *Presidential Suite*. Calmly, confident that he would not be disturbed for some time, John-Paul sat down and considered how best to kill Klaus Krenk.

Half-an-hour later, a plan clear in his head, he left the royal splendour of the hotel for the humbler reality outside.

CHAPTER FIVE

It was an hour before midnight in the luxurious calm of the Presidential Suite and Klaus Krenk had retired to bed to begin reciting his memoirs. His beautiful secretary, Grace, although never again to be trusted to accompany him to official meetings, was apparently worthy enough to inscribe all the secrets of his life. To ensure that not a word was missed or misconstrued, a tape machine complemented the swift movements of her pen on notepad. She had just written:

"For many years I have tried to find a title for my life story that accurately describes it, and I have chosen *King of the World*."

Grace had not objected to her employer's strange working timetable and she was not disconcerted by the fact that he lay there like an invalid, in yellow and black silk pyjamas. The title of the book was followed by sections, as though Krenk, in his usual methodical way, already knew every word to be dictated.

"Section One will be *Early Years*. That's when the character of a man is made. As you'll see, Grace, I went to a tough school. The next section will be called *First Things First*. That will illustrate what the priorities of life should be. Mine was like being on a raft at sea. Learning the essentials. Food, water, shade from the sun, warmth against the cold. And I'm still on that raft. But more later. Next, *The True Measure of Success* and, the final section, *How to Rule the World Without Being Discovered*."

Krenk's cold blue eyes stared over a bed and perhaps ten metres of carpet as though all his past triumphs were on display, there to be enjoyed, exulted over. It had been a long battle and he had won. Yes, once the habit of winning and profiting was established, one simply continued winning and profiting. And now, allowing himself the indulgence of taking stock, of considering where he was going and what he had achieved, he was about to record why he should be seen as *King of the World*.

A number of factors had prompted this decision, this urge. First, he had passed sixty and therefore had to admit that he was at that point of swift decline known as old age. Secondly, he had become aware that his wealth and power were such that he could affect the destinies of peoples, their countries and even whole regions of the world. The old empires of the British, the French and all the others, had disappeared but his own, without a line or a tint showing on any map, quietly expanded and flourished.

But there was one reason for this urge to record his life story that he was not prepared to admit or even to allow to surface in his most secret thoughts. It concerned the young woman sitting a metre from the bed and who, with apparently total obedience, was setting down his claim to immortality. She was to be his witness. Without her presence, if he had simply been speaking into a dictaphone, an important dimension to believing in one's purpose would have been missing. Grace, then, unknown to herself, and despite being treated as a lowly secretary, enjoyed the status of being both witness and inspiration.

"The only precaution I'm taking against your future treachery, Grace, is to give false names to the countries and the personalities involved." He held a notebook that contained lists of coded names. "I want to begin with an episode from section three. That's how I'm going to do it — recount the parts that come to mind, then we sort them out later."

His calmness and his thoughtfulness were a little exaggerated because he wanted to reassure his secretary that he was only concerned with his story. Yes, the story was, would be, one of the most important undertakings of his life, but there was another motive to the occasion, which was no less than the seduction of this unsuspecting young woman. In a little over an hour, if his plan was successful, her notebook and pencil would slip from her hands and she would lose consciousness. What followed would depend on his ability to transform his fantasies into the actual seduction.

Without guilt, he said: "Adventures in Equatoria. How the narrator saved the independence of an African country when the president and his army were about to surrender."

The lovely hand of the young woman scribbled away with a certain animation as if she, too, was about to be excited by the story. Her long fair hair, with her head bending forward, seemed to flow down the front of her shoulders. I have no regrets, thought Krenk. Once she has recovered from the outrage, she'll realize how much she has to gain; and with his conscience assuaged, though speaking more quickly than usual, he began his narrative.

Certain events of war and peace changed the world for ever, he dictated as an introduction, and one of these had been the granting of independence to a quarter of the colonized countries of the world in the space of a few years. The retreat of the great imperial powers had not always been responsible and well-meaning, he continued. Some had departed like ravaging armies, loaded with booty, other colonies had been abandoned like helpless infants, having to survive as best they could. And, like the poor and the starving in times of disaster, neighbour had turned on neighbour, tribe on tribe and armed bands on armed bands.

"I had hardly arrived in the capital of Equatoria to sell them a load of Second World War junk, which I'd bought for a few dollars and was going to exchange for a copper mine abandoned by the French, when the neighbouring country, Boronia . . ." He paused to check the substitute name in his notebook. "Yes, Boronia, sent its army across the frontier and seized the border territory."

Grace was transcribing tidily and dutifully, and the recording machine was rotating with quiet efficiency. The King of the World, though not in the days to which his mind had now returned, began to describe that moment when the rabble of a Boronian army had advanced on an even more absurd collection of untrained soldiers and he had witnessed the terror of the president and government of the threatened capital. At the time of independence, the Equatorian president had been a post office clerk, his ministers, at best, schoolmasters and small traders, and his generals promoted directly from the rank of sergeant; and now, thirty years later, Krenk remembered the exact words he had used in turning them from trembling fools into something approaching, if not a government, at least a collection of adult administrators.

"Put me in a room with a telephone," he had commanded. "And don't interrupt. Just have faith in me."

There was really no alternative to having faith in him, he now recounted. In two weeks the Boronians would have stormed the capital, the government would have been tortured then thrown to the crocodiles, and their wives and daughters seized by the victors. And he went on to dictate a panegyric on the wonders of the telephone.

"There we were in the middle of Africa, yet those telephone wires, crossing forests and deserts, going under the sea and then spreading out to reach any city in the world, carried my appeal to all those I knew would help."

In those days he had been, perhaps, a Prince of the World, not yet a King, but his powers, his contacts and his reputation, had been enough to mobilize parties in half a dozen countries, from government ministers to the international underworld, from banks prepared to risk their customers' money to European mercenaries eager to kill, and to have them begin an immediate rescue operation. There descended on the single airport of Equatoria, really no more than an area of parched ground, a constant succession of aircraft, some with national markings, some without them, some of mysterious origin and design and others that should never have been allowed in the air.

"Within a week," continued Krenk, his voice animated by memories, "the army had rifles and artillery, the approaches to the capital were mined, chemical war experts came in with supplies and an earthquake frightened half the Boronian battalions into retreating. Then it was the turn of the Equatorian army to advance. They captured a quarter of the neighbouring country, slaughtered most of the men, carried off the women into slavery and sold off the children to Arab traders. It was considered a great victory, the beginning of the country's history. Streets were named after me and baby boys were called Krenko-krenko."

After an hour of describing his adventures in Africa, however, Krenk picked up the telephone and ordered refreshments, tea for Grace and coffee for himself. Before the order arrived he went on to explain a most important technique for poor countries burdened with debt, as Equatoria had been after its victory on the battlefield. He called it the art of inviting banks to get blood out of stone. As with governments, banks were controlled by directors who were never satisfied with their present wealth. Krenk had perfected a proposition whereby these directors were persuaded that it was in everyone's interests, within a few years, to have the loans written off. Particularly in their own interests. Frequent development grants for backward countries from the Bank of Mankind, encouraged to be generous by the Community of Mankind, adequately covered private arrangements with the venal directors and his own six per cent.

"Come in," shouted Krenk.

A uniformed member of the night staff of the Hotel Royal Splendor pushed a trolley into the Presidential Suite. Krenk and his secretary paused while tea was poured for Grace and coffee for himself. Before the young Indonesian withdrew, he bowed slightly to Krenk, a gesture that was simultaneously understood and ignored. In the short interval of sipping their drinks, Grace spoke animatedly of the native temple she had visited, the wonderful handicrafts, the charm of the people and the beauty of the women. Krenk listened with every appearance of being interested.

With the beverages consumed, Krenk turned from the young woman's tiresome chatter to his memoirs. In no way must he seem to be preoccupied by other thoughts.

"The advantage of an influential individual like myself to governments is that I can operate on their behalf with total anonymity," he continued. "I can say to leaders, tell me what you'd like done but dare not do for national and international reasons. Then give me a free hand. In this secret capacity, I have undertaken commissions for the late Chairman Mao, the late President John Kennedy, the late General de Gaulle, and the late Shah of Iran . . ." Krenk was about to give details of these remarkable yet secret associations when he found it difficult to speak. He was suddenly very tired. He looked, with some bewilderment, at Grace. She was as bright and alert as ever. "I call it the art of indispensability . . ."

The lights of the well-lit principal bedroom of the Presidential Suite began to dim.

"Are you all right, Mr Krenk?" he heard Grace enquire.

"Of course I am," he managed to exclaim. But it was more a sleepy protest at what he suspected was going wrong. "Oh God, those idiots, those idiot niggers . . ." he murmured. But the sleepiness had become too overwhelming to permit a furious outburst of rage. "Oh God, those idiots . . ."

As he fell asleep, Grace looked at him with concern, as if deciding whether he was ill or simply too tired to continue. Seeing no evidence of anything but an ageing man fast asleep, she switched off the recording machine, gathered together her papers and prepared to leave. As she did so, however, she became aware of a noisy uproar in another part of the hotel.

It was now a little after midnight and the walls of the building were very solid but they hardly served to quieten the shouts and the commotion. It seemed, as she tried to identify the noises, that they were travelling along all the floors and corridors simultaneously, up the elevator shaft and even from the hotel entrance far below. She felt she was suddenly exposed to the dangers of a strange and not quite civilized country.

Instead of leaving, the terrified Grace turned to the sleeping figure of Krenk, and asked: "Can you hear all that? What is it?"

But her elderly employer, from his long experience in foreign parts, was unable to reassure her. He had begun to snore.

There was a big public square in front of the Hotel Royal Splendor but since Jakarta was a city in one of the earlier stages of modernization, it meant that the neighbouring perimeter was composed of crumbling old colonial buildings, wooden shacks, demolished spaces serving as temporary car parks and a few modern office blocks already completed. Facing the hotel that offered royal splendour at a price was a small café-bar called the Bandung Peace, its neon strip lighting shining down on a few plastic tables set out on the unmade pavement.

The hour was nearly midnight, the earlier city crowds had disappeared and there was only one customer seated at the outside tables. He was John-Paul Bonuomo. That young man had been steadily drinking Ginseng-Fire Soda for some time and contemplating the hotel entrance across the sixty metres of the square. An unexpected occurrence was making him consider whether it would affect his plans. A high level reception by the government was being held in the hotel, and the guest of honour, the Minister of Education, was important enough to justify special security arrangements. A dozen heavily armed police stood on the hotel steps, and two military vehicles were parked with the government limousines.

John-Paul was not carrying a briefcase. He had decided to wear a safari jacket because of its large and loose pockets, both of which were filled with bulky objects to conceal the fact that one of these was a loaded pistol. He felt well and confident and was waiting for midnight. This was the most important moment of his life, he reflected, as he sucked at the straw in his fourth bottle of Ginseng-Fire. If he did not succeed in ridding the world of the tyrant, Krenk, and restoring Grace to a life worthy of such a very special young woman, he had no wish to live himself.

The calmness of the words he used to himself in no way reflected the intense fury of his feelings. He had now carried this obsession inside himself for weeks, and though on occasions it had subsided, those moments had been brief and usually brought on by exhaustion. As he was considering his state of mind and whether he should order another bottle of *Fire*, he became aware of the square filling with people. There was something almost drilled in the way they had suddenly emerged from the many streets radiating from the open area. And there was another curious feature. They were all young, mostly males in white shirts, and they had begun to assemble in front of the hotel in remarkable silence.

John-Paul did not order another bottle but decided to join the crowd, or rather to find out what was happening. His enquiries would not be those of a curious bystander but of someone whose purpose could be affected by what had every appearance of being an organized demonstration. To his relief, the presence of an alien European did not create hostility and he was soon having the reason for the gathering explained to him.

"The government's closed all the universities. They say

they're hotbeds of communism, independence, atheism, drugs and disrespect for our leaders," a fluent English-speaking student explained. It was difficult to believe that such pleasant and friendly faces could be roused to such anger and such action, but there was no doubting their purpose. "We're going to change things. They say that until we stop thinking for ourselves, and get such unpatriotic notions out of our systems, we can't continue our studies."

"That's awful," said John-Paul. "But what are we here for?"

He realized that he was already one of them. The solidarity of students and the young was worldwide and he was told that the object was to confront the education minister now being fêted in the *Grand Salon* on the top floor of the hotel. If he did not receive a deputation, then they were forcibly going to deliver an ultimatum. This information made John-Paul understand why so many of them wore masks and protective clothing against batons or clubs. He pushed his way further into the crowd, to the centre of it, where a masked student with an old-fashioned megaphone had begun to stir the crowd. The earlier silence gave way to a series of cheers and roars and what sounded like angry threats.

"What's he shouting?" asked John-Paul.

"Student rights," he was told.

Banners were now waving over the heads of the packed square of students, trumpets were sounded, the megaphone gave off even more excited slogans and shouts, and the roars became even angrier.

"Student rights," shouted John-Paul, imitating the local language. Then, picking up another chant, said: "And what's that one? What are they shouting?"

"Freedom of thought!"

"That's not much to ask, surely?"

"Too much. We'll never get it."

And John-Paul, again picking up the local words, began to shout: "Freedom of thought!"

The demonstration had lasted some time when the patience of the students, as though it was a stretched cord getting tighter and tighter, snapped. There was a movement forward that forced all those in the square, whether they were willing

or not, to push towards the hotel. On the steps of the Royal
Splendor, as if this development had been anticipated, the
handful of security police had been joined by fifty others,
reinforcements cleverly concealed. Their appearance was a
further provocation, and from the front of the crowd could be
heard cries and scuffles.

"Student rights!" shouted John-Paul, adding his efforts to
the surge towards the hotel.

But a different sound rose above the crowd, that of weapons
firing. From the front, the cries became louder, turning to
shrieks and screams. Instead of retreating in terror, however,
as if they had passed the point of fear, the students, like a single
enormous body, hurled themselves forward. And since they
had been brought up to believe that to die for their religion
meant glory in Heaven, the idea of death for a good cause was
not strange to them.

"Student rights!"

"Freedom of thought!"

By the time John-Paul had reached the hotel steps, the
security police, all of them, had been overwhelmed, trampled
on, killed or pounded in their turn by the invading army of
students. From the darkness outside, the youthful crowd
advanced into the brightly-lit foyer of the hotel, their mood
very different from the one in which they had first assembled
in the square. And as they moved among the horrified guests
and the staff, those privileged people reacted as if overtaken by
an unimagined disaster. The sky-high tariff, it seemed to have
been assumed, also meant protection from all the threats of the
outside world. To which a service charge was added. But it did
not.

Not that night. At the long reception desk, as the white-
shirted students stormed the foyer, the pretty young women
screamed and dropped out of sight. The uniformed porters, six
or seven of them, always on duty and at the service of the
guests, this time forgot their duties and fled towards an
emergency exit, while the duty manager for the night, step-
ping out of his office, instantly retreated and locked the door.

On the ground floor there was a restaurant, the best in
Jakarta, its chefs from France, the waiters from Italy, and the
maître d'hotel from Switzerland. It, too, found itself invaded

by angry and irreverent students, the elegant diners choking in alarm on their food, glasses of vintage claret and the very best armagnac spilling over white table cloths and on to silk dresses and the fine suits of the male guests. And the Italian waiters, like the hall porters, felt it prudent to hurry for the emergency exit.

It was the worst emergency in the short history of the hotel, with the guests as alarmed as if the fire bells were ringing or the country's tiny communist party or small Chinese minority had seized power. Meanwhile, John-Paul was being forced upstairs, from floor to floor, from first to second to third, one of an invading army determined to occupy every inch of the building in its determination to find the culpable government minister. And instinct played a part, as if those students had returned to an earlier stage of evolution, when the senses picked up primitive intuitions long since lost. Everyone knew where they were going, what had to be done.

"Student rights!"

"Freedom of thought!"

The banquet for the Minister of Education, who was also Minister for Culture, His Excellency Mochtar Saleh, was taking place on the top floor of the Hotel Royal Splendor. The *Grand Salon* covered half of the sixteenth floor, enjoyed a magnificent view of the city, particularly at night when the areas of squalor had disappeared, and had what was called a Palais de Versailles décor. The waiters, under the glow of priceless crystal chandeliers, had just served the last of seven courses to a hundred and fifty guests, when the noise rising from below caused the distinguished diners to stare at each other. First with puzzlement; then with apprehension.

But John-Paul did not join the other students as they poured into the *Grand Salon*. There was an even higher purpose for his invasion than student rights and freedom of thought; the killing of Klaus Krenk. As he walked towards the Presidential Suite, he pulled the soft fabric mask given to him by one of his new friends over his face. All along, in the square below, he had sensed that the student demonstration was providential, that if it led to disorder, his mission would be made easier.

Behind John-Paul, in their rush into the *Grand Salon*, the crowd of students had spilled towards the Presidential Suite, but not so close that he could not separate himself from them. He had almost reached Krenk's suite when the door across the corridor opened and two massive Europeans appeared to investigate the noise. Seeing what was happening, they hurriedly produced a key for the suite opposite and opened one of the double doors. John-Paul, seizing the opportunity, pulled the pistol from the pocket of his bush jacket, pushed against Krenk's bodyguards and pointed the weapon at their faces.

"Inside," he ordered.

The threat of the masked and armed intruder reduced the two giants to trembling obedience. John-Paul closed the door behind him and ordered them to lie face down. As the men obeyed, it seemed he had been presented with an incredible source of power.

"Hands behind your backs."

He encouraged obedience by prodding their necks with the pistol then, having foreseen such a need, tied their hands with nylon cord. He then warned them that a single sound out of them would be their last, and went in search of Krenk.

In the next room of the Presidential Suite, unbelievably, a white-haired old man had continued to sleep through the commotion. In Krenk's unlikely choice of pyjamas, exotic yellow and black silk, it took John-Paul a moment to accept that here, all alone, waiting to be shot, was his adversary. His target. He raised the pistol to the level of Krenk's cheek then found himself, without nervousness, with no sense of urgency, studying the sleeping face, intrigued that a man of such power, such dominance, could seem so guiltless in sleep. The helplessness of the sleeping man, however, troubled John-Paul.

"Open your eyes, Krenk — open your eyes!"

The pistol was prodded into a pink cheek. Sleep still claimed the man. But surely only the dead could be so still; and why did he seem not to be breathing? Well, decided John-Paul, as innocent as Krenk looked in sleep, he had to be shot.

In this moment of hesitation, however, he was unaware of a young woman creeping towards him. She was carrying a long malachite vase lifted silently from its stand, and held like a club. Too late, John-Paul turned, but before he could recognize Grace, the vase came down on his head. The blow was heavy enough to have smashed his head to pulp but, her aim not quite accurate, the oblique impact simply brought instant unconsciousness.

Grace's fortuitous presence was because the alarming noise outside had caused her to hesitate to leave the sleeping Krenk. To descend to her room on the floor below would have exposed her to unimagined dangers, particularly in this strange, foreign country. And, confirming her alarm, the moment she had seen Krenk's bodyguards forced into the suite by a masked gunman, she had slipped behind the floor-length curtains.

With the gunman now slumped at her feet, however, her single act of heroism had exhausted her courage. Her only concern was to untie the two guards so that they could take control of the situation.

"Well done, Grace," said the freed Manoel. "You were great."

But she had probably not heard the compliment, having collapsed into the nearest chair.

In the *Grand Salon*, along the corridor, a similar brave mission was coming to an inglorious end. Instead of being intimidated by the invaders, the Minister for Education and Culture, His Excellency Mochtar Saleh, had simply waited for the enormous dining hall to fill before standing on his chair at the top table and demanding silence. He was one of a majority of government leaders who had been army generals, and he spoke to the assembly exactly as he had to prisoners captured in campaigns against native nationalists fighting for the liberation of Timor and Irian Jaya, except that the fate of the students was not to be as bloody as that suffered by the rebels.

"When you leave this hotel, you'll find it surrounded by the army. You're all my prisoners." The Minister's remarkable self-assurance, and the harsh facts of what he was saying, quickly subdued even the noisiest of the students crowding into the spaces between the tables and in some cases snatching insolently at silver dishes of petit-fours and tropical fruits. "Further, from this moment, you have lost your university places. Every one of you. It's a privilege to have a university education and you've betrayed that privilege. Yes, if you can't be trusted to be loyal to your rulers, to be devout Muslims and worthy citizens, you're not the sort to lead our great country into the future."

As he finished his brief speech, a roar of approval and applause filled the *Grand Salon*. But it had not come from the students. As well as the army waiting for them in the square below, the crowd of young men had to face the abuse and the blows of the privileged guests.

The deaths of twenty students and the immurement in a mountain camp of nearly two thousand of them did not, as the country's leaders would have preferred, remain simply a matter of local news. There seemed always, in modern times, to be a foreign cameraman or reporter to capture an event that should not have been their business and to send round the world what should ideally have remained hidden.

At the headquarters of the Community of Mankind, Signora Modeste was not particularly affected when she first heard of the outrage. Day by day, as reports of massacres by governments, arrests of political opponents, closures of newspapers, legislation against minorities and the banning of religions, were brought to her attention, she had to decide which might most concern the international organization. The articles of a number of covenants and treaties specifically outlawed such actions by governments but the gap between solemn obligations and what happened in practice was as infinite as the universe. There was also, among those same articles, one that rendered all the others meaningless. It stated that there should be no interference in the internal affairs of a country.

Nevertheless, the security action in Jakarta caused Signora Modeste to concentrate more than usual on what, on any comparative scale, might be seen as a minor atrocity. It was the coincidence that her son should have been in that city at the same time and that he had been arrested for the attempted murder of an important international businessman. If there was one consolation in the awful news, it was the fact that an attempt to murder did not amount to murder. On the other hand, an evil man like Krenk, in a part of the world where the law was simply the wishes of those in power, could easily arrange for John-Paul to disappear.

Without trace. That dreadful possibility kept recurring in Signora Modeste's mind, forcing her once again to seek the advice of Count von Baum.

"Damn," said the Director, his seniority usually sparing him the day-to-day problems of COM. "What happened?"

"We traced Krenk to Jakarta four days ago. We knew that my son, somehow, would follow soon after," Signora Modeste explained defensively. "When his arrival was confirmed by our man out there, who has his contacts, we were going to apply for the repatriation of one of our employees, a Mr Bonuomo, on grounds of mental health and because of certain financial misdemeanours. Unfortunately, the situation has been complicated by this murder attempt."

"We can still try," said the Director. "A crime like that means nothing out there."

"But it makes it that much harder. And who knows what they might do to him in prison."

"It won't be difficult to guess, my dear Carla," said the Director, a little cruelly. "What carrots can we hold out?"

"It may not be so simple," his deputy replied, a despairing mother in both her manner and her appearance, "since we often criticize that country for its human rights violations, they may make this a show trial. To show that we're as corrupt as many others." And she went on to mention another aspect of the problem that was troubling her. "How can I keep up the pretence that he's not my son?"

"Very easily."

And Count von Baum proceeded to reveal the qualities and qualifications that had made him such a success in his position. In ascending order of effectiveness, they could have been described as versatility, opportunism, amorality and deviousness. The obvious solution, as a first step, proposed the Director, was to regularize John-Paul's position. Their power to negotiate his release would be infinitely stronger if he were a genuine COM official. It would be their duty. After all, every organization was allowed to have the occasional madman.

Signora Modeste made the inevitable protest.

"But he's not one of us, Konrad," she said. "We could finish up, you and I, by being kicked out of COM ourselves."

"Really," murmured Count von Baum, a voice of tolerant

condescension. "Then let me tell you this. The young man started working for us three years ago, as a researcher. Don't you remember? If we haven't complete records of his appointment and his progress, then there's been palpable negligence, a total breakdown, in our system. And if we cannot trace the culprits, then we will have to introduce severe new measures for tightening up our procedures."

With admiration, Signora Modeste listened while her superior's imaginative mind appraised all the variations of his plan. Yes, a researcher was free to travel anywhere in the world, to any one of a hundred and sixty member countries. If there wasn't much evidence of the young man submitting reports, well, he would not be fulfilling his duties and merited dismissal. And if no one in the organization seemed to have heard of him, with offices all round the world and the headquarters building in New York crammed with representatives of all humanity, should that be so surprising?

"We now come down to the practical details," the Director said, at last. "Carla, you will get out a list of all the documents to regularize his employment. Take three years off today's date, to keep it nice and tidy. I'll sign whatever documents you put in front of me. If they need countersigning, you simply add yours. But what are you frowning about?"

"You've overlooked the fact that his history isn't in the databank, that there'll be no proof that he's ever drawn a dollar as a salary . . ." And Signora Modeste continued with a list of all the details that Count von Baum appeared to have overlooked. "So how do we take care of all those?"

"As the Director," Count von Baum said coldly, "my job is to direct. As I've said, I'll sign anything. And now, carry on. Carry on."

His deputy carried on. In two days, her son, or rather a certain John-Paul Bonuomo, was an accredited representative of COM, the status of researcher on international assignments freeing him from a specific location. The computer operators obeyed orders, records were revised, the fury of the Director himself, at such negligence, was conveyed to those members of staff held to be responsible, and COM's personnel was eventually complemented by one extra researcher.

The moment this had been achieved, Signora Modeste

departed by air for Jakarta. She felt more confident, though not totally confident. John-Paul's plight was serious though not catastrophic. Besides, she was visiting the country for another reason, to convey to the government the regret of a number of member states at the deaths of twenty students and the continued detention of over a thousand others. She knew, of course, what the reaction of the authorities would be, a mixture of indignation and a reminder that the matter was not the concern of COM any more than was the electric chair for murder in the United States, the persecution of Kurds in Iraq or the denial of women's rights in Saudi Arabia.

But the international outcry on behalf of the students of Jakarta was as good a pretext as any for starting the process of talking. When she was moved by conviction, she could be eloquent; when she knew her arguments to be weak, she could hardly put words together. But this time she would be fighting for her son; perhaps for his life.

The next day, even before she had recovered from her flight, she had insisted on an early audience with the Minister for Political and Security Matters, his Excellency Bustanil Wardhana. Her request was granted.

The idea of a crisis or a major problem in the life of Klaus Krenk had become, with success, a rare embarrassment. He was in good health, he had wealth beyond calculation, his commands brought obedience and his profitable occupation as an arms dealer promised to continue for so long as nations were prepared to fight and kill each other.

But this morning was that rare occasion. Of crisis. Or a sense of it. It had begun, on waking, with an awareness of a severe headache, of feeling drugged, of fighting to restore his usual self. What had happened? Where was he? What had gone wrong? With a disciplined effort, he answered the questions simultaneously. His plan to seduce his desirable young secretary had not only been a farcical failure; it had rebounded on himself. Then came the uncomfortable realization that even an innocent like Grace must have suspected what had happened. Would she refer to it?

A little later, the sense of crisis worsened. He learnt that soon after falling into unconsciousness, because it could hardly have been described as sleep, there had been an attempt on his life. Not that the would-be killer had actually struck, because a courageous intervention by Grace had saved him, but murder had been the man's intention.

What had made the information even more troubling, infuriating, was that it had not come in the first place from one of his bodyguards, or from Grace, but from a high-ranking police colonel. The man and two of his juniors had suddenly descended on the Presidential Suite and had begun questioning him as if he might know the reason for the event; or to direct them to suspects. The information of what had happened was upsetting enough; to be interrogated was unbearable. The colonel's questions were countered by angry ripostes of his own.

Why should they assume that he might have enemies? Why couldn't the intruder have been an ordinary burglar, a thief-in-the-night? And if they felt it unusual that a European should be the culprit — so what! Were Europeans above crime just because they were in a foreign country? Krenk had then told the colonel that the best way to solve the mystery of the man's real intentions was by methods at which they were experts; and on those methods, they hardly needed advice.

Once the police had departed and sufficient of the morning had passed for him to recover some of his composure, Krenk faced the fact that someone wanted to kill him. But who? Almost as important as defeating an enemy, was to know their identity. He gave orders to his bodyguards and Grace that not on any account was he to be disturbed, and settled himself to consider who might wish to kill him. It was an exercise, as his mind went back in time and over all those with whom he had recently been involved, that was both startling and frightening. Could he really have made so many enemies?

In the way of a financier setting out his columns of profits and losses, Krenk compared the great wealth he had made in life and all he had achieved with opponents or competitors he had defeated, outwitted and perhaps ruined. But how could one become the most successful of arms dealers without leaving a trail of those who considered themselves victims, who felt betrayed, cheated and even defrauded! At the end of the exercise the debit column of names lay like a shadow along the full length of his triumphs. Yes, there were many who could have wanted revenge.

Later that morning Klaus Krenk had recovered enough of his sense of importance to telephone the Vice-President. Number Two in the country of one hundred and seventy million, one in thirty of all humanity, a retired army general who could be relied on to take the same view as himself.

"The would-be assassin, Excellency, could be associated with one of your subversive organizations. In that case, my death could set back the timetable for our arms deal. I'm sure you'll agree that the murder attempt is also an attack on the security of the state."

It was an argument that Krenk knew must succeed. No bonds between men were as firm as self-interest. Or survival.

"Say no more, Mr Krenk," the V-P assured him. "Extracting a confession will be no problem. An attack on you is an attack on us."

The troubling day passed; the following night also. Krenk was divided between the obligation to leave Jakarta and proceed to his next destination, South Korea, or to delay his departure in the hope of discovering the would-be killer's identity. But security came first. How could he leave the place without knowing his enemy!

His dilemma, however, was resolved later that day; and in a manner that was beyond, outside, remote from, anything he could ever have imagined. He received an unexpected call from Grace. What was troubling her, he wondered, as he waited for her to state her purpose. She had certainly, since the attempt on his life, seemed in a state of shock, even red-eyed, as if from crying; but surely this was taking distress to an unbelievable extreme?

Or perhaps, Krenk reflected, having long experience in the unpredictable ways of women, the thought of his dying had made her discover she was in love with him. It was a pleasing thought. After all, one of the universal truths was that the most attractive of men were the rich and the powerful.

★ ★ ★ ★ ★

They sat at opposite ends of the classical French sofa in the Presidential Suite and Klaus Krenk realized that Grace's misery was giving him great pleasure. And there was something sexual in the satisfaction, this chaste and normally composed young woman displaying her vulnerability.

"But why are you in this state, my dear?" he asked, curious for the explanation. "Come along — what have you got to tell me?"

Grace gave what he thought was a guilty glance at the sky outside, sighed, and made her confession.

"The man who tried to kill you was my fiancé, John-Paul. He tried to kill you because of me," she explained quietly, then went on to make an equally unbelievable request. "He's in prison, as you know, but the only person who can free him is yourself."

There had been events in his life, not many, that had briefly stunned Krenk into both speechlessness and paralysis, and this was one of them. But recovery usually followed quickly; as it did now. He was able to reach both a conclusion and a contradiction in the same moment.

"He could only have followed me here if you've been informing him of our movements, Grace." His voice and manner were ominously restrained. "Have you, all along, been doublecrossing me?" But before she could reply, he offered her, in fairness, the contradiction. "On the other hand, if you were a partner in crime, why did you save me by knocking him senseless?"

Her response was immediate; and vehement.

"I never told him we were here! You must believe me, Mr Krenk." As she pleaded, the rims of her reddened eyes filled with tears. "I'd already struck him before Manoel pulled off his mask. I was as shocked as you are now. In fact, I fainted."

"But how did he know I was here?" insisted Krenk. "You haven't answered that!"

"I don't know. I really don't. He found out for himself."

It was not in Krenk's nature to believe such explanations if it suited him to do otherwise. There were many advantages in having the other party suffer guilt and doubt. But for once he was reluctant to turn it to his advantage. He was not negotiating with businessmen and officials as tough as himself so perhaps, for once, a sympathetic hearing might yield the best results . . . Yield? The word appealed to him. There were those who yielded — and those who conquered.

"All right, Grace, let's assume you knew nothing about this. Tell me, why did he want to kill me?" Krenk paused, as if she would appreciate that his reasoned approach was as helpful as he could allow himself to be. "You must have an explanation. What is it?"

"He loves me," said Grace.

"But that's not an answer," Krenk protested mildly. But it was an answer. To his own fears. A feeling of relief followed. So the young man was not on that long list of enemies, had not been sent by a powerful organization which would persist and persist until they had succeeded. "Unless you mean that his motive was jealousy?"

There began, on the pale green sofa, a restrained, and really very sensible discussion. However innocent Grace might have seemed, she had an instinctive understanding of male weaknesses. And jealousy. John-Paul had feared for her safety, she confessed, all the travel in dangerous foreign countries and, yes, since it was only natural, he had felt that being with a man of Krenk's reputation, he would soon make use of her. In other ways. So, yes, his reason could only be jealousy.

"In other ways, Grace? What would he have meant by that?"

Her careless words, too good to waste, were instantly seized. And Krenk thought: Why does she even trouble to reply! If she were a little older, and a little more confident, I would simply be told to stop being unkind.

But Grace was neither older nor more confident.

She said: "John-Paul was sure you would want my body."

"Want your body?" He expressed his indignation with convincing horror. "Does he think I'm a cannibal — that I was going to turn you into a pot roast?"

This time the attempted provocation was ignored.

"Please help, Mr Krenk. Please." And a sob; not so choking that it prevented her pleading, but a despair from the depths of her torment. "Surely you have influence with the authorities. You're so important . . . Whatever you ask, they'll agree to!"

To have his power and influence expressed so clearly was pleasing, even to a man who hardly needed to be reminded of them; and Krenk listened in a mood almost of compassion while Grace assured him that it would never happen again, that she could guarantee John-Paul's future behaviour . . . Guarantee? What a strange term to use, thought Krenk. Guarantees were pledges, were binding . . . But had they not also to be honoured, whatever the cost?

He said, now a little excited: "This requires careful thought. Tonight we'll dine together. If I decide to help you, I can. If I don't, I don't. Understand?"

Between moments of brief sobs and trembling, she indicated that she understood. At least in the literal sense.

And so the ageing arms dealer, Klaus Krenk, having escaped the assassin's bullet by the brave action of his secretary, found that his survival had presented him with an unexpected advantage in his efforts to overcome Grace's reluctance to submit to him. His frustration had been all the more infuriating because he had always, almost sadistically, enjoyed winning what he called uneven contests. The powerful prevailed over the weak, the cunning over the naive and the rich over the poor. A good arrangement, a happy fate, in which he was always on the victorious side.

When Klaus Krenk, in his role of man of the world and connoisseur of lovely women, led his young secretary into the Starlight Room of the Hotel Royal Splendor, the best of its five restaurants, he was already anticipating another uneven contest; and one that would end in triumph. For himself. As usual.

He had reserved the most secluded table in the restaurant, where they would be concealed should Grace lose her self-control and entertain other diners with a display of tears or tantrums; and when, with exaggerated flourishes, the Italian waiters had settled them in their gilded seats, it seemed that a variation of chess was about to begin. One advanced one's pieces, there was attack and defence, silent moves, hidden strategies, subtle tensions and, when the contests were so uneven, a sense of wonderful power.

Krenk allowed the first courses of a dinner that almost qualified to be described as a banquet to pass pleasantly and quietly, Grace permitting herself to be tempted, despite her troubled expression, by the *haute cuisine* of the French chefs and the choicest wines of their country. And he further encouraged the sense of a social occasion by recounting stories of his earlier life, brothers and sisters disappearing into the concentration camps of Central Europe, mother escaping to Amsterdam, where she supported her surviving child, and that child eventually becoming a determined young man and emigrating to New York and in turn supporting his mother. Until, not really old, she had died after falling from a tenth-storey window. Accidentally, it was said.

But the pretence could not be perpetuated beyond the Cotellete de Veau en Papillote and the Château Margaux. A consuming sense of purpose, infinitely more satisfying than anything offered in the Starlight Room, was at last allowed to dominate him.

Krenk said: "Let's get back to this unhappy affair, Grace. You're right to recognize how much I can do for him. But persuading people at the top isn't just a matter of lifting a telephone. If a favour is granted, even by a government, a favour is expected in return. Sometimes a lot of money has to change hands. In this case, of course, it would be mine."

He stared a little challengingly at Grace while the information was considered. She returned his stare, not with her own challenge but as if the obligation was for practical suggestions.

"I see what you mean, Mr Krenk. You're talking of bribes," she said quietly. "Well, we have to take the world as it is. Whatever it costs, I'll find the money."

"I mean real money, Grace," he said with deceptive gentleness, her optimism briefly amusing. "A hundred thousand dollars. You couldn't produce that immediately, could you?" Then, his manner suddenly changing, he explained with threatening emphasis: "Because if we're to help him, it's got to be done immediately."

"What do you mean — that he might be harmed?"

Her fear was ignored.

"Then don't forget how much this delay is costing me, Grace. Consider how I've had to reschedule my programme. I can no longer give firm dates, appointments with ministers have had to be cancelled, not to mention travel and accommodation plans."

"I'm sorry." She apologized as if recognizing for the first time the wider consequences of the situation. "But to get back to money — you know my father. There's no shortage of money. Then there's John-Paul's mother. She loves her son . . ."

"Which mother doesn't," Krenk murmured, not without sarcasm. And, in the one-sided chess match in which he was so frequently involved, he imagined his hand settling on a piece and moving it to a winning square. "Time is crucial, Grace. Really, you simply have to consider what I said earlier. That a favour can be repaid by another favour."

Tears, but not an audible sobbing, came at last. He felt no compassion for the creature now visibly and silently succumbing to a kind of terror, glistening lines on her cheeks.

"You can't mean . . ."

But Grace could not put the thought into words.

"Mean what?"

His calm question, his face without expression, concealed a wonderful sense of triumph. To have the beautiful, the wayward, the young, at his mercy came close to an old man's rejuvenation. Power and wealth, after all, could close the gap between the ageing and those in splendid youth.

"Well?" he insisted.

She replied with her own question. Which answered itself.

"You mean you want me?"

In reply, Krenk smiled. At the neighbouring tables a hundred and twenty diners were enjoying the best cuisine in Jakarta, the air seemed animated by conversation and laughter, and maroon-jacketed Italian waiters danced like a corps de ballet. And in this happy setting, Krenk moved to terminate the uneven contest.

"Don't you think you're putting a high price on something that most modern girls are ready to give away by the time they're eighteen?"

"Oh, God," murmured Grace.

"Or perhaps you don't love him enough?"

"Oh, God," she repeated.

A little later, he guided her between the tables, her misery conspicuously apparent, but he managed to talk animatedly until they were out of sight of the diners in case they might think that he, Klaus Krenk, was with a woman who was not elated and honoured by his company. But alone, in the elevator, his irritation found expression.

"Don't make a tragedy out of it, Grace. It's all part of life. If you want something, you pay for it."

They reached the fortress of the Presidential Suite and he wasted no time in enjoying his conquest. Near the enormous bed, he undressed her, and she began to sob at the first touch of his hands. He stared at her nakedness for some moments; and she sobbed. He lay her on the bed; and she sobbed. He undressed himself and a gross white shape emerged from the black dinner suit; on his side, he settled next to her.

"Don't be so upset," he said, impatient at her distress. "It's nothing."

But it was not nothing. The Hotel Royal Splendor was a monument to guests who commanded, who had wealth to insist on every whim, and staff whose role as servants compelled them to obey and to be ingratiating, but no extremes were greater than the contrasting fortunes of the couple who that night shared the large bed in the Presidential Suite. The lovely but ingenuous Grace suffered an outrage that violated every part of her, the ageing arms dealer indulged in a passing pleasure that was only a little more meaningful than usual. And when Krenk had completed what he regarded as a conquest, and beneath him his victim apparently lay lifeless, he silently congratulated himself.

It had been a well-conducted seduction.

CHAPTER SIX

Despite the oppressive nature of the local government, and the swiftness with which the summary justice of that country could be administered, the tempo of Paradise Prison was one of casualness and inefficiency. And so John-Paul, although his offence merited stern punishment, with or without a court trial, was fortunate that nothing dreadful happened during his first three days. Nothing dreadful, that is, if one overlooked the fact that he had been chained to a wall for the whole period, that the cell was like a furnace and that a guard had fed him clumsily and painfully.

This curious period in John-Paul's life, when he wondered if, in reality, he was a side of beef in a butcher's shop, was further prolonged by the arrival of Signora 'La Mamma' Modeste, deputy-director of COM, though the fact of her initiative was unknown to her son. Also unknown to the prisoner was the information that the country's vice-president, on hearing of the arrival of the deputy-director, and wanting to avoid unfavourable publicity in New York, Paris and London, had ordered that the interrogation of the COM employee should be delayed.

But hanging from the wall, crucifix fashion, was not the only cause for John-Paul's despair. Krenk was still alive, unharmed, while he had to face the prospect of some severe form of punishment for his failed attempt. As if failure wasn't enough! And though his body was chained, his tormented mind was not. A series of images of Grace as the pink-faced brute's mistress, of Grace beginning to enjoy the luxuries that went with being Krenk's secretary and companion, went constantly through the young man's head. And, as the hours of hanging on the wall passed, and exhaustion developed into fever which, in turn, brought on hallucinations, the images of

Grace as the old man's possession were so real that he was driven to fits of screaming.

At the lowest moment of suffering, however, when he was almost demented, the prison authorities appeared to relent. The sequence of events that followed his release from hanging on the wall was such a relief that it seemed a form of clemency. First, two guards led him to a wash-house where he cleansed himself of all the bodily excretions accumulated under his clothes, then he was given time to scratch away the lice and bugs adhering to his skin, then allowed to sit on a lavatory pan and, lastly, presented with the luxury of a clean prisoner's uniform. His relief was complete when, instead of being returned to the dark dungeon, he was led to a cell that contained such blessings as daylight coming through a barred window, a little fresh air, a bunk with a straw mattress, a floor covered with tiles, and a central electric bulb.

In the euphoric mood of this change in his fortunes, John-Paul was quick to introduce himself to his cellmate, a small, oriental man who might have been a middle-aged politician, a schoolmaster or perhaps the respectable proprietor of a high class brothel. And his introduction to that gentleman was so warm that the Eastern courtesies of bows, polite gestures and a minimum of words soon gave way to pleasant conversation. In English. In a careful but educated English.

"Are you from a ship, sir?" asked the polite gentleman, whom John-Paul took to be Chinese.

"You mean a passenger?" asked the puzzled young man.

"No. Seaman."

"No, sir."

"Tourist, sir?"

Even though John-Paul was reluctant to be questioned, in this mood of relief it was a pleasure to have someone interested in himself. And to address him so politely.

He said: "In a way, I suppose, you can call me a tourist."

"Ah, drunk and disorderly," said the Chinese gentleman knowingly. "I hope the police didn't bruise you too badly."

"But why do you think I was drunk?"

"Well, you're a European. Why else would you be here?"

"It's not difficult in this country to finish up here," said John-Paul, again puzzled.

"Well, that's true, sir. It could be drugs, theft, politics, vice — all kinds of things. But you don't seem that sort."

"I could be here for something much worse. The crime of attempted murder."

John-Paul, as the words slipped from him, was astonished at his own carelessness or, rather, recklessness. Somehow he needed to make that simple confession. To someone sympathetic. And the respectable Chinese looked at him, if not with sympathy or understanding, certainly without condemnation.

"And you didn't succeed?" he suggested, after some moments of reflection.

"No, I failed."

"We pay for our failures," the Chinese gentleman said philosophically. "I know. And perhaps we pay for the failures of others. When we know each other a little better, I shall tell you my story."

And in Paradise Prison, at least one of the inmates was considering himself very fortunate. Not only had he been unchained and allowed to clean himself, decided John-Paul. He now had company, someone with whom he could converse, not a brute or a ruffian or a rogue or a killer, the company one expected in prison, but a cultured gentleman. Even in the most threatening of situations, he reflected, harsh fate could relent a little.

What John-Paul did not know was that fate was relenting not by a little but to a considerable extent. Not by any lessening in the seriousness of his crime or any qualities of mercy on the part of the authorities but by the discreet arrival of the deputy-director of COM. This good lady had two missions in mind, one the serious matter of the deaths of so many students and the detention of a thousand others, and a second purpose of finding a formula that would permit the release from prison of her son. She felt a little guilt, being of high principles and conscious that concern for John-Paul should seem the more important, but she firmly forced herself to keep to the priorities that would be proper for someone in her position.

Five kilometres away from Paradise Prison, at mid-morning, she began her talks with the Minister for Political and Security Matters, His Excellency Bustanil Wardhana, her manner relaxed but the deepest part of herself a turmoil of anxiety and tension. Yes, she agreed with the minister, it was a pleasure to meet in Jakarta rather than in New York, where life was just one mad rush and, another pleasure, to have the chance, even if only briefly, to see a little of one of the loveliest countries in the world.

"If you would like to visit Bali, signora, or Yogyakarta, you are welcome to be our guest," said the charming, young-ish and really very handsome minister. "Our hospitality is, you might say, infinite."

"That is most kind of you but I shall first have to consult my diary."

"Then there is Bandung, so famous in the history of those many countries that suffered under the old colonial powers . . ."

"Quite," agreed Signora Modeste.

And the minister went on to explain that his facility with five languages owed everything to years at the Sorbonne in Paris and at Sandhurst in England, where that military academy had trained him not only to be an officer and a gentleman but also to appreciate that the army was the backbone of a country. No backbone, no country. At least not one worth respecting. Did she agree? She agreed.

At last, however, having enjoyed coffee, further expressed her admiration for the country, its leader, its achievements and its people, she felt that protocol and discretion permitted her to introduce the purpose of her visit.

"This is an unofficial mission of mercy," began Signora Modeste, and made herself comfortable in a chair wide enough for two, the carved teak arms and back being covered with dragons and other mythical monsters. "I accept that COM is not entitled to interfere in matters that are the internal affairs of member countries, which is why no publicity has been given to my visit . . ."

She was interrupted. Gently but firmly.

"Our policy has always been to reject any form of interference or outside influence except, of course, when it suits us," Wardhana said, with brief severity. "A country's freedom is more important than the individual's."

"Quite, Minister," agreed Signora Modeste, checking the impulse to state that a country was the sum of its individuals. "However, we are permitted to convey to countries the sentiments within COM."

"I appreciate you are simply a courier, signora. A messenger. And those sentiments, provided they're not critical, will be carefully considered."

Signora Modeste felt a little relief. She was on firm ground, familiar ground. The diplomatic *jeu* was being played to the rules. Anything that might provoke discord would be a clumsy gaffe on her part, particularly when the fault could always appear to lie with those not present.

"Our Director, Count von Baum, who has met your President, has asked me to convey certain information. He, of course, like myself now, is simply a messenger."

"Quite," said the handsome minister. "Let me hear what these interfering delegations have to say." He assumed a bored expression. "There are so many do-gooders in this world, don't you agree?"

She agreed and, in her most diplomatic language, went on to explain that pressures were building up among member-states to bring the matter of the Jakarta students before the General Assembly. Both she and the Director had always been of the opinion that public debates and protests achieved little, except to strengthen the resolve of the country being accused, and that she was hoping that this visit to His Excellency would help the Director and herself to make a pacifying statement. And she allowed herself to seem helpless, bewildered, a practised expression meant to appeal to male gallantry.

It did. As with most handsome men, the Minister enjoyed flattery, and made the surprising admission that, though the reports had greatly exaggerated the matter, he was prepared to admit that there had been a small, insignificant demonstration of students. But didn't they occur all over the world? She must remember Paris in 1968? It was all the fault of parents, of course, particularly fathers who had not disciplined their sons to the great virtues of obedience and loyalty to their country. And then, displaying not only gallantry but his own contribution to the diplomatic game, he suggested that . . .

"We should get our heads together, signora, to find a form

of words to satisfy the delegates in New York. After all, let us admit, they're only responding to protests at home. Like ourselves, all they really want is a quiet life."

At the end of half an hour a statement had been drawn up that would satisfy all parties, asserting that states were sovereign authorities within their own frontiers, that the Minister's country had always been among those honouring treaty obligations and human rights charters, but out of respect for member countries who might have been misinformed by misleading reports about protesting students, the government would begin an official enquiry forthwith.

"And now that is out of the way, signora," said the minister, as though very satisfied with the meeting so far, "I am sure there's another matter you wish to discuss."

Signora Modeste smiled appreciatively. She was not surprised. In fact it was possible, she reflected to herself, that the man had understood all along that the real purpose of her visit was to intercede on behalf of one of her own COM employees.

"There is," she sighed, a tragic sigh that might have issued from the stage of the San Carlo in her beloved Napoli. "I'm afraid there is."

"A very strange case indeed," the minister observed. "From our preliminary investigations, it would seem that the young man has travelled all these thousands of miles to kill this distinguished gentleman, a guest of my country. But why here?"

"Terrible," agreed Signora Modeste. "He has been missing from his duties for some weeks."

"Missing? You mean he disappeared?"

"This is a highly sensitive matter, Excellency. I wish there was some way we could discuss this confidentially, off the record, so to speak."

"Please, signora. You have my word."

Although Signora Modeste had definite ideas of the worth of statesmen's pledges, she was confident enough in her story to recount in a calm and factual manner the case of a promising young man who had suffered a nervous breakdown and had disappeared when Count von Baum had pressed him to have psychiatric treatment. Equally upsetting, explained the deputy-director, was the misappropriation of a large sum of money.

"In anticipation of our discussing the matter, Excellency," continued Signora Modeste, "I have brought along documents and medical reports to attest to the young man's mental condition." She did not choose to mention that all COM representatives were covered by the usual diplomatic protection, even the crime they were now discussing, and handed the papers to the minister. "You will find psychiatrists' reports, one from our financial director, a letter from the Director himself and a brief resumé of the man's career with COM."

The minister gave her a suspicious stare before accepting the folder of papers, as though long training had taught him that nothing was as it seemed to be. Not even the plea by someone so obviously above suspicion as the woman now seated at the other side of his desk.

"I'm pleased you brought these papers along, signora. In fact, we were wondering whether his passport was genuine. All our usual tests proved it was but we were still doubtful."

"Of course; naturally," said Signora Modeste. "In a case of attempted murder, you can't be too careful."

She wondered, as the papers were studied, whether her son had been tortured, what his prison conditions were like, and how such a sensitive boy was surviving the dreadful experience. But she kept her motherly concern disguised and hidden, even when the minister observed that he was in a high security prison, one especially for terrorists, heretics, subversives and anarchists.

As he was reading, hoping the minister could read and listen simultaneously, the deputy-director said: "I've never met him myself and normally I would have left the whole matter in the very capable hands of Mr Singh, our local representative, but since I'm here . . ."

"Say no more, signora," said the minister, looking up between one document and another. "It's your duty to see the young man. A visit presents no problems."

When the meeting was over, on her return to her hotel, she felt modestly encouraged. Her instinct told her that there was a deal to be made. Governments, good or bad, liberal or oppressive, were motivated by the same priorities. In ascending order of importance they were — the lowest — matters of principle, the interests of the poor, social stability, national prestige and — the highest priority — that which benefited the country's ruler or rulers. If something was to be gained by putting her son on the next flight from Jakarta, an arbitrary order would be enough.

That afternoon she was informed that a Ministry car would collect her on the following day and take her to Paradise Prison.

But tomorrow did not come.

A sequence of remarkable events occurred which prevented Signora Modeste from visiting her son. They were set in motion by the earlier decision of the prison authorities to move John-Paul into the same cell as the polite Chinese gentleman who, on properly introducing himself, confided that he was one of the country's disaffected academics and very sympathetic towards student protests.

"My full title is Learned Professor Cheng," said the gentleman, "but you may address me as Professor Cheng." And, displaying an even greater informality, added: "Let us forget we are strangers and become acquaintances. It will make it easier for us to share this small cell."

With formality set aside, Professor Cheng, philosopher and linguist, was soon able to expand on his favourite subject, the injustices inflicted on the small Chinese minority in a country dominated by Islamic practices and beliefs. The plight of the Chinese puzzled John-Paul, as he now admitted. Since they were the oldest civilization in that part of the world, were the most cultured and hard-working, created wealth for everyone wherever they settled, why was it that they were not appreciated by the local population? Particularly since that local population clearly preferred a leisurely, even indolent, way of life?

"The world has made advances, young man, in every direction but one. With a few honourable exceptions, people cannot accept those who are different. The divisions, whether between yellow and white, brown and black people, between one religion and another, one nation and another, one area of a country and another, are exactly as they were hundreds of years ago. We may not go to war at the slightest provocation, we may not express our prejudices openly, but the inner hostility remains exactly as it was. And so, in what is now the country of our birth, we Chinese are made to feel like outcastes, inferior, like lepers."

"You mean you are here in prison because you're Chinese?" John-Paul asked, a little disbelievingly.

"Yes," said the learned professor. "But let me explain. We are not allowed to publish books in our own language, the oldest of written scripts in the world, we cannot send our children to Chinese schools or write or print or display Chinese characters, particularly in public, such as shop signs. This fate we have been forced to accept. But although we are the most patient and long-suffering people in the world, there is the occasional revolt."

"Which is why you are here?"

"Indirectly."

And Professor Cheng went on to explain that although he had held a high appointment at the city university, he came from a small village fifty kilometres from the capital, where he was regarded as a leading mandarin by the Chinese population of two thousand. In this position, on many occasions, he had to negotiate problems with the district governor and military commander, a Colonel Nuryadin. This severe commander, determined to be a good servant of his government, had cast a permanent shadow over the village, prosecuting those who committed the slightest offence, having regular burnings of Chinese books in the village square and flogging those he suspected of discriminating against the few Muslims who had remained there.

"History had taught us that it was better to accept small injustices rather than face really heavy penalties. Bravery was one thing but when you are a fraction of the whole population, what can you do? However, a certain Wang Yun, who owned a large store in our village, had other ideas. He was an elderly Confucian, and since it would not be long before he departed on the great voyage to join his ancestors, he decided to revolt against those who had persecuted him and his people all his life. He did this in the most open way possible. He hung a sign of Chinese characters, large and red, over his store. They simply stated CHINA FOODSTORE. Then he placed his chair by his front step and waited for trouble."

Trouble came within the hour. First it was the arrival of a sergeant in the security police who reminded the old man that it was an offence to display Chinese characters, and when the warning was ignored, went on to say that the sign would be confiscated and the offender arrested. A little later, a higher official arrived, his purpose to make a senile old man see reason. Not only was it an offence to display Chinese characters but since the store was not in China, Wang Yun was committing a second crime of misleading the public because the name CHINA FOODSTORE implied that it was in China. The correct name should be INDONESIAN FOODSTORE -- CHINESE STYLE.

"The old man did not trouble to reply to such finer points of meaning so they took down the sign and forced him to close the store for a month. The official had decided that this loss of income would be worse than imprisonment or a fine in court and would also save the state the trouble and the expense of supporting a man in prison," went on Professor Cheng, in English that was fluent and in a voice that was gravely gentle. "But the Chinese have learnt to live with adversity and, once darkness arrived, often after midnight, his old customers showed their support by creeping to the back entrance of the store and buying their usual provisions. This went on for a week until, without warning, the police arrived and everyone was arrested — the old man, seven women, a number of children and two youths buying illicit alcohol."

In face of such communal lawlessness, recounted the professor, the authorities then decided to 'cleanse the village', as they called it. A hundred soldiers arrived and went from store to store, purifying anything with a Chinese character on a label, on a box, on a leaflet or on wrapping paper, by removing or obliterating them. Cans and packs of favourite foods, usually imported or smuggled in from outside, were suddenly without identifying labels. Beans could therefore be taken for lychees, meat for ginger, Szechuan delicacies for ginseng and noodles for joss sticks. It was not Wang Yun's customers who were confused, however, because his store was officially closed, but those at the other five shops in the village.

"By nature and conviction, and as a philosopher, I should have remained outside minor disputes," Professor Cheng went on, "but it is this kind of unpredictable crisis that brings people together. And so we began to agitate for the release from prison of Wang Yun's customers."

"Ah," said John-Paul, overwhelmed by admiration. "Now I understand. You're here because of a principle."

"Oh no. However it might have started, I finished up by committing a dreadful crime. We Chinese have a saying that the longest journey begins with but a single step. In the same way, the worst of disputes begins with but a single disagreement."

And he went on to describe how the dispute of the CHINA FOODSTORE was taken up by the most active group in any society, the youth of the village. From being the least conscious of their Chinese heritage, because their short lives had been spent in this foreign country, they were suddenly the fiercest in its defence. This took the extraordinary form of bands of youths forcing their own people to restore Chinese characters, and not only those that had been discreetly tolerated by the authorities but in new places as well. Hand-written labels went back on cans of beanshoots, on packets of tea, on bottles of soya sauce and on the pharmacopoeia of imported medicines in which the Chinese trusted to relieve every conceivable ailment, but the wild youngsters insisted that Chinese characters also went up outside barbers and butchers, cafés and drapers, clubs and temples.

"This," sighed the professor, as though the follies of the world never ceased to amaze him, "was the beginning of what the village called the China Foodstore War. War? Well, decide for yourself, young man. There was an early phase when our youth clashed with the police. No deaths, just a lot of arrests, broken heads from the truncheons and beatings in the military camps before most of the boys were sent home. Then we heard that poor Wang Yun had died in prison and had begun the long journey. The violence in the village worsened. The hatred towards the authorities reached fever pitch. The students formed a committee to raise funds for the fight. There were two purposes to the fight. One was to have freedom to display Chinese characters, the other for defence reasons."

"But a minority in a country like this can't win," John-Paul observed, when the professor went quiet and contemplative for a few moments. "I thought the Chinese were the first to recognize a useless fight."

"So did I," said Professor Cheng, "but youth is youth. They're the only group in any society that can fight for what they believe. And why? Because the consequences, even if they lose everything, are not so bad for them. They don't have wives and children to suffer, they haven't reached the point in their careers when they must hold on to them at all costs, they don't have pensions that are at risk . . . And then . . ." He gave a deep and prolonged groan. When it had exhausted itself, he said: "Because I was the best-known, and possibly the most influential, and, besides, the Chinese respect age, they made me the head of the defence organization."

Professor Cheng had made only one condition. That he was not involved in violence. Unknown to him, however, some of the youths had got hold of explosives. These they placed outside the police headquarters. When they were detonated, half the front of the building was blown up, a dozen security men were killed and, another serious offence, the national flag over the building finished in the gutter. At this point, the district commander, Colonel Nuryadin, took direct control, coming from a neighbouring small town to announce local martial law and to set up his headquarters in the village's only hotel.

"From that moment, young man," continued Professor Cheng, "we really experienced what the state can do to a defenceless population if it really wants to. And, of course, if they give ultimate authority to a sadistic brute. First of all, those of the young men not arrested for the explosion were conscripted and sent to the distant island of Sumba to work on the roads, then the prettiest of our girls were taken away for questioning, which lasted days. When they returned, their stories were too horrific to repeat; some had been mutilated — you know where — some could not bring themselves to leave their houses for months, others were pregnant, others went mad. Then Colonel Nuryadin, on the pretext that we were not paying taxes, ordered his men to search every house in the village."

After the search, the colonel had become a very wealthy man. In true Chinese tradition, having little faith in money or banks or government securities, but knowing that the value of gold increased with time, hoards of coins, trinkets and small and large ingots had been buried in the ground, hidden in walls, even painted to look like cheap ornaments. The soldiers, however, had come with metal detectors, about which the villagers were ignorant, and within hours the life savings of the whole population had been discovered and removed.

John-Paul had listened attentively, growing more curious than ever about the reason for the professor's presence in the prison. At last he was permitted to ask.

"Yes, all right," replied Professor Cheng, as though he could no longer avoid a question he would have preferred had not been asked. "As the head of the defence committee, I felt I had a special responsibility. Violence is not in my nature but I was suddenly driven by the need to murder an evil man. And so I borrowed a gun from one of the defence committee and killed Colonel Nuryadin."

"You killed him?" It was difficult for John-Paul to believe that the quiet scholar could have been moved to murder. "Murdered?"

Professor Cheng nodded.

"He didn't deserve to live. I am against violence in all its forms and yet I felt this had to be done."

John-Paul could not speak for some moments. His eyes were bright with admiration and he felt moved by a sense of kinship. So others, too, could be driven by desperation to rid the world of evil men. Even the gentle and the non-violent could be seized by primaeval emotions. Even the intellectually sophisticated.

"I shall pay the penalty three days from now," said Professor Cheng, almost as an afterthought. "Then I'm shot." The calm statement was followed by a question, a sudden curiosity about the young man who had listened so intently. "And you? What have you done?"

It was John-Paul's turn to recount his story. He began by saying that, in his case, it had been a murder attempt that had ended in failure. When he had finished, though conscious that his own motives were not so admirable as the professor's, they settled down to a discussion on the justification for violence. It was soon obvious from his observations that Professor Cheng had spent many hours rationalizing his crime, setting out as though lecturing a class of students all the points in favour and all those against. But he had not quite finished drawing a comparison with the legalized violence of the state against its citizens, when there was a loud explosion in a distant part of the building.

"Ah," said the professor, his calmness not changing. "That could be the diversion." Then, noticing John-Paul's alarm and confusion, added: "We Chinese may be a relatively small minority but that doesn't mean we're helpless."

Within seconds of the explosion, and with acrid dust beginning to drift through the cells, two guards appeared outside the iron door and unlocked it.

"I'll be leaving, young man," said the professor, holding out a hand then withdrawing it. "Or perhaps you might want to come with me?"

The quiet suggestion was almost inaudible because of the growing turbulence of noise, guards rushing past them towards the scene of devastation, shots being fired and every occupant of the corridors of cells screaming with either terror, encouragement or pleasure. But John-Paul did not hesitate.

"Let's go," he said.

The two uniformed guards took the arms of the prisoners as if they were under special duress and led them down the corridors, across an open space and through a number of doors, apparently having keys when they were necessary. Suddenly, John-Paul and the others emerged into the open sunlit street. A car was waiting, a large Chevrolet from an earlier era and which was therefore roomy enough for them all; and it began moving, and moving fast, before the rear doors had been closed. Only then did John-Paul observe that the bogus guards were removing their uniforms and that they were paler-skinned Chinese, not typical of the local security forces.

"Where are we going?" he asked.

He was ignored. The numerous occupants of the car were

talking and shouting in their own language, half in argument and half in celebration. Only when, after having travelled through the city suburbs and into a crowded urban area of dilapidated houses divided by canals and open sewers, was anyone prepared to give him attention.

"The first thing we shall do with you," explained Professor Cheng, "is put you through an inauguration ceremony. My colleagues are angry that I encouraged you to leave with us."

"But what sort of inauguration?" asked a bewildered John-Paul.

"The escape was organized by the Iron Hand Triad, with which our local defence committee is associated. Only not until you have been sworn to secrecy and loyalty, can you be accepted and helped."

John-Paul was not less bewildered by this explanation. Was all this really happening to him? But it was, the car bouncing over unmade roads, bodies thrown together because of broken shock absorbers, the brakes being applied every twenty metres.

"And what's the alternative?" he managed to ask.

"The alternative?" The professor paused, as though having to make a difficult decision; or perhaps having to announce it. He came down in favour of a merciful concession. "Well, if you don't agree, we'll let you get out here."

John-Paul glanced out of each of the car windows. At the crowded slums.

"I'll stay," he said.

Triads such as the Iron Hand flourished in every major city of the world where large numbers of Chinese had settled. As with many organizations of different immigrant groups, its origins were noble and its purpose to protect vulnerable minorities. But times had changed; and noble ideals with it. The Iron Hand, as with those in New York, San Francisco and London, had descended to crime and plain gangsterism, activities only redeemed by the occasional quixotic gesture such as helping John-Paul escape with Professor Cheng.

The young man, in the weeks that had passed since his departure from New York, had undergone a period of painful but intense education in the ways of the world. Among the lessons he had learnt was that within every country there were many powerful individuals who could descend to such depths of savagery that he wondered whether they had ever lived within a society and whether they had ever known parents, family and friends. Then there was corruption, the readiness of people to be bribed, bought and perverted. And the authorities. Ah, what a lot they were, he had decided, after his many confrontations with officials, police, administrators and their parasites.

The result of his recent harsh experiences was to make the young man more of a realist, and more prepared to ignore minor principles for the sake of major ones. He therefore allowed himself to go through what he regarded as the absurd ritual of being inducted into the Iron Hand fraternity, a ceremony that included long periods of chanting in an unfamiliar language, the rubbing together of blood oozing from his lightly cut thumb with that of the triad chief, and having a small fist-shaped tattoo incised under his left arm.

But rewards followed. As someone who was now one of them — though not really one of them — and had been accepted out of loyalty to their respected professor, the Iron Hand was immediately concerned with getting the unwelcome member out of the country. Within a few days, John-Paul possessed a modified Australian passport, previously that of a young tourist from Queensland, an air ticket to Hong Kong and a sum of money in American dollars that was adequate rather than generous.

Professor Cheng seemed genuinely upset at bidding farewell to the young man and, being a linguist, hoped that *l'avventura d'uno Bonuomo* would have a successful end. And when John-Paul requested a last favour, that of persuading his Iron Hand brothers to discover Klaus Krenk's next destination, not a difficult task for such a network of informants, it was instantly granted. They would have the information when he contacted them from Hong Kong.

And so they had. Exactly two days later.

After the conquest of his lovely young secretary, which was how Klaus Krenk saw her despairing submission, the merchant statesman was determined to show her that being a rich man's mistress could bring rewards greater than any of the sweet illusions of love. And his generosity was motivated by other considerations. In the thirty years he had travelled from country to country, secretaries or young women who had worked for him had remained exactly what they were — paid servants. Now, after only a single night of love, and hardly with a woman who had entered into the spirit of it, in fact she had lain like a corpse, he was wondering whether, for the first time, he could develop her into a companion.

A secretary who was also a loving companion . . . But the morning brought an early prompting of what was expected of him, not expensive gifts but simply the keeping of a promise.

"Of course, of course," Krenk said, with quick assurance. "I've always prided myself on keeping my word."

"But today," insisted Grace. "He's in prison. They could be doing the most awful things to him."

Krenk assured her that she was being unnecessarily troubled, that John-Paul would be well treated and that, in any case, he would soon be ringing the Vice-President of the country, who was a good friend. When she appeared to doubt such comforting words, he sent her back to her room on the pretext that, when speaking to the V-P, he must have privacy. Alone, Grace having departed with an anxious face and showing no evidence of having enjoyed a night in a man's arms, Krenk was instantly restored to his daytime self, that of a tough man of action.

"Krenk, V-P, Krenk," he half-shouted into the telephone. "In great form — and you?"

"I'm fine," said the Vice-President pleasantly. "This call is not unexpected. What's your proposition?"

"It's about that young fool who tried to kill me. What's it going to cost me to have him put on the next flight to New York?"

"Well . . ." The Vice-President pretended to be shocked by such brazenness. "That's an unexpected request! You're giving me the impression that in this country we can ignore the due process of law . . ."

"I was hoping that the matter need not get that far. That it could be settled before it ever reached the incorruptible and excellent men who manage your legal system."

Krenk seldom committed himself to propositions he knew to be doubtful or hopeless. There were always two factors in approaches of this kind — the individual involved and the country itself, its traditions and its morals. And so, after a few moments, the V-P, as Krenk expected, reverted to custom.

He said: "You're lucky, my friend, that you're in a country where those who govern it are above the law. Imagine if this had happened in the States or Holland or Australia! This little matter would begin as headlines in the press then go on to embarrass the government itself. They might even find a sex angle to it."

"Ah, yes, V-P. There's nothing lower than Western journalists. However, since you are ensuring that it can be done without publicity, I would like to make a generous contribution to the welfare of the poor."

"Well, my good friend, that's very kind of you. In that case I'll let you have my bank details in due course."

"In Switzerland, if you wish."

"Ah — well, we'll see."

Krenk replaced the telephone and once more, because he had a high opinion of his resourcefulness, congratulated himself on the ease with which he overcame life's problems. As continuous as time itself, they followed each other, problem after problem, and they were always neatly and satisfactorily resolved. He called Grace back to his suite. He had good news for her. The Vice-President's word was as good as his bond. It might take two or three days but that should hardly be upsetting. And he promised the anxious young woman that they would stay in Jakarta until her fiancé was safely flying on his way.

"And now, Grace, I have a pleasant surprise for you," Krenk announced.

A little later he led her from the hotel to where the government limousine placed at his disposal was waiting. Manoel, who had joined them, and who had obviously been given his instructions, whispered an order to the driver. A short journey followed; when it ended, Krenk led Grace into the Jakarta branch of a Place Vendôme jeweller, the smartest in the city.

"There," said Krenk grandly, moved to impress the young woman, as he might have behaved at half his present age. "You can have whatever takes your fancy."

The Chinese manager had been warned of the visit. He had greeted them with a bow and now waited with some expectation, and servility, for this young white concubine of the old man, as he would have seen the relationship, to make her purchase. Even if her expression had been sullen and disinterested on entering his establishment, he appeared confident that she would soon be tempted by his glittering showcases.

"Perhaps she might like to see these," the manager quietly suggested, his instinct acute. "They are all original pieces and created by the best French craftsmen."

They were led, his customers, to an upright glass display case. In the folds of purple velvet, three bracelets had been laid both in and on the soft fabric. They glittered with large sapphires and rubies, and smaller diamonds. Krenk smiled happily. They were all the same, these women, when temptation was placed within their reach.

"Priceless," said Krenk. "You can have whatever takes your fancy."

The manager, with silent discreetness, produced a key and opened the case. A female assistant appeared from the establishment's interior, as if an expensive object, even though the piece might be small in size, might need her help.

"Try them on, Grace," suggested Krenk, guessing he would soon be parting with a quarter of a million dollars. And happily. "Here, try this."

And he raised one of her arms by the wrist. Her summer dress was without sleeves. He looked at the lightly tanned skin and from an artistic impulse unusual for such a man, picked up the bracelet he considered most suitable.

"Put this on, Grace."

Her arm dropped as he released it. An unmistakable reluctance compressed her mouth. Was she about to embarrass him, Krenk wondered, both puzzled and uneasy. And glanced at the Chinese manager. The appeal was answered immediately and that good gentleman, with great fluency, proceeded to tell them of the valuable bracelet's pedigree, as if it were a prize animal, the best stones of Burma and Brazil and Africa, the design from the treasures of the old Russian royal family.

When he had finished, Grace simply said: "I don't want anything. Thank you, all the same."

As she walked away, Klaus Krenk checked an angry exclamation. But in the company of people for whom loss of face, as they called it, was so important, her behaviour had to be treated as unsurprising. And he smiled at the Chinese manager. Absurd young woman. The smile was returned. Think nothing of it, sir. It happens all the time. But not a word spoken.

"We'll take it," Krenk said. Then, to Manoel: "Fix it up. We'll be waiting in the car."

It was a relief to be again in the limousine, away from public humiliation, spared the defiance of a wilful young female. When Manoel returned to the limousine, his light tropical suit bulged with the shape of a package. And as they continued to their next destination, Krenk again considered the possibility of elevating a secretary to the role of companion. Not mistress. He hated the word. Also, it implied she had been around, slept with dozens of men. No, companion. It sounded — more acceptable, select? He thought of the first virtue he required in a woman. Obedience. With obedience, everything was easy. After all, what was the point of a rich man supporting a companion in luxury if his generosity brought tensions and arguments and squabbles?

"Here it is," said Manoel.

The limousine had stopped outside a shop too stylish and select for its surroundings. In discreet gold letters were the words *Parfums de France*. Inside the clear glass entrance, a woman of some magnificence was visible. She appeared to be hovering, vulturelike, for an expected party of customers. As Krenk emerged, she smiled.

"Come along, Grace," he said, turning, endeavouring to show gallantry — and forgiveness — by extending a hand to help her from the limousine.

"I'm not getting out. I don't use perfume," said the young woman, contradicting a liberally scented presence.

For the second time that morning the urge to violence was

controlled just before Klaus Krenk became a bellowing specta-
cle to the mild-faced natives walking by and already finding
enough reason to stare at the party of Westerners. To be
humiliated again, in public, would be insufferable. But avoid-
able. When he retreated into the limousine, because retreat it
was, he seemed to have experienced an unfamiliar defeat. And
brought on by himself, by his assumptions.

"Back to the hotel," he ordered.

Behind them, through the glass doors of *Parfums de France*,
the face of the regally sophisticated manageress displayed
bewilderment. But her disbelief hardly equalled Krenk's.
Sometimes defeats had nothing to do with lost deals, being
outsmarted in negotiations, making bad investments. Subtle
areas of a man's pride could be hurt, too.

And all he could say was: "Foolish girl. You could have had
anything."

He sulked for much of the day, banishing Grace from his
presence until, just before midnight, he called her to his suite
where, sitting up in bed with notebook in hand, he was ready
to continue with recounting his life-story. As she resumed her
role as attentive secretary, a little of the normality of life
seemed to have been restored. Why was he inviting problems
for himself, particularly emotional ones, by imagining this
naive creature, absurd child, could become his companion?
And, in this philosophical mood, Krenk turned to two aspects
of life that made sense, seemed of the utmost importance.

"I want to dwell on the uses of wealth, how great fortunes
are spent, and particularly the desire to accumulate material
possessions ostentatiously, as proof of success," he began.
"And, secondly, if we have time tonight, the true measure of
greatness."

If Klaus Krenk could be regarded as having a virtue it was in
his refusal to imitate those of comparable wealth, the well-
publicized few, who spent great sums of money on the highly
visible extravagances of the ridiculously rich. To live well was
one thing. Particularly when it was honestly earned. But to
preside over an empire of material acquisitions was simply to
admit the deeper doubts and inadequacies of one's nature.

"I have always avoided the ostentatious," Klaus Krenk
observed for future readers of his memoirs. "There are those

who have six or seven homes in different countries, castles, estates, villas and ranches, who fly between them in their private planes, who have an enormous yacht lying idle for most of the year in a fashionable resort, who buy works of art because of their high price rather than their appeal and who make generous donations to so-called worthy causes because of the publicity this brings; but I am not among them. I do not need to fortify myself with illusions; how can a man be rich if he is begging for praise and attention? Beggars are beggars no matter how they disguise their motives."

When Krenk had finished criticizing his peer group of the wealthiest individuals and had defended the relative anonymity of his own mode of living, he went on to explain to the busily scribbling Grace how he planned to hand it all back on his death. Hand it all back? And he revealed a second admirable side to the greed, the dishonesty, the heartlessness and the brutishness that had characterized the way in which he had accumulated such wealth. It — wealth, riches, fortunes — all came from society, had been drawn from the labour and the pockets and the bank accounts of all the individuals who made up that society. If success, in the course of a working lifetime, had been so remarkable that a few of the most victorious — because wealth was synonymous with victory of a certain kind — had taken for themselves a thousand times more than others, then the return of that wealth was the ultimate and honourable justification of all that had gone into making it.

"And expiation," he concluded. "Make sure we use that word, Grace. I can't turn to God for forgiveness, because I know he doesn't exist, but I can turn to myself for that expiation. It's like paying off a debt. A man of great wealth takes and then, on his death, he returns it all. It's my way of ensuring I go to Heaven. My own Heaven." He looked at his watch, suddenly aware that a whole hour had passed. "We will leave the measurement of greatness for another time."

Exhausted, he lay back and did not speak for some minutes. When he had recovered, which he did with remarkable swiftness, he turned to the waiting young woman still sitting there. Except that she was no longer his secretary but his companion. Promoted in a moment. On impulse. With a smile.

"Don't look so nervous, my dear," said Klaus Krenk. "After all, it's nothing new to you now, is it?"

The tape machine was switched off, her notebook closed, her folder carefully packed before Grace could bring herself to look up, to stare back at the elderly man half under the yellow counterpane.

"I'm tired, Mr Krenk," said Grace. "Really, I am. Surely you'll let me go to my room?"

"For tonight, this is your room."

"But I'm tired." Her voice sounded resigned, an admission of helplessness. "Wasn't last night enough?"

He laughed at such innocence, pleased that she might think him so virile.

"Now, Grace, you know I'm doing you a great service, that I've kept my promise about your fiancé," he said, as kindly as he could. "Get your clothes off and come to bed."

She turned away as she began to undress. Good, thought Krenk, as her arms went reluctantly from garment to garment, she's learning obedience. When she was naked and slowly approaching the bed, her nervousness as much as her beauty added to his excitement. Yes, he decided, I can turn this one into a companion.

The following morning, when they were dressed and ready to descend to the dining room, the telephone rang. Instinct made him reach for it rather than allow Grace to answer. It was the Vice-President. After greeting him with appropriate respect, Krenk heard with disbelief a story that sounded so unlikely that he instantly thought it was a trick to extract further concessions on the arms deal just concluded with the man's colleagues. Apparently the prisoner, Bonuomo, had escaped. A hundred heavily-armed men had invaded the prison to secure the release of a gang leader and the young European had taken advantage of the confusion to make good his escape.

And Krenk heard, still restrained from interrupting the V-P in case the story was true: "It's possible that if we don't get our hands on this dangerous individual, he may make another attempt on your life. I've therefore arranged for you to have an armed guard for the rest of your stay in Jakarta."

The receiver was replaced before Krenk could reply.

"You bastard," he said to the instrument. "You oriental bastard."

With Grace at his side, Krenk considered the new situation, the threat, his ability to take independent action. After some moments, he called Manoel. He was to make arrangements for their immediate departure. If there were no direct flights to South Korea, the next stage of his programme, he should make reservations on the regular service to Singapore; then on to Seoul.

"I want to be out of this place by this afternoon," he added, indicating an urgency his bodyguard would understand. With the man departed, he turned to Grace. "Change of plans. We're leaving."

Her intuitive question was immediate.

"Is it to do with John-Paul?"

His own instinct, in turn, was to tell her to remember her position and not to ask questions but an uncharacteristic sense of fairness forced him to admit her involvement.

"He's escaped from prison, Grace. There was a mass breakout or something. The V-P seems to think I'm in danger. The best way to avoid it is to put this country behind us." He smiled to cover his own nervousness. "Come on, let's go to breakfast."

But there was no willingness to follow him. A heavy frown distorted Grace's young face, which showed the fatigue of a second distressing night.

"That means he's being hunted," she said, as if slowly going over the implications. "They could shoot him. Isn't that a favourite excuse — shot when trying to escape? We can't just abandon him like this." Then, defiantly, she announced: "I'm not leaving."

"Really," murmured Krenk, calmly sarcastic.

"No. I'm going to the police. I'll cooperate in finding him. Don't you realize, I love him? He's here because of me . . ."

Krenk, too, had greeted the morning in a more fatigued state than on retiring the night before. Now, after his forced respect towards the V-P and the pretence of composure on giving Manoel his orders, the need was to express his real fury. And Grace had given him justification.

"You mean you're telling me what you'd like to do . . ."

The exclamation of disbelief rose in volume to an uncontrolled roar. "You impertinent child! You'll do exactly as you're told. Forget about breakfast. Go down and pack your things. Get out of my sight!"

But her brave defiance was not yet exhausted.

"No, Mr Krenk. My duty is to stay," she said quietly. "It's the least I can do for John-Paul."

He refrained from striking her. There was a dignified courage in the young but tired face that convinced him that persuasion rather than threats was the only way to influence her. To bring her back to a state of obedience.

"Let me explain the situation, Grace," he said.

And went on to inform her that she was one of his party, that they were the guests of the government and that they had to conform to protocol. Which meant departing together. There was also the fact that he held her passport, that without his support she could not survive a day in this foreign country and, lastly, the reality that if she introduced herself to the police as the escaped prisoner's fiancée, she was inviting . . .

"Well, you know what, Grace. You wouldn't have a chance. They go mad out here for a blonde, blue-eyed European."

As he had spoken, her defiance had retreated into irresolution. When she replied, it was the voice of the defeated.

"You make me feel like your prisoner, Mr Krenk."

"Not prisoner, Grace. I consider you my responsibility."

It was the only pleasing moment of the morning, the fact that she appeared to accept that she was his responsibility. In return for what seemed her obedience, he placed a consoling arm across her shoulders and suggested that, after all, they should have breakfast together.

At about the same time as Grace was expressing defiance, the government limousine was arriving at Signora Modeste's hotel. The place hardly compared with the Royal Splendor but it fairly represented its name, the Grand Hotel. It was a journey that seemed to be a slow manoeuvring of a leviathan through a blockage of smaller cars and orange-coloured taxis, motor tricycles and pedal tricycles but, when the limousine arrived, it was not at the gates of Paradise Prison but at the ministry.

To her surprise, she was immediately taken to His Excellency Bustanil Wardhana's office, noticing at once that the man greeted her with excessive formality and then hastily retreated behind his desk, as though something urgent needed their attention.

"A disturbing event occurred early today," he said at once.

The deputy-director's immediate interpretation of the man's words and manner was to assume that her son was dead but this fear was quickly allayed. She received a graphic description of an attack on Paradise Prison. The guards had fought heroically but had been outnumbered by five to one. In the confusion, a number of prisoners not associated with the attacking left-wing guerrillas had also managed to escape. Among them had been the COM representative.

The long and dramatic account had given Signora Modeste time to formulate a number of questions.

"Could he not have been kidnapped — for a ransom, Excellency?" she asked. "Or is being held to negotiate the release of other prisoners, comrades in another prison?" And, seeing the minister listening politely, observed: "This is a very serious matter for COM. And your country, as a member of the organization, must be concerned for his safety — no matter the charge against him."

"Naturally, signora," agreed the minister with dishonest reassurance; then added. "On the other hand, I have certain duties."

"Duties? Of course you have. But such as what?"

"Such as discovering if there were political motives to the attempted murder. Could this COM fellow, for example, be a communist, a pacifist?"

And Signora Modeste had to suffer an interrogation on the COM employee, assuring the minister that COM had not been infiltrated by international gangs, neither political ones nor associates of drug cartels, the Mafia, Chinese triads or Timorese terrorists. It was obvious, from the documented evidence she had earlier placed before the minister, that Bonuomo was suffering a breakdown, a total nervous collapse . . .

"Which can happen to any of us," she added in a motherly way, giving the minister a glance that conveyed her warm concern for all the unfortunates of the world. "Have you given orders that this man must be treated well when he's recaptured?"

"Of course, signora. Unless a culprit resorts to violence, our police always behave with admirable restraint." The handsome minister frowned, an indication that he was about to change the course of the conversation. "We have some evidence that makes us feel we are dealing with a mystery man. We intend to find out more about him."

"You mean you are widening your enquiries?" asked Signora Modeste. "Of course."

The minister's disclosure, however, brought on an attack of vertigo. Was she going to faint, she wondered, determined to resist the sensation. But her determination was not enough to prevent her from fainting. When she recovered, she was aware of the minister pouring water between her lips and lightly slapping her cheek.

"Are you all right, signora?"

"Perfectly all right," she replied quickly. "Do sit down, your Excellency. I've suffered all my life from these attacks."

The ease with which she had lied, and a sudden conviction of being with a flexible and sympathetic individual, gave Signora Modeste a strange and most unprofessional idea. What if she told the man the truth? All over the world, she considered to herself, children were taught that honesty was the best policy. At the highest level of governments and international organizations, however, that old-fashioned concept was — or would be, if it ever happened — the response of fools.

"Do you believe, Minister, that honesty is the best policy?" she found herself asking.

Such an undiplomatic question clearly bewildered the minister. When he nodded, it suggested he was preparing to hear an outrageous lie.

"This young man, Bonuomo, is really my son," confessed the deputy-director.

"I don't quite understand," replied the minister, a predictable diplomatic response to give him time to consider the information. "Will you please repeat that?"

Signora Modeste proceeded to give the minister a restrained, detailed account of what had occurred, from John-Paul's first appearance in her office in New York to when he had flown off with a COM passport to rescue his fiancée from the despicable arms dealer, Krenk. Committed to the strange experience of complete honesty, it was difficult to control such a proliferation of truth. Her confession went on from the issue of the passport to the later deception of giving the young man an authentic status within COM then, and for which she now apologized, her flying out to Jakarta for the purpose of deceiving the minister and his government.

She concluded by stating: "I can only excuse myself by saying that my feelings as a mother overcame my principles and my professional duty. If you think I've behaved foolishly, I could not disagree with you. But a mother's love can be right and foolish at the same time."

"I don't know what to say," the minister admitted, when a pause permitted him to speak. "I really don't know what to say. This is extraordinary."

She guessed, La Mamma, that the minister was both confused and uncertain, an experience not dissimilar to what she herself had suffered, the conflict between a deeply felt emotion and the call to higher duty. And when he next spoke, this confusion was confirmed.

"You have placed a terrible responsibility on my shoulders, signora," the minister confessed, his manner gentler than at any moment during the meeting. "Do you realize that your career, in fact your whole future, is in my hands?"

"I do. But I have to admit that I feel better, Excellency. You must decide yourself whether I deserve to hold such a high position at COM."

There was silence for some moments before Wardhana said: "But what puzzles me is that he's called Bonuomo. That's not your name."

"No," agreed the deputy-director. "I forgot to explain that."

"Then you must have married again?"

"No. In fact, I'm divorced."

"Then he was the son of your first husband by another wife?"

"No," she said, still committed to honesty. "It was all part of the deception. But, tell me, Excellency, do you posibly have a son around the same age as mine?"

"I have," the minister said, proudly.

"Have you ever known him to commit a folly of the utmost gravity?"

"He could never do that. He has been brought up as a good Muslim."

Signora Modeste, already exhausted, found a little more strength.

"But if your boy fell madly in love? Young men aren't any different whether they're in your country or mine . . . Couldn't he behave with the same madness?"

"You are wrong, signora. Young people are not the same," said the minister with conviction, a face without doubt. "My son would not fall in love the way you Westerners do — just like that." His hand made a careless, or carefree, gesture of dismissal. He seemed to be enjoying a moment of superiority; of faith, of culture. "Besides, we parents are obliged to watch over our children until they marry."

"And they listen?"

"Of course they listen. Or should I say they have listened all their lives and are therefore created in our image. My boy is twenty-two. He can take up to four wives, but there will be nothing like your Western courtship." He hesitated, as though considering the propriety of a further observation. Then he surrendered to it. "There can be no trying the goods before they've been bought."

Signora Modeste's concern, however, was with finding her son and not in winning arguments. When she had conceded a vague agreement with the minister's views, or at least indicated her understanding, she asked what he proposed to do.

"How will you find him? He could be anywhere. Your country is enormous."

"Enormous or not, signora," said the minister, "he cannot leave it without a passport. And that we've seized. On the other hand, since he escaped with a band of Chinese, and they're the most lawless and cunning of all our minorities, we can't rule out anything. Tell me, could he be involved in the drug trade, is he violent, could you imagine him stealing . . .?"

"Excellency, I'm not being a silly trusting mother when I say that he couldn't possibly be involved in anything like that. All he's after is rescuing his girl. It's as simple as that."

The minister stood up. It indicated the end of the meeting. Or as much as he could tolerate.

"Leave this with me, signora," he said, guiding her from the office. "We get quick results in this country. We have thousands of agents, you Westerners would probably describe them as informers, and we'll soon be on his trail."

In her room at the Grand Hotel, Signora Modeste was not too tired to consider the consequences of the meeting. And her astonishing attack of honesty. What had possessed her! And what could be the dreadful consequences of such honesty? If long experience was anything to go by, the minister would have reverted to his strictly professional role the moment his door had closed, her son would be pursued more relentlessly than ever, COM would be accused of involvement in the attack on the prison, possibly being in the pay of the Chinese, and her own career could be at an end.

As she stared out of the window at an untidy skyline of buildings being both constructed and demolished, she felt she had never before been so vulnerable. It seemed that she, too, was now sharing John-Paul's fate of being pursued.

CHAPTER SEVEN

Crowds were demonstrating again when John-Paul arrived in Hong Kong, not the students who had been protesting in Jakarta about their rights or the Nigerians in Lagos furious about food shortages but half the population of a small enclave of a Western colonial power terrified at the prospect of being returned to their country and people of origin. But since the demonstrations were disorganized, more like noisy protests, and there was no violence, the authorities could conveniently pretend they were not happening.

For the thousands of tourists it was sightseeing and shopping as usual but the young man whose name had changed yet again to Anthony Hitchbottom, a student according to his Australian passport and a year older than John-Paul, had other priorities. First, he needed an address and a telephone number to convey to the good Professor Cheng or one of his colleagues so that information on Krenk's movements could be received; then, a second priority, he had to adapt to living as cheaply as possible.

Within hours of arriving in Hong Kong he had fulfilled his first purpose and made good progress with the second. On the tenth floor of a shopping complex called Chungking Arcade he found a cheap *pension* with the grand name of Dowager Empress Hotel, settled himself in a room without a window but with a bed and a single chair, and waited for something to happen. Below him, however, on all the floors down to the street, much was happening including the busy operations of Night-and-Day illegal brothels, All-Hour illegal gaming dens and one or two traditional but now illegal Anytime drug parlours. At ground level, however, the respectable activities of brightly-lit shops, at least respectable by giving the customer something approaching value for money, continued only until midnight.

It was unlikely that the formidable Dowager Empress, had the building existed a hundred years earlier, would have condescended to set one of her tiny bound feet in such a place but one of her remote descendants, a comparably dominant woman by the name of Alice Wong, had been a guest at the pension for some weeks. It was with this young person, on emerging from his small cell, and beginning to feel lonely, that John-Paul felt compelled to converse. There were only three chairs in the lobby of the pension, and since no one else was present, they were soon talking in a friendly and easy manner. As well as being pleased that Miss Wong spoke fluent English, John-Paul was also aware that she was very pretty and was fashionably dressed; she was also, he guessed, only a little older than himself.

After half an hour, Alice Wong suggested that they should leave the depressing ambience of the lobby of the Dowager Empress for the liveliness outside and that, being free for the rest of the day, she would be happy to introduce him to Hong Kong. It was an offer which John-Paul accepted with gratitude and the afternoon was spent traversing the harbour on ferries, riding on the upper decks of tramcars, being pulled in a rickshaw, and climbing above the city area on the funicular railway. Between these colourful adventures, they had their fortunes told by different kinds of soothsayers, ate numerous small but tasty snacks, visited temples and burnt incense to the revered ancestors of both the Wong and Hitchbottom families.

It was a fast-moving metropolis, Hong Kong, and it seemed to John-Paul that his friendship with Alice was being similarly infected with an almost reckless compulsion. Too much was happening in a short period but there was no way — or will — to resist or dissent. For the first time for many weeks, he was enjoying himself. And when, that evening, she suggested visiting one of the tolerated but illegal gambling houses, she easily overcame his objections. If he had no money to gamble, okay, they would watch others lose theirs. If he was troubled by principles, why hadn't he objected to visiting Buddhist and Taoist temples when he followed another faith? And, besides, since he had been so generous during the day, she insisted on paying the admission money.

And so, on a day that seemed to have been an escape from

reality and from the serious purpose of pursuing Klaus Krenk, John-Paul found himself standing by a roulette table, partly fascinated by the lively personality of Miss Alice Wong, as she occasionally referred to herself, and partly intrigued by the assembly of faces concentrated over the green baize. It seemed that every slightly sweating gambler had placed his life savings on the next spin of the wheel, that winning would bring eternal happiness and losing eternal ruin; and that all that had happened in their lives was not so important as this particular moment. With wonder, appreciatively, he smiled at Alice.

"What are you thinking?" she whispered.

"Truthfully? Well, apart from thinking I'm witnessing a kind of communal madness, I'm thinking how useful a lot of that money would be," he admitted.

"The Chinese follow their instincts. Do you feel this is your lucky day?"

It was a question that first caused John-Paul to laugh, dismissing whatever superstition she had in mind. Then, seized by an absurd recklessness, he said: "Well, let's see."

There began a remarkable half-hour in the life of the reborn Anthony Hitchbottom. As John-Paul Modeste, he had once spent a few days at Las Vegas, a similar period at San Marino on a visit to Italy and a weekend in Monte Carlo. At the tables of the casinos of those places, he had quickly lost all his money, though in total no more than three hundred dollars, but it now seemed that an even greater wheel of fortune had suddenly decided that his luck should change. Beginning with a modest handful of tokens, he quickly needed both hands to carry his winnings. Then his pockets. Then Alice's hands.

"What a night!" he gasped, in a state of disbelief. "How much longer can it last?"

He was aware, turning from giving his new friend a grateful squeeze of the arm, of a further triumph. Some of the habitual gamblers were glancing at him watchfully and suspiciously. Glances that were not missed by Alice.

She said: "They think you're on a lucky streak. They'll put their money on your numbers."

"Is that good or bad?"

"It means that the wheel will soon be fixed so you can't win."

"But that wouldn't be fair."

Miss Alice Wong contemplated the eager face of the inno-cent foreign devil and appeared to come to a decision as determined as any taken by her remote ancestor, the Dowager Empress. Taking John-Paul's arm she tugged him away from the table.

"But I might have gone on to make a million," protested the young man.

"Be satisfied with part of that million."

And he compliantly followed her commands, offered the cashier at the *bureau* stack upon stack of tokens, allowed Alice to count the high-denomination American dollar bills and, with his pockets bulging, further submitted to being led from the air-conditioned interior into the hot and humid air outside.

It was only a short walk to the pension and in the elevator to the tenth floor John-Paul was moved to seize Alice's hand. It had been an exciting day, his new friend had added at every moment to the colour and the liveliness of the place; and now this success at the casino. And with a further desire to express appreciation by physical contact, he squeezed her waist and kissed her cheek. In his room, they counted the winnings. Twenty thousand Yankee dollars, to be exact. And Alice revealed the preoccupation of most of the five million Chinese of the British colony by observing that it was enough on which to live for two years in Australia, four in the Philippines and six in Indonesia.

"Take this, Alice," said John-Paul, giving her a quarter of his winnings.

"Why should I take it!" she protested at once, sitting on the edge of the bed. "I didn't win it."

"But you deserve it."

"I don't take money from a strange man."

"But how can you call me a stranger after today?"

"Did I know you a day ago?"

Her argument prevailed. He remembered that he had been out all evening and that a message might be waiting for him at the desk. An old man was asleep, with his head on the counter and an unlit cigarette between his fingers.

"Any message for Anthony Hitchbottom?"

The old man opened his eyes, took moments to wake up to

the question, then muttered: "No mess."

"Are you sure?"

"No mess."

When John-Paul returned to his room, Alice was reclining rather than lying on the bed. She had removed her blue silk cheongsam-style dress but not her shiny black underwear. He concealed his surprise and sat at the foot of the bed. When Alice smiled, she seemed to be saying that it had been understood all along that the day must end in each other's arms. Then honesty overcame his surprise and he realized that he, too, had been expecting the same. It seemed, after these weeks without Grace, perhaps also the lateness of the hour and being enclosed in a hot and small room, that just for once he could abandon himself, forget his fiancée and consummate the experience of a single day that was too extraordinary to belong to his life.

But thoughts of Grace refused to disappear. Alice's smile continued, as if she intended it to remain until he took her in his arms. And with thoughts of Grace, everything else returned. The monster Krenk, the need to kill the man, to rescue his fiancée; and, yes, not to be diverted or distracted or tempted.

"I want to explain, Alice," said the handsome young man, sadly accepting that the day had ended and that reality must again be faced. "Of course I want to take you in my arms. You're beautiful, you've been wonderful and I trust you."

It seemed important to state how much he trusted her because, with only the slightest hesitation, John-Paul felt compelled to talk about himself, to confide in this new and understanding friend. Also it would soon be morning, another day, when he might have to disappear without a word of farewell. He began, as he had begun with Professor Cheng, by trying to convey that he was ready to die for the woman he loved, that if she, Alice, could not understand how a person could be seized by such an extreme emotion, then all that he was about to tell her would seem foolish, reckless, mad. Without waiting for a reply, however, he went on from event to event, from country to country, from one unlikely situation to the next until, his story uninterrupted by a single question, he finally waited for her response.

It came, a response not to what he had confided but about herself. The earlier smile had disappeared and in its place was an expression of anxiety and despair, the face older, not really beautiful, changed by a private agony.

"I've been using you, Anthony," she said. "You've trusted me. Now it's my turn to trust you."

"But how can you say you've been using me!" protested John-Paul. "We've had a wonderful day, I'm now a rich man and . . ."

Again, in her interruption, the decisiveness of her remote ancestor the Dowager Empress was evident.

"If you'll let me explain, I'll tell you how I would like to use you. I need your help to bring my husband from China."

The day, or rather the night, seemed for John-Paul to take yet another astonishing turn. Alice proceeded to introduce him to her own world of dangers and compelling missions; in fact to what others would see as a madness equal to his own. Hardly more than twenty kilometres from where they were now sitting was one of those frontiers between countries that separated two totally different societies. Every day hundreds of people tried to escape from the great mother country of China to this tiny bit of territory. They had only one purpose in mind. To lead their own lives. But between them and this desire for freedom were frontier guards prepared to kill, minefields and high barbed wire fences and, if they chose to come by sea, patrol boats ready to shoot them on sight.

"I will explain," said Alice; and the tone of her voice was a command not to be interrupted. "Two years ago . . ."

And she explained how she had slipped into Hong Kong during one of the periods when relations between great China and the tiny territory had been more relaxed, and though it had never been lawful to cross the frontier without a permit, at least it had been easy to bribe the frontier guards on one side of the wire and the local police on the other. But now, with relations again going through a bad period, bribes were actually being refused, the illegals seized and imprisoned, and the repatriation laws rigorously enforced. Alice's husband had been unable to follow her.

"I have now, however, prepared a new plan," Alice continued. "All I need is a European to pretend to be my friend or lover. He will help me to sail my boat halfway across the Pearl river, where my husband will be waiting. Once we pick him out of the water, he will hide below deck. If the patrol boats pick us up in their lights, all they'll see is a European enjoying a night out sailing with his Chinese girl."

"And I'm to be that European?" inquired John-Paul, as she waited for a reply to an unstated question.

"You now see how I've been using you."

"Perfectly."

"And what do you say?"

For John-Paul, it was not a difficult decision. And the warm-hearted young man wondered how anyone, in his situation, could possibly refuse.

"Of course I'll help, Alice. Tell me what I have to do?"

The neat Chinese girl stood up and reached for her dress. It was three in the morning. When she was ready to leave, she gently kissed his cheek. Alone, John-Paul reflected on the possible consequences of his decision. But it was too late to change. After all, they all belonged together.

The following morning, John-Paul learned more of Alice's preparations; the kind of boat it was, a six-metre craft that had cost every cent of her savings, where it was moored and what their timetable was to be. She also explained that she was now expert in sailing it, steering it, following the charts and checking directions by both the night sky and the dark contours of coastline and mountains. John-Paul was impressed.

As if to convince him that she had not drawn him into an ill-conceived venture, Alice hastened him to the harbour near Tuen Mun to see the craft, to step on it to prove it was hers and to start the motor to reassure him that it was mechanically sound. The cabin, which covered two-thirds of the boat, contained two bunks, an assortment of ropes and lamps and flags, and looked to be in a state of readiness. There was a seat across the stern and the rudderpost came high above it; and if they were caught in a beam of light from a Marine Police launch, the impression would be that of a romantic couple seated together, one of them displaying the privileged status of being European, enjoying a night far out in the bay. Alice's boat was called *Friendly Faces*.

They returned to the Dowager Empress in the afternoon. The old man at the desk waved a scrap of paper at John-Paul. The message was brief. The spelling was bad but the meaning was clear and, corrected, read: *Your friend is now in Seoul. South Korea. Met by minister.*

"Is everything all right?" asked Alice, who was still at his side and who had noticed John-Paul's change of expression.

"Yes," said the young man. "It's good news."

Once alone in his room, able to consider the information, it was certainly good news; except that he could no longer respond immediately. He was about to pay a high price for Alice's friendship. It would probably be two days before he could fly to Seoul. Possibly longer. And that was assuming the mission was successful. On the other hand, he was indebted to her for his unexpected wealth; and the freedom it permitted could make all the difference between pursuing Krenk and urgently needing money.

"The sooner it's over, the better," said John-Paul, on meeting Alice later. "When can we start?"

"I've already made contact," she replied. "I don't want to give you time to change your mind."

And so, later, in the company of this very determined young woman, John-Paul steered *Friendly Faces* away from the jetty and out of the crowded little harbour near Tuen Mun, two hours to midnight and the streetlights providing enough illumination to delude the many curious faces that here was yet another instance of a barbarian round-eyes carrying off one of their desirable womenfolk for his depraved satisfaction. And, among those watching, as Alice reminded her companion, would have been a couple of government informers.

It was one of those humid nights which had a caressive tangibleness of its own, the craft slipping through the still water, the sky placid yet crowded with stars, the bay and the distant mouth of the wide river stretching darkly in front of them. After a little while Alice took the rudder and began to steer a course which, to John-Paul, had no recognizable bearings but which evoked from her sounds of approval.

After an hour they passed through a number of scattered

lights which Alice explained were stationary fishing boats, one of the few areas of the bay which seemed to be neutral, without a frontier, and where men from both Hong Kong and China could cast their nets. From time to time, lights on the horizon rose into visibility, then receded, not villages on a shore but large cargo ships sailing to or from the major city of Canton at the head of the river. Then Alice turned *Friendly Faces* to the north, indicating by the care with which she checked her chart and the darker contours on the landward horizon, that this was one of the crucial points of her course.

"Good," she murmured.

"Which side of the line are we on?" asked John-Paul.

"The Chinese, of course. The danger is from the Hong Kong Marine Police launches. Once we start back and enter their waters, you'll soon see them come out of nowhere. We'll be stopped at least once."

The information did not unnerve John-Paul. He had seemed, on starting his pursuit of Klaus Krenk, to have moved from an existence in which prudent behaviour and the conventional idea of responsibility had changed to the freedom to act courageously and to follow his convictions. The oppression of people, he had discovered, took many forms. His impetuous and innocent Grace, seeking an adventurous and well-paid position, must surely have become Krenk's slave and mistress. A Chinese husband and wife were denied their right to be together in a country of their own choosing. And what had he seen in Jakarta? And Nigeria? And Colombia? Being with Alice on the boat *Friendly Faces* was all part of a wider involvement in a world that had not existed until he had discovered it. Or stumbled on it. By that first blind rage against Krenk.

"We're almost an hour early," he heard Alice shout. "This is about the spot."

The engine was switched off, a miniature anchor thrown into the water and a signalling lamp and a rope made ready. Then John-Paul was commanded to join Alice on the aft seat.

"We'll have some tea," she announced, drawing a thermos from a plastic bag of supplies. "Then I'll tell you about my husband. The kind of man he is, good and brave . . ."

The world seemed to go silent, as if wanting to listen, too, and the almost black sky and the tiny bright stars and the very still water surrounding the small boat drew them into a vast but invisible presence. Mysteriously.

". . . and high-minded."

He had been an army captain, Alice's husband, obedient and loyal and, like almost everyone in a country with the largest population in the world, keeping his opinions to himself. Her story began three years earlier, she explained, when the good captain had been chosen for a special duty.

"It was a great honour," said Alice. "And it was this."

That year, the leaders of the country had held an international congress that was attended by almost fifty presidents, princes and prime ministers. For the great occasion, a special venue was constructed at a cool hill station a hundred kilometres from Shanghai. It was a congress to celebrate the achievements of the Chinese people and their mighty and supreme leaders, and though most of the visiting presidents, princes and prime ministers, would have been against the political and social system of the host country, they were not against spending a week in luxurious palaces or villas, in gardens that had been carefully prepared by thousands of the descendants of those who had set out the glorious royal parks of centuries earlier, and where they would enjoy the tastiest foods and the finest wines that the fields and the vineyards of the planet could produce.

The mission of the good captain was therefore of the highest importance. From the quaysides of the port of Shanghai, and from the storehouses packed with imported provisions specially sent by rail from Hong Kong, his convoy of trucks had to pick up the supplies for the congress and deliver them to the hill station. It had taken fifty men a whole day to load the trucks, and when the task was complete, the captain had led the convoy out of the city.

It was not a straightforward story for Alice to tell. From time to time, correctly assuming the young European's ignorance, she digressed to explain certain characteristics of the system. For example, its reliance on the army, the way it served as an auxiliary public service, the way it was above the law and the absolute authority of the officer in charge of the convoy. Once the loaded convoy was outside the city, however, Captain Wong had changed direction and headed for the agricultural community of Tseng Po.

Why Tseng Po? Alice asked rhetorically.

"My husband's *heung ha* or ancestral home had been absorbed into the community so he always considered himself a son of those parts. For the previous year he had been deeply upset because a drought had brought near starvation to the two thousand people of the community. Some had even died. Appeals to the government had brought only promises. You know how it is with governments."

John-Paul agreed that he knew how it was with governments and was then told of what happened next. The convoy had driven two hundred kilometres in a different direction, arriving at Tseng Po just as the community was rising in the morning and ready to depart for the parched fields and the withered shrubs. The captain had at once called them into the communal square to make an official announcement over the loudspeaker system. When more than half the people had gathered, he told them that the government was responding to their appeal, that he had brought them the finest foods and wines, and that they were to have a week-long feast to celebrate the achievements of the party and the country.

It was an honour for such a poor community to be visited even by an army captain, and though the generosity of the government was beyond belief, the good comrades of Tseng Po did not hesitate to obey the directive. There were also thirty soldiers under the captain's command, and they were given a similar order. Eat, drink and be merry! There was not a single case of disobedience. It was doubtful whether, in all the experience of hard-working and loyal peasants, and in that of the conscripted soldiers, any order had ever been obeyed with such enthusiasm and joy. Men and women who had tasted little more than rice and a few vegetables, the occasional chicken and a little dried fish during all their lives, now feasted on the most succulent meats, the rarest of shell fish, crates of fruit from Africa and Australia, and canned luxuries from France and America. And for those who liked a glass of alcohol and who had tasted only the roughest of rice wine, there were whiskies and cognacs, still wines and champagne, German beers and Spanish sherries; and to be drunk by the bottle rather than sipped frugally from small glasses.

No one could say that the good folk of Tseng Po had not feasted as well as presidents and princes but whether the banqueting lasted a week or not, the good captain was never able to verify. On the second day, satisfied that his orders were being obeyed, and that in fact the desire to be obedient was even accelerating, he had waited for night to fall, changed his uniform for the clothes of a farm labourer, and walked out of Tseng Po and into the darkness.

The first Alice knew of what her husband had done was when the police and the army had descended on their modest home and taken away all the good captain's possessions; and stolen a few other valuables as well. To the bare story given to her by the authorities, she gradually received clandestine messages from trusted friends and relatives. Her husband would not be returning to Nanchang and she must prepare herself to leave as soon as he summoned her.

"A month after his disappearance, he called me to the mountain town of Kweiyang, where we made plans for the future. Since what he had done would bring the death penalty, we had to leave the country. But leaving the country meant finding a lot of money. Well, as you'll have guessed, we had only enough for one, and being a good wife, I didn't argue when he told me I should go first."

And Alice went on to describe how she had escaped by boat, in the same clandestine way that her husband was now attempting, and that after a miserable few months in Hong Kong, she had learnt how best to make a living, a good living, she admitted, then went on hastily, and a little guiltily, to say that much of the money had gone to China to support her husband and to help him pay for his escape. And even the naive John-Paul, though not quite permitting the idea to become a firm conclusion, guessed that she had supported herself in ways about which he did not wish to hear.

A little later, he said: "The fishing fleet seems to be getting closer."

Six or seven dull orange lights sending reflections across the water had advanced without seeming to be in motion.

"It won't be long now," said Alice. "Just keep your eyes open."

He kept them open. And all his other senses, tensely alert. Then there was a slight splashing sound followed a moment later by the pale arms of a swimmer emerging regularly from the water. When he reached the side of *Friendly Faces*, he was helped into the boat and lay gasping without speaking for some moments. Not a word was exchanged between husband and wife until the middle-aged man had recovered, at least could rise to his feet and embrace her. A conversation followed, not a word understood by John-Paul, but the minutes of being totally excluded ended when Alice, in a mixture of English and Mandarin, introduced him to her husband.

The motor came to life again, filling the universal silence with sound. The orange lights of the fishing fleet were left slowly behind. They crossed into Hong Kong waters, and Alice mentioned the fact, as if they had sailed over a printed line on a map. And when John-Paul asked how far they were from the coast, she did not reply with a calculation of distance but with the time it would take to swim to the shore.

Then she said: "At any moment a police launch is going to turn on its lights. Then we swim for it. You stay on the boat and cover for us."

"Cover?" John-Paul enquired, confused. "But I thought your husband was going to hide below? And you and I were going to sit at the back?"

"Change of plan. My husband's orders," said Alice. Her voice was sharp and a little nervous, unlike the charming young woman of the Dowager Empress Hotel. "You make sure you keep *Friendly Faces* between the launch and ourselves. Once we enter the water, we'll need a couple of minutes to swim out of the light."

"But what if they smash into the boat?"

"That would be the best thing of all," replied Alice. "They'll have seen you're a European so they would stop and rescue you."

She proceeded to remove her cotton blouse and trousers, leaving John-Paul to steer the boat. At a command in Mandarin, her husband emerged from the cabin. Her prescience was timely and exact, the result of months of planning, and when the Marine Police launch sent its wedge of daylight across the darkness, she and her husband went silently over the side. As they swam away, John-Paul gave the engine full throttle, not seeking to escape but directing the boat at the oncoming launch.

The young man needed neither seamanship nor practice. Like animals just born that instinctively struggle to their feet or stretch their heads to take milk, his steering was exact and certain. He was also helped by the element of surprise. The helmsman of the launch was hardly prepared for someone on a suicide mission and, unwilling or unable to change course, smashed into *Friendly Faces*. It was carried some distance before sinking and, as it did so, a siren sent out a continuous wail. Or sound of fury.

"You bloody fool!" exclaimed an English officer, as John-Paul was pulled on to the deck. "Are you mad?"

His staring Chinese PCs seemed to share his conclusion. Police Launch 65 had been patrolling the coastal waters for many years and had been involved in hundreds of pursuits; but not one had ended like this.

"Take him below," ordered the officer.

With his arms gripped firmly, John-Paul was pushed along the gangway.

As the interrogation of the young man proceeded, there were others who also considered John-Paul to be mad. His responses to the questioning that had begun immediately he had been put ashore were so provocative, brief and uncompromising, that he was quickly passed on to higher authorities. He would not have received this fairly considerate treatment had he been Chinese; in fact, he would have been taken to the Lo Wu bridge and roughly pushed to the other side, but as a European his offence could not be resolved in such an arbitrary fashion.

The first stages of his questioning by a board of Marine Police inspectors were therefore concerned with establishing his identity and discovering his real purpose. Had they uncovered the tip of an international operation? Was this fellow part of a drug racket — even associated with a Chinese triad? Could he be a political troublemaker, particularly in view of the sensitive relations between the colony and the neighbouring mother country, which would soon be absorbing it under its rule? After two days, the authorities seemed satisfied that he was neither a drug trader nor a political activist but they still could not accept the bare report submitted by the commander of Police Launch 65, that he had probably been assisting illegal immigrants.

"This nonsense has gone on long enough," Deputy Regional Commander Fanshawe said, beginning the final interrogation before handing the case over to the public prosecutor. "Let me explain the powers of this inquiry. If we're satisfied that you've simply been involved in a misguided humanitarian action, we can recommend you for immediate deportation. On the other hand, if you're involved in something more criminal, well, it's a court trial and a long prison sentence." He leaned, fatherly-fashion, over the desk. "Come on, lad, we want to help you — so how about helping us?"

John-Paul was a very different individual from the young man who had entered his mother's presence many weeks earlier and announced his intention to kill Klaus Krenk. The remarkable experiences in a number of oppressive countries, like the forced maturing of plants or animals, had concentrated a normal life-span of years into a couple of months. Deputy Regional Commander Fanshawe and the two colleagues on his board were therefore faced by an accused person who refused to be intimidated and, worse, who seemed not to accept that he had committed a crime.

"All I've done," John-Paul now repeated, standing between two Chinese police constables, "was to help a most admirable man and wife . . ."

"Admirable?"

"Why not?" John-Paul replied to the chief of the board. "Can't you imagine that people seeking freedom by an illegal method could be admirable?" He stared from one pink, clean-shaven, middle-aged face to another. A hard lot, concluded the young man. But he was determined not to compromise, not to be untruthful. "I wasn't paid for my help, my action wasn't some kind of protest against the colonial system and I'm not likely to repeat what I've done." In his mind, however, he felt his last remark had been cowardly, and quickly added: "But I would if I had to."

He was being interrogated by three senior officers in pale-green twill uniforms with badges of high rank on their shoulders. Although, like himself, they were the product of European civilization, they seemed infinitely more alien to his nature than the Chinese he had met. They carried about them an authority that was neither cruel nor vicious but seemed equally formidable because of an assumption of absolute rightness and of being the appointed representatives of eternal justice.

"Hitchbottom," said DRC Fanshawe, who was clearly in charge, "I'm prepared to believe you're a well-intentioned young fool but that doesn't alter the fact that you've committed a crime. A very serious one."

Above his head, a portrait of the crowned queen of his colony smiled approvingly at the words of her representative. Or so John-Paul saw it. She might even, in his imagination, have murmured: Good show, Fanshawe.

"The really serious crime has been committed by yourselves," the young man was impelled to reply. "They were trying to escape from tyranny, they wanted to reach safety. Who was trying to stop them — you or I? In fact, we should be on the opposite sides of this desk. You're the ones who should be on trial."

Two of the three senior officers went red with fury but one of them responded like a human being. At least he smiled and nodded in half agreement with what John-Paul had just said.

"Okay, Hitchbottom, from a moral point of view you may be right. But think of how things are in the colony. Where do we put all these thousands of refugees? We're a small island — well, not much more. We've got to house them, feed them, find work for them, absorb them into our society . . . Come on, now. Be sensible."

His queen continued to smile approvingly. And again John-Paul seemed to hear her speak. And say: Sound sense, Commander. Sound sense.

The young man, however, did not respond to the plea to be sensible. He made the most outrageous suggestion that any of the senior officers had ever heard. He said:

"It's a matter of priorities. There are luxury hotels all over the place. Thousands of beds for the tourists. Why not choose to help the desperate and the threatened rather than those visiting this place for a good time? Take over the hotels and give the beds to the illegal immigrants."

There was a silence of disbelief, then the officer who had not yet spoken said: "You can't be serious . . . That's one of the ways we make our living — by tourism!"

But John-Paul was serious. These were the men who administered the law, who upheld, were supposed to repre-sent, all the values and good sense of a caring civilized society. Alice and her husband, on the other hand, were . . . What? Without rights because they were on the wrong side of a line on the map, on territory which regarded them as aliens. Aliens! Human beings alien to an area of their own planet!

The young man was becoming angry but he managed to suppress the evidence of this. He thought of the way patrio-tism possessed otherwise decent and kindly people, of whole countries for whom a few words and a national anthem were sacred, for which men died, soldiers, rulers, whole societies . . . There was the Marseillaise, Deutschland Uber Alles, God Bless America . . .

John-Paul glanced at the portrait on the wall, and said: "God Save the Queen."

Stunned expressions appeared on the faces of the three senior officers and one of them murmured: "What did he say? Did I hear correctly?"

But DRC Fanshawe had not only heard. He had come to a conclusion.

"This fellow should be turned over for a psychiatric report," he said. "Listen, Hitchbottom, I want an honest answer. Have you ever had any . . . Well, emotional prob-lems? A nervous breakdown?"

"God Save the Queen," repeated John-Paul, having at last decided that honest replies would be misconstrued and that silence could be provocative.

"He's being impertinent."

"He's insulting the Queen."

"I've a good mind to thump the little shit."

The concert of hostility from those across the desk served to remind the young man that he was totally at their mercy. If they decided he should face trial, to be followed by a prison sentence, how could he possibly continue his pursuit of Klaus Krenk? For a few moments, as he faced the reddening angry faces, he was pulled in two directions. Grace had to be rescued but, on the other hand, how could he admit to guilt for having been involved in another kind of rescue which was even more compelling?

"God Save the Queen," he repeated again, ignoring the need for prudence.

If John-Paul had imagined that he had chosen the least provocative course, his mistake was quickly apparent. His further impertinence towards the portrait of a lady wearing a jewelled crown caused the officers to put their heads together and exchange muttered comments. One audible suggestion seemed to find general agreement, that the young man in front of them needed to be taught respect for the monarch.

"Well, Hitchbottom," said DRC Fanshawe, as if the half audible exchanges had taken place in another room, "we don't like your attitude at all. Helping illegals or drug smuggling is one thing. Disrespect towards Her Majesty is a more serious matter altogether. A little lesson in respect won't be out of place."

And with that short announcement, the senior officer stood up, left the office and returned moments later in the company of a heavily-built junior European officer and two more Chinese constables.

"You'll be going to the cells for a bit, Hitchbottom, while we consider what to do," said DRC Fanshawe. "Since you've refused to cooperate, we've got to consider very carefully what is the best course."

In the cells, or rather in one of them, John-Paul received his lesson in respect. The three senior officers had been gentlemen of a sort, their demeanour suggested that by speech and manner they could decently represent in public the lady in the gilt-framed picture above their heads, but the young officer in charge of a brief course of education seemed to have come from a rougher background altogether. His first action, as John-Paul was held against the cell wall by two constables, was to punch him in the stomach; then to repeat the blow a little lower down.

John-Paul, however, was not the only one receiving a lesson. The junior officer, with each swing of his fists, appeared to be passing on his expertise to his Chinese subordinates.

"You must never leave bruises. If you do, and a medical report shows the prisoner's been beaten up, we're all in the shit. Okay?" And he proceeded to hit the young man with the flat sides of his fist, with his knee and with his elbow, in the fleshier parts of his body. "Here and here and here!"

John-Paul did not lose consciousness but he was not aware of what was happening. There was the painful sensation of his body receiving blow after blow, and that he was too winded to breathe and too weak and helpless to be able to defend himself; but he vaguely knew he was neither dead nor unconscious, as if the junior officer was even trained in that, the art of severely beating prisoners without their feeling they were actually going to die.

"There," said the tough European at last. "Now give him some water."

And he smiled at John-Paul, as if expecting appreciation for such a benevolent gesture, and encouraged the young man to drink up, to sit down if he wished and, seriously, to consider himself lucky that it had been no worse.

John-Paul was left in solitude for half-an-hour. Then he was escorted back to the presence of the three senior officers. He was surprised that he could walk and stand erect when his body was suffering so much pain, and considered whether there would be any point in making a complaint.

But DRC Fanshawe's bland greeting quickly made it apparent that it would be a wasted protest.

"Ah, Hitchbottom," he said, "But you look a little shaken, old man. Are you all right?"

"Perfectly all right," John-Paul replied, again aware that what really mattered was the decision of the three senior officers in front of him. And, bravery demanding he remained nonchalant, asked: "Let me know the worst. Have you decided to put me on trial?"

His words were greeted by smiles, as if a more kindly set of officers had replaced those of earlier.

"We've given your case careful consideration, Hitchbottom," said DRC Fanshawe, "and we've reached the following conclusions. First, you were probably motivated by high principles but you were totally ignorant of the consequences of your behaviour. Then you were unaware of the seriousness of adding to the overcrowded conditions of Hong Kong and failed to appreciate the heavy responsibilities we British carry in the colony. However . . ."

In the pause that followed, John-Paul suddenly realized that all the senior officer was saying could be stated in a few words. And before he could check himself, he had uttered them.

"You mean I'm rocking the boat."

John-Paul had instinctively used a phrase that he knew would find favour with his interrogators, one that they probably used repeatedly themselves. The result was a line of pleased smiles, as if a particularly obtuse pupil had passed a test.

"Now you've got it!" said Fanshawe. "In fact the image isn't as fanciful as you might think. Hong Kong may be a fairly big boat but it can capsize if we behave stupidly." The DRC leaned forward. "Now I'll let you have the good news."

John-Paul was to be deported immediately. From what the police had seized at the Dowager Empress Hotel, discovered by going through the register of arrivals in the colony, he appeared to have a considerable sum of money, which meant that his deportation would not be a charge on the state. Which was to his credit. And when the young man, realizing that everything was to be gained by his cooperative attitude, asked for a favour, it was immediately granted.

"Instead of sending me back to Australia, may I fly on to South Korea? To be with old friends?"

The high officials agreed. Pleasantly. And advised him, once he had arrived in a country where the police were particularly severe on lawbreakers, to watch his step. The penalties could be very painful.

With his body aching in a dozen places, John-Paul promised to take their advice.

CHAPTER EIGHT

At about the same time as John-Paul was enjoying the sights of Hong Kong in the company of Miss Alice Wong, Signora Modeste was in a state of despair. What new folly was her son perpetrating? What further misfortune had overtaken him?

Her agony, however, was ended by Mr Singh the Sikh, the COM representative in Jakarta. There were many Sikhs in the region of the Far East, and almost as many Singhs, but this gentleman was always given his full title out of respect for his dedication to COM and his admirable reputation. In this instance, when he called at the Grand Hotel to inform the deputy-director of the fate of the missing representative, a John-Paul Bonuomo, he clearly deserved that reputation.

The missing COM man was not dead, he assured Signora Modeste, nor had he been kidnapped or cut to ribbons by knives, cleavers or kukries. In fact, he had escaped from Paradise Prison with members of a Chinese triad and they, for reasons he had not been able to discover but which were probably connected with money, had enabled him to leave for Hong Kong on a false passport.

At first, the deputy-director dismissed Mr Singh the Sikh's information as one of the colourful stories of the local community but he soon convinced her that his twenty years in Jakarta had permitted him to set up a network which was even better than that of the local police. Who else, except the COM representative in Jakarta, could hope to gain the trust of communists and criminals, the Chinese and other persecuted minorities, free-thinkers and all the others regarded as enemies of the state?

When Mr Singh the Sikh's honour had been placated by her eventual acceptance of his story, he went on to state how worried he had been that one of their representatives should have been arrested and, while not approving of his crime, that it was a relief to have him out of the country. Signora Modeste replied by admitting that she shared his relief and that, to show her appreciation for his undoubted abilities, she would be recommending him for promotion when she returned to New York.

The turbaned and bearded Sikh bowed happily and departed. Left to herself, Signora Modeste enjoyed that deep relief known only to mothers, that her child was not condemned to a dreadful fate, and considered the new situation. It would obviously be foolish, if not impossible, to try to trace the boy to Hong Kong. Similarly, she would be well advised to keep up the pretence to the local officials, and the minister, of knowing no more than she had been told by them. On the other hand, there was the considerable relief that her son was no longer travelling on a COM passport and that no further favours were required from His Excellency Bustanil Wardhana.

As her heavy body relaxed further, her mind indulged in the extraordinary desire to relax with it. Her years with COM had been one long period of commitment, of dedication, of duty. Now, far from her headquarters in New York, and with the connivance of Count von Baum himself, she could extend her absence and enjoy a brief period of freedom. A few days without obligations. Yes, actually take a holiday. But she had hardly come to the decision to take a complete rest from her work and the demands of her high-principled life when she became aware of a sensation she described as THE DREAM.

The sensation was neither sudden nor unfamiliar. Throughout her career with COM, she had carried a secret fantasy as others carried ambition, a hidden love or perverse desires. And what was this secret fantasy she had never dared to put into words? From time to time Signora Modeste had negotiated with, or simply sat with, some of the most evil oppressors and national rulers of modern times. As she had talked and stared at these present-day tyrants, and on occasion even dined with them, she had wondered if they could ever be persuaded to change their characters and their ways. In THE DREAM, she was suddenly possessed of the power to turn them from evil to good, from cruel to kind. Yes, in dreams one could hope for the impossible.

Signora Modeste, at heart, was a simple woman and close to the warm and expressive ways of her native Sicily but, with COM, it was the head and not the heart that had come to dominate her life. The dream had therefore remained not only a fantasy but a guilty secret. Even if the idea of changing evil people into good was accepted as impossible, the same ridicule would have been the response to suggesting its desirability. Now, however, in Room 627 at the Grand Hotel in Jakarta, the deputy-director succumbed to the dream. What if . . .

Quietly she considered the fact that she was sitting in a room in a part of the world where almost every country was ruled by either a tyrant or a form of government that could be described as oppressive, where people were told how to lead their lives rather than being able to decide for themselves. Suppose, she thought to herself, I had to choose a country in this region to put my dream to the test, which would it be? One by one, the worst were eliminated from her mind. Tyrants, too, could be divided between the inhuman and the slightly human; and she finally decided on Angladesh.

All that day, and the next, delaying her departure from Indonesia, Signora Modeste fought to suppress the absurd dream. But why not Angladesh? It was ruled by a genial tyrant, a military general who had survived rather longer than those other generals who had been regularly assassinated during the previous thirty years. For how long had Chowdhury ruled? Three or four years, she calculated. And who better to visit? They had met occasionally in New York, they had dined together, they had laughed together and they had even discussed the remote idea of Angladesh honouring its obligations to the COM charter.

But even after two days, Signora Modeste remained infected by the madness. If she followed the dream, she would be guilty of the worst crimes that officials and administrators could possibly commit, those of idealism, visions, the taint of principles. On the third day she surrendered to the dream. At worst, the genial tyrant would dismiss her as someone temporarily deranged or, since Angladesh was that kind of country, that it was only what could be expected of a woman.

There was no direct flight from Jakarta to Acca, the capital of Angladesh, so she had to pass the night in Singapore, the travel centre of the region. If she hoped that a change of surroundings would cure her, she was wrong. The dream was as pressing as ever. From Singapore, the flight to Acca took four hours. She found her own hotel, then called the local COM representative, a surprised Mr Islam, and announced her arrival. Would he come round at once? Her instructions were brief and revealed nothing. Would he arrange a meeting for her with the President? The bewildered representative said he hoped that he had done nothing wrong and that no complaints had been passed back to COM headquarters, then, when reassured, hurried away to obey his instructions.

After his departure, Signora Modeste stood at the window high above the city. A little like Jakarta, though much smaller, she looked down on the desolation of centuries, the desolation greater the more modern the buildings. Crumbling structures of faded grey and fawn, a conglomeration of rooftops so untidy that they might not have formed streets and squares, a few multi-storey office blocks like giant tombstones, and palm trees drooping despairingly, seemed to confirm what she knew about the country. It was the poorest, most miserable place for thousands of miles in every direction. It was constantly flooded, with half the crops destroyed by that yearly catastrophe; famine and plagues and popular uprisings suppressed by military rulers were all part of a regular cycle of events; and the heat and humidity, the malaria and the dysentery, debilitated without discrimination the population, society, the rulers and even the functions of the state itself.

She had chosen well, decided Signora Modeste. This was the most wretched place on earth. Later that day, she learnt that the President had graciously invited her to dinner on the following evening.

It was part of the earthy philosophy of Klaus Krenk to proclaim that the best things in life were free. This was not an argument to vindicate his great wealth but because in rare moments of humility it was clear that relieving a full bladder, enjoying a good night's sleep, quenching a thirst with plain tap-water, being spared toothache and many other aspects of human frailty, were more important than money. Similarly, after a long and tiring journey, particularly when one was getting old, to have reached his destination and to be able to rest and relax were among the great comforts of life.

Another stage of his world tour was over. The visit to Seoul had been brief but successful. With a wealthy country like South Korea, there were none of the involvements of raising international loans, doubting its ability to honour its commitments or of having to watch every manoeuvre and analyze every word as though one were bartering in Alexandria or Bombay. Happy the country that could pay cash for its own military strength. And, relaxing on his arrival at the government rest house just outside the city of Acca, he contrasted this rundown, impoverished, dirty country of Angladesh with the one he had just left. Yes, there was all the difference between the healthy and the sickly, the lively and the torpid.

Among the delights that came to an old man at the end of a tiring journey was that of having a beautiful young woman as a captive servant, Grace transformed from waywardness to obedience by a few days of harsh experience and the realization of her dependence on him. It was a greatly pleasing development. It restored — dare he imagine it? — a little of youth.

"My slippers," commanded the man who could privately see himself as one of the kings of the world, not ruler of a palaceful of menials but, perhaps even more satisfying, of a lovely girl who, after defying him, had now been conquered. "And some iced water. See it's bottled. Nothing from the local taps."

And in this indulgent mood, Krenk allowed himself, with uncharacteristic generosity, to consider Grace's situation. She appeared to have recovered well from the upsetting events in Jakarta and, if she was suffering inside, she was sensibly not displaying it. Also, to his relief, she seemed to have taken an optimistic view of her fiancé's escape. He wasn't in prison, therefore he couldn't be tortured. The country was a collection of islands, so he could find a boatman to sail him away; or he could stow away on a ferry. Why not? She had faith in him . . .

Grace returned with his requirements, the iced water, his slippers.

"There," she said dutifully, removing damp socks and

shoes too heavy for the climate, and pushing slippers over his bare feet. "More comfortable?"

"Good girl. Now tell the boys I won't need them this evening. They can go into town — that's if it appeals to them."

The internal telephone system, like half the country, had broken down so Grace left him alone while she crossed to the rooms of the two bodyguards. In her absence, he decided to encourage her further with a reward, not a material one but that of status.

"I'm very pleased with you, Grace," he announced on her return. "Now that you've got a better understanding of how I work, the discretion that's needed, you can again take up your secretarial duties. Are you pleased?"

"Yes, Mr Krenk. Thank you."

He glanced at her in case her politeness indicated mockery. There was none. He decided to be even more munificent by pretending to be concerned about her fiancé.

"Don't despair, Grace. If the security forces find the young man, they won't torture or kill him. I've paid for him to be sent back to New York." Then Krenk added what he considered the most convincing proof of all. "The money is already in the minister's Swiss account. At the level I work at, it never pays to cheat."

At ten o'clock on the following morning, Krenk took his place at the negotiating table in what was called the Old Palace and which now served as the headquarters of the Ministry of Defence. He was in the company of four uniformed generals, two civil servants and his secretary, now restored to favour. In the interval of waiting for the President, General Chowdhury, the conversation dwelt on the terrible floods that were devastating the country and the ingratitude of whole communities that were protesting about the government's failure to help, as if acts of God could be blamed on their great ruler. There was even violent unrest in the remoter parts of the country, all of which Krenk deplored as heartily as the others round the table.

Any indications of internal unrest, possible civil wars, border disputes between countries and outright invasions were, in fact, always good news to Klaus Krenk and he waited confidently to conclude the package deal which had been prepared over a period of months. The air conditioning of the Old Palace had broken down, as had the water supply and the sewage system, but the overhead fans, relics of the old colonial days, created a cooling draught; and a white-robed servant holding a silver tray of mineral water and orange juice stood behind every chair.

Half-an-hour late, General Chowdhury, in the company of two aides, came through doors held open by liveried attendants. His flowing white moustache contrasted with his slightly brown skin, and his bulging eyes suggested a thyroid complaint. His khaki uniform, a type worn for combat, was decorated by six rows of medal ribbons and, instead of taking his seat, he stood behind it and announced that he was declaring a state of emergency. Further stretches of the principal river of the country had overflowed, the death toll had risen by a hundred thousand and five million more of the population had either lost their homes, were marooned or were heading for the safety of the hills.

"I'm sorry to call off this meeting," the President announced with crisp authority. "But as father of the people I have a duty to help. As you are my guest, Mr Krenk, I will honour you by allowing you to accompany me."

It was an honour, as the helicopter rose magically but noisily from the lawns of the Old Palace, that Krenk would willingly have forsaken but the cunning trader in him recognized that the father of the people, in this manic mood, would have taken refusal as an insult to the dead, the dying, the living and the unborn. He felt a little abandoned without Grace, who had been left behind, and a little frightened by a first experience of seeming to float in the air rather than to be flying. But movement they were making because the rooftops of Acca were soon left behind and the first brown stretches of water gave way to what seemed a vast muddy sea.

"I am not called the Light of Angladesh for nothing, Mr Krenk," said the President. "When I descend from the heavens, people in remote areas think I'm God. Perhaps they're right."

"I'm sure they are," Krenk said.

"He is," said one of the accompanying generals. "Our president has given us peace and order and pride in our country."

The helicopter eventually descended on the largest of the islands in the light brown sea. It was a town that had been submerged to about a quarter of its normal size, mostly a collection of small box-like buildings with mosques rising above their flat roofs. In the centre of the unflooded area, the surviving population of the town had assembled in the market square, a cordon of police keeping them in order. A temporary platform had been erected for the President's visit and two amplifiers pointed at the crowd from telegraph poles. When the President spoke, his voice was heard by everyone.

"He's telling them that supplies will be dropped this evening," explained one of the accompanying generals to Krenk. "He's assured them that the floods are now falling, the town will be rebuilt and everyone compensated for their losses."

"A great leader," Krenk said readily, wondering whether in fact a single brown face in the crowd believed a word. "They obviously see him as God."

"They certainly do."

But the police remained alert for any demonstration against God; or even the odd shouted heresy. Then a number of mullahs came forward and led the crowd in prayer, finally embracing the Father of the People before he flew off in his helicopter.

"You saw how they loved me and why I must always do my duty," said the President. "I reminded them of their good fortune in being alive and in having a leader who put their welfare above all else, even his own life. I also told them they needed faith. That it's better than comfort and riches."

Krenk added his agreement to the voices of the President's party. Apart from the two pilots, there were six passengers, the interior crowded but offering remarkable views for all of them, the helicopter flying low enough to recognize that the tiny floating islands were bloated cattle or uprooted trees or human bodies. But Krenk remained nervous for two reasons. He could not conquer the fear that the flimsy shell in which they were flying would suddenly drop into the water below and, the second reason, that the President was even crazier than he had imagined.

Then Krenk heard: "Siddiqui, change seats."

"Of course, Mr President."

The quiet aide who had sat in the companion seat to Krenk's, and who had been a reassuringly calm neighbour, stood up and moved forward. In his place, and a much bulkier figure, the President settled himself. His manic smile suggested a sudden impulse to correct any neglect of the important visitor to his country and a determination to impress him.

"Well, Krenk," said the President, "what better place to discuss our affairs than out on a field mission! You've observed my dedication to the needs of my people, haven't you!" The presidential head turned to the right. "Just look below, Krenk. If it wasn't for all the flooding, we'd have the most fertile land in the world. Better than Egypt with its River Nile. Don't you agree?"

Krenk proceeded to agree with everything the President said but what he most feared, that the man would eventually turn to business, was a fear soon fulfilled.

"What've you finally come up with?" demanded the President, his voice booming into his guest's ear. "Anyway, you must admit that we've escaped one of those drawn-out sessions at the Ministry of Defence. Who wants to sit through all that detailed stuff, this clause of the agreement, that sub-clause, substituting one word for another with exactly the same meaning . . . Don't you agree?"

Klaus Krenk had always hated the feeling of being under pressure, of being trapped, of not having the opportunity to manoeuvre, avoid, delay and escape. It required considerable courage to reply in the manner he did but he felt he had no alternative.

"With respect, Mr President. This isn't the way to negotiate. Without your advisers, without the documents . . ."

"Who needs advisers? Who needs documents?" demanded the booming voice. "I'm not president for nothing, Krenk. I make the decisions."

In his most diplomatic manner, Klaus Krenk proceeded to treat the President as if he were a child, which he was not, and a rogue always seeking advantages, which he was.

"Mr President, I propose to tell you a few things in confidence," Krenk said, in a low voice. "Strictly secret, you understand?"

General Chowdhury's manic manner, at such an inviting prospect, moderated at once. High above the brown floods below, and the devastation of a thousand villages, he nodded and whispered like a bazaar trader settling a deal.

"Not too loud, then."

"Angladesh is getting the best deal I've ever put together, Mr President, and I'm going to tell you how I've done it."

And Krenk, to spare himself the pressing questions of the manic ruler, went into a long explanation of how he had persuaded international banks and other creditors to lend enormous sums of money to a country without resources, without gold reserves and without prospects for the future. The President frowned at such a truthful picture of his country but he managed to retain his composure. And to listen in silence.

"It is a great balancing act, Mr President. The arms manufacturers, in these times when the world is going through one of its misguided periods of disarmament, are only too pleased to reduce their prices, even to make small losses, particularly when payment is guaranteed by major banks rather than by a poor country. In turn, the banks can't lose because of other arrangements I've made. Apart from the safety net of being able to write off losses for non-payment of debts against their national taxes, I have made a further provision."

And he went on to describe his excellent relations with some of the directors of the Bank of Mankind. After three or four years, which was a short period for international banks, Angladesh would receive from the international agency large sums of money in the form of interest-free loans and aid. Instead of this money being used for urgent development projects, it would be used to pay off the creditor banks. There would also, of course, Krenk explained to the President, have to be discreet gifts to the directors of BOM, a few million dollars . . .

"Call it a commission. For help, Mr President. One per cent. It's nothing," said Krenk.

"It's nothing," the President agreed. "And we get the latest missiles?"

"Of course."

"And fighter planes?"

"The best."

"And two modern submarines?"

"Nuclear-powered."

"And chemical weapons?"

"Enough to paralyze half your neighbours."

"You make me very happy, Mr Krenk," murmured the president. And stared dreamily out of the helicopter window until, noticing a figure waving from a marooned rooftop, he shouted: "Pilot, drop down and pick up that poor fellow. Otherwise he's finished."

The helicopter descended steeply, the co-pilot lowering a rope with a harness attached to it, and soon a gasping middle-aged man was being laid on the only available space on the floor.

General Chowdhury bent over him.

"I'm your president," he said. "The father of the people." This he repeated in English for Krenk's benefit. "I've saved your life."

The man responded by closing his eyes. The co-pilot felt pulse and heart.

"He's dead, Mr President."

"Well, we did our best. But we're not undertakers," said General Chowdhury. "Open the door and throw him out."

Krenk watched until the body made a tiny splash below and, as if the distraction had served to turn the President's thoughts to other matters, he was spared having to discuss business for the rest of the flight. By the time the helicopter had reached Acca, and there was now no danger of crashing from a few thousand feet, the successful arms merchant was in a mood of some euphoria. The city rising towards them might not have a decent water supply, adequate electricity or enough schools and hospitals, with a transport system augmented by ox-drawn wagons, donkeys and sweating porters, but the people would soon have one of the best fighting forces in the region.

Which was exactly how he explained it to Grace, once he had returned to the government rest house and that sensibly obedient girl had instantly applied herself to making him comfortable after his tiring day.

"Grace," he confessed honestly, "I'm finding everything about you a delight. I don't know what I'm going to do when I lose you."

It was a confession that invited a reciprocal response; but none came.

At about the same time as Signora Modeste had been informed of the invitation to dine with the country's leader on the following evening and Klaus Krenk was congratulating himself on the prospect of the biggest arms deal in all his career, John-Paul had learnt once again that his pursuit of the enemy who had carried off his beloved fiancée had been frustrated.

If he had begun his travels in a state of innocence, however, that often blissful condition had been changed by harsh experience. On discovering that Krenk had left Seoul, he had found without difficulty a corrupt high official of Korean Airlines who was prepared to take a sizeable sum of dollars for going through all the passenger lists of the previous week. By this simple method, John-Paul had been able to learn of the movements of Krenk and his party.

He had arrived in Acca as Anthony Hitchbottom, no longer the possessor of a useful diplomatic passport but still the holder of one issued by a country regarded as one of the friendliest in the world. But this time he carried no murder weapon in his luggage. Apart from the fact that he was travelling light, which meant a single canvas bag, he no longer enjoyed immunity from searches by customs officers. On the other hand, with so much wealth, and in the form of ready cash, he was confident that whatever might be required, he could buy it.

On his first day in the city, John-Paul discovered that part of it was called the European quarter, after the old colonial days, and that this was now the superior residential suburb. It was also where the rest house in which Klaus Krenk and his party were lodged, information obtained from a newspaper editor who needed a little extra money to feed his family. It was the district with the two best hotels in Acca. Acting on this information, John-Paul proceeded on a reconnaissance of the European quarter and by the evening of his second day in the place, had taken a room in the International Hotel.

The attraction of Room 1009 on the twelfth floor was its commanding view of miles of suburbs, including the three hundred metres that separated it from the bungalow-style buildings of the rest house. The open 'field of fire', as he knew that marksmen would have called it, confirmed the soundness of his latest plan. A high-powered rifle with telescopic sights, with a single shot, should claim its victim provided he remained still for a few seconds. Powerful binoculars, bought that day, brought the rest house near enough to touch with his hand. The main residential part faced the hotel, and its wide verandah, typical of colonial-style bungalows throughout the tropical East, extended from side to side.

As well as a weapon able to kill with one shot at three hundred yards, John-Paul needed two personal attributes. The first was patience and the second a renewed conviction in the rightness of his mission. Having studied every corner and window and door of the rest house, he lay on the bed to consider this last factor. Was he as determined to kill Krenk as he had been on first setting out? Had his travels and travails in any way lessened his love for Grace or the need to save her? At the end of a long period of reflection, in which he had considered his mental state, and whether he was mad, he still came to the same conclusion. He loved Grace enough to want to kill her master.

With his doubts settled, the next pressing need was to find a high-powered rifle. And, again, he realized how much he had learned in such a short period of time. With much of the twenty thousand dollars he had won in Hong Kong still in his possession, he only had to make the right contact to be led to the market for such weapons. One of the basic truths of the universal system of supply and demand was that if there was a need, somehow, certainly for those with money, that need would be met.

John-Paul left the International Hotel wearing the kind of bush jacket favoured by past generations of colonial adminis-

trators and white African hunters, one with large patch
pockets, four of them, and a belt with a brass buckle. His cash
had been divided so that it did not bulge suspiciously, or
invitingly, and he carried a tourist map of the city. He took a
taxi to the part still called the Native Quarter, which was
almost all of the centre of Acca and, on descending, assumed
the manner of an Australian visitor, showing a friendly
openness that either shocked or amused the populace but
which invariably meant that he was tolerated as a vulgar young
European.

The roads were noisy and crowded and fouled by the less
fastidious residents, by passing mules and donkeys, and by the
occasional camel. There were open sewers but they were
neutralized by a stench that hung heavily over everything. The
population itself appeared to divide between the well-fed and
prosperous and scrawny beggars and lepers stretching out
imploring hands, and women who were either lovely in bright
saris or crones in black rags. John-Paul walked on, hoping to
find an area which might seem more promising for his
purpose, and eventually came to streets with small red lights
shining from darkened passages and doorways.

Here, from first floor balconies, smiling young women
shouted greetings. Where was he? He wondered. Should he
take another direction? But as John-Paul considered the situation, a man's voice, more compelling than the others, claimed
his attention.

"What you want, Joe?" he called in English, coming
forward to pluck the young man's sleeve. "You from a ship,
eh? Listen, I got the best girls in town. Clean. No sickness."
Sharp eyes in a constant state of watchfulness appeared to
search the tourist's face for private tastes. "Or you like to see
donkey love woman, two women together . . . I got everything."

The middle-aged pimp, balding, stout and brown-faced,
paused hopefully. John-Paul decided he had never before
confronted anyone who looked so dishonest and wicked. But
it was an appraisal that encouraged him. Had he found his
contact?

"As a matter of fact, I am looking for something," the

young man said pleasantly. "But I don't know whether you can help me."

"Not help you!" exclaimed the pimp, as if he had heard the inconceivable. "Listen Joe, Abdullah will get you anything. Maybe you want heroin? I got."

"I want a gun," said John-Paul.

The man's suspicious eyes showed neither surprise nor reproach.

"A gun? I got."

The ready offer momentarily locked the two men together, like wrestlers silently testing each other. Then John-Paul smiled. The stalemate ended. The contest continued.

"I want a special kind of gun, not an ordinary revolver."

"I got," repeated Abdullah, a little excited, it seemed, by the prospect of a customer. "Whatever you want, I got. But have you got the money?"

"Plenty."

The information excited the pimp even more.

"Come. Come," he repeated, taking John-Paul by the arm.

Apart from a couple of rebel movements confined to the hills and a group of armed religious fanatics who killed three or four recusants a day, Angladesh was probably the most peaceful country in the region. Its capital city therefore served ideally as a minor market place for all kinds of weapons, an illegal trade that was profitable both to the dealers and to the government officials who encouraged it. The actual market was near the river, by the port installations, and it was to this area that John-Paul was guided by the quick-moving and quick-talking Abdullah.

People were bathing in the mud-coloured river and there was a coinsiderable traffic of decaying wooden boats rowed by half-naked men, rusty cargo ships and high-sided old ferries, but it was the groups of grim and intimidating individuals standing outside the entrances to what appeared to be warehouses that reminded John-Paul that this shopping expedition was not without risk.

"Here," said Abdullah, raising a canvas awning.

In the shade of the warehouse, a row of seated men were drinking coffee, five or six to John-Paul's quick glance, and behind them were so many stacks of weapons that it seemed that the place had been the scene of the mass surrender of an army. Abdullah immediately began to explain the purpose of the visit in his Angali language, an explanation that was received in silence though the eyes of all the seated men, most of them elderly, remained suspiciously on the stranger. But the silence was followed by questions, not in Angali but in a fluent English, and not to Abdullah but to himself.

"What sort of weapon do you want?" asked one of the elderly, white-robed figures.

"A rifle," said John-Paul. And, with some confidence, recognizing that these men were not interested in morality, only in money, explained: "I want to kill someone at about three hundred metres. I'll need an accurate telescopic sighting on the rifle, accurate enough to get him with a single shot."

It seemed, from the silence that followed, that he did not require a reply, or that he had not been heard. He glanced round the warehouse, now noticing that the stacks of weapons along three of the walls or hanging from the ceiling included the obsolete as well as the modern, the museum pieces of tribesmen long since dead in their beds, automatics and mortars and anti-tank guns as well as unopened wooden crates with the markings of different country of origin.

"How much can you pay?"

"How much do you want?"

"Five thousand American dollars."

"You're asking too much," said John-Paul, not so naive as to believe that the first price should be taken seriously. "I'll offer you a thousand."

"Our price," said the spokesman of the group, "includes secrecy. Perhaps protection. We may in your eyes be a bloodthirsty lot in this part of the world but murder is still murder."

"Show me the gun," said John-Paul.

The spokesman raised his voice and two younger men appeared from behind a curtain. More commands. A deadly looking rifle with telescopic sights was handed to the old spokesman.

"Here. Try it."

John-Paul's experience with rifles was limited to the toy

ones of his childhood and those he had used in fairgrounds but he managed to examine the weapon with a pretence of expertise. And, since he could read, he was able to comment that it was German and that it came from Essen. Eventually, he agreed a price of two thousand.

He experienced a first uneasiness, however, as his hand went into his bush jacket pocket. What he did not want to do was pull out an enormous roll of hundred dollar bills and count out the agreed sum. He would have liked to retire for a few moments of privacy but such a request would only have increased the suspicion with which he was being watched. He decided to trust in the saying that there was honour among thieves, produced a sum of money three or four times that of the agreed price, and separated twenty one-hundred bills from the roll.

He was aware of whispering among the men as he handed the money to the spokesman, and realized that he was suddenly afraid. As calmly as his fear permitted, he placed the two thousand on the long low table in front of the grim old men, then asked whether the rifle could be dismantled and wrapped for the return to his hotel. But the whispering in Angali continued, coming to a climax in a shouted command to the young men standing to one side. Three of them advanced on John-Paul.

"Leave me alone!" he exclaimed, recognizing the threat. Then, when his arms were seized, he shouted: "You can't do this to me! We've agreed the price!"

But neither agreement nor price appeared to influence the purpose of the three young toughs as they dragged him behind a ragged curtain, threw him to the floor and went through his pockets. Once they had removed all four rolls of money, they helped him to his feet, a brief gesture of decency, then indicated politely that he could leave.

When John-Paul faced the elders of what seemed a tribal gathering, his fury had overcome his fear.

"You bunch of rogues! Give me back my money!" His eyes went from one face to another, then to Abdullah, preoccupied with lighting a well-earned cigar. "You crook — you knew all this in advance!"

The old men — and the young — listened to John-Paul's

tirade with great patience, as if, in return for his wealth, he had every right to express his feelings. Then, during a breathless pause, the leader of the old men spoke.

He said: "If there's been a crime, go to the police. You know where we are." Then, when he received no reply to the suggestion, he added: "Otherwise, if you don't stop these insults, you'll be thrown into the river."

"Okay, throw me in the river!" shouted the enraged young man. "I don't care! You've robbed me . . ."

The old man nodded to the waiting ruffians and said in English: "He wants to be thrown in the river — throw him in the river."

And John-Paul, without the rifle he had just bought, had the incredible experience of finding himself lifted by a number of strong hands and arms, carried across the rough open area in front of the warehouse, and hurled over the quayside. As he went into the water, and under it, his single instinct was to save himself from drowning. There were steps a few metres away, and as he swam towards them, he was thinking neither of being robbed nor of the outrage to himself. Further away, hundreds of people were enjoying bathing in the holy waters of the muddy river, but for John-Paul survival came first.

On the quay, and again able to think, he considered his situation. There were a number of people, mostly standing in silent groups, staring at him but since not a single face displayed anything except sullen hostility, it seemed pointless to expect their sympathy. He began to walk back to the centre of the city.

Darkness had descended and his progress seemed to be between one ring of light from streetlamps to the next, but since it was a very hot climate, water soon ceased to drip from him. His splendid khaki jacket had lost its elegant line and was now darker in colour, and his trousers seemed to drag at his legs with every step, though compared with the local population, he still remained a well-dressed European. And, just as survival had been his only instinct when he had been thrown into the river, his single desire was now to get back to the shelter of the International Hotel. It seemed a thousand miles away.

As he approached the centre of Acca, the streets became

lighter, the darkness less threatening. He had just reached the main square, which was further illuminated by a number of extravagant neon signs, when he noticed the reassuring presence of another European head among the crowds of uniform black ones. Then, that it seemed that of a fair-haired young woman and was distinctly familiar. To himself, he thought: 'God, I'm suffering from hallucinations!' There was an unbelievable resemblance to Grace.

"Grace!" he called out, though still thinking he must be mistaken.

But he was not. The fair-haired woman turned. Recognition came without a word. In a moment they were in each other's arms. When their faces drew back to stare at each other, their eyes were filled with tears.

"But it can't be . . ."

"It is, it is!"

They were repeating similar exclamations, the same words, the delight exactly the same. Then an even longer embrace followed, a blinking neon sign over their heads adding to the sense of this being a magical moment, in defiance of reality, apart from it. But when the embrace ended, and Grace pulled away, her joy had changed to alarm.

"You haven't followed us here to kill Krenk, have you? Be truthful . . ." But she immediately supplied her own answer. "If you have, you're going to find it impossible. He's been arrested."

"Arrested!" exclaimed John-Paul.

"Yes. I don't know why, except that he has. And I've been ordered to leave the country within the next two days."

John-Paul was prevented from asking further questions, or indeed continuing to hold his fiancée in his arms, by the arrival of a government limousine. As it drew up, two heavy European men stepped down, took Grace's arms, and almost lifted her into the vehicle.

"Wait!"

But John-Paul's bewildered cry was stifled by the fact that Grace neither protested nor resisted what had seemed a minor assault on her. Krenk's bodyguards, he decided. And there had been nothing he could do. He waved after the vehicle but because the windows were of almost black glass, he was not sure whether Grace had waved back.

For some minutes, he could not move. The neon overhead continued to blink; but no longer magically. It was a thousand miles back to the International Hotel. There was no second miracle. The walk did not seem any shorter.

CHAPTER NINE

The events that led to the arrest of Klaus Krenk began the evening before, when Signora Modeste dined with General Chowdhury, president and absolute ruler of fifty million souls, as he preferred to describe his people.

The table at which she sat was many metres long, with the President and herself at opposite ends. In front of them were hand-woven place mats, gold cutlery and the best crystal glassware. Between them were bowls of plants trailing to the floor, ornate dishes of delicacies and two gold candelabra. The salon was vast and high-ceilinged, with the walls lined by traditional oil paintings of victorious battles and warriors, and the uniformed servants outnumbered the diners by about five to one.

Signora Modeste was not discomforted by her surroundings nor was she any less purposeful about her mission. She had refrained from even hinting at what she called "the dream" during the brief and formal welcome over fruit juice disguised as cocktails, judging it wiser to wait for the long and uninterrupted period of dinner. And she was pleased that the President not only remembered their meetings in New York but actually quoted what they had discussed. They were not, therefore, meeting as strangers.

It was remarkable, considering Signora Modeste's life, that the dream had survived. Reality had been harsh and demanding. In marriage she had soon been abandoned for a tart of a beauty queen, she had struggled against male domination to attain her high position at COM, and her dedication meant putting the needs of others before her own. That was her nature. And, lastly, she was a woman. She had often thought of the great disadvantage of being one of the sex that conceived, gave birth to and nurtured the human race, and having a body designed for that purpose, but to have expressed her

feelings about the unfairness of fate would only have preju-
diced her chances of a successful career.

There was, however, one advantage in being a woman that
had served her well, or in being a certain kind of woman, and
that was what was variously described as being the 'motherly
sort' or 'very maternal''. And for that favoured status she had
had to wait for middle age. Conscious, however, of the subtle
power given to her by nature — because hadn't even the
general now facing her loved his mother? — she was determined that it would serve the dream.

"Mr President," she said, with smiling directness, "what is
your opinion of the Community of Mankind, of which your
country is one of its most distinguished members?"

A little hypocrisy was permitted, she thought; or perhaps it
should be called flattery. Feed them with flattery, lowly men
or exalted leaders, and the effect was the same. A softening. At
least.

"Well, I'm pleased you should think so highly of my
opinion, signora," said the President, the praise causing him to
lean back with satisfaction. "Our organization is all the world
possesses to maintain the peace, create just and contented
societies and to ensure respect for the individual. These are all
enshrined in the COM charter and it's the duty of all members
to honour them."

Signora Modeste allowed the tyrant to continue in this
manner for some time. A plate of delicacies was set in front of
her, food and flavours she could not recognize, but which she
bravely ate, keeping a fixed stare of admiration on the figure
facing her and who was ignoring his own plate of food to
expand on his lofty theme.

"Let me conclude, signora, by stating that the spirit of our
organization is like that of the military academy where I
trained as an officer. Our motto was: 'All for one — one for
all!' — or was it the other way round?"

"Mr President," said Signora Modeste, "I feel you are one
of the few heads of state with whom I can speak openly and
honestly."

The President had chosen to wear large rimless sunglasses,
even though the lighting of the salon was subdued, but not
even they succeeded in masking his delight at the compliment.

"Thank you, signora. I take that as an honour." He was dressed in a magnificent white uniform on the chest of which were rows of medals and the winged emblems of both pilot and parachutist. He was further decorated by his president's blue silk sash and gold braid on shoulders and cuffs. "You know you have a sympathetic listener."

"I realize that, Mr President," said Signora Modeste. "But if I were to speak in a private capacity, as a woman rather than as deputy-director, would you still be so sympathetic?"

"Oh, signora," exclaimed General Chowdhury, extending both hands in a gesture of gentlemanly protest. "How could I be otherwise!"

Signora Modeste smiled in gratitude at a leader who had never allowed a word of opposition, who had killed or imprisoned his political enemies, who had arrested journalists and broadcasters the moment they departed from the cult of worshipping the country's leader, and who lived in ostentatious luxury while most of his people starved.

"I can speak to you, also, because I know you love your people and do all you can to make their lives happy and fulfilled," she now said, convincingly. "But I believe you could do even more, Mr President, which is why I have visited you."

The President frowned, visible despite his large sunglasses, and shifted uneasily in his large dining chair. Then he remembered the food in front of him, and began eating hurriedly. Signora Modeste was quick to recognize a nervousness at the prospect of unwelcome questions, and annoyance at being obliged to be polite to a foreign and influential guest.

Gently, continuing with flattery, she said: "Your people have given you absolute power, they love you as their leader, even their religious leader. In all the world, there are not many presidents who enjoy all that; and of course deserve it . . ."

She paused as the stewards served the next course. They did so with some ceremony, as though it was something special, which it was because the President's frown changed to a smile; one of pride.

"You will enjoy this dish, signora," he said. "It's tiger's meat. Good for courage and bravery. And cooked in its own blood." Then he laughed, as if he felt more confident about facing whatever embarrassing questions this visitor might ask. "Not that you are short of courage. But come to the point — what is the real reason for your visit?"

With this encouragement, and observing that the man was now more relaxed and had begun devouring tiger meat as if he were the same species of animal, she calmly confided her dream. On occasions, in history, she explained, there had been a number of benevolent rulers, kings and princes, who had become dedicated to making sacrifices for their own people, who had given generously and who regarded the nation as one great family. But nowhere in today's world was there such a generous and heroic ruler. No, she added hurriedly, not even in Angladesh.

She was not interrupted and she sensed that her manner was serious and respectful enough to avoid provoking the tyrant. From his own people, not a word she said would have been tolerated but, encouragingly, she felt her own status was just enough to persuade him to behave as if this meeting was taking place in the COM headquarter building.

"Could there, Mr President, be such a benevolent ruler in today's modern world?" she now asked. "The answer must be that it would be more difficult because the number of absolute rulers is less than it was. But there are still a few."

Her pause, and the fact that her kindly, motherly face seemed to be inviting a comment, caused the President to swallow hastily the last of the tiger meat, and give a half-choking reply.

"And you think I'm one of them?" he said, his tone one of mild protest — and disbelief. "But, signora, you force me to remind you of how irregular this is. I'm sure your motives are admirable but international organizations are simply not per-mitted to interfere in the affairs of member countries. After all, who would want to become a member if we were being told what to do?"

"I concede that, Mr President," said Signora "La Mamma" Modeste with the utmost respect. "But I understood you to agree that I could speak to you as an individual. As a woman. Or do you now withdraw your consent?"

Again she used her motherly expression, a polite reprimand for a man who had disappointed her. General Chowdhury, wearing rows of medal ribbons and other awards for heroism and distinction, allowed himself the unique experience of surrender.

"Go ahead," he sighed in defeat. Then added: "But wait. Let's get these idiots out of the way."

The attendants were ordered to leave and, once they had departed, he pushed aside the plates in front of him and leaned over the table as if he were preparing to enjoy a new experience. As it probably was. That of honest discussion. He even removed his sunglasses, a barrier between himself and a threatening world, and smiled encouragingly.

Without a single witness, not even that of the lowliest servant, who in any case would not have understood a word of English, he said: "I'm beginning to understand why you've come, signora. You are expecting me to create miracles. Well, I hope I have a sense of humour — so carry on. Say whatever you wish."

Signora Modeste pretended to share his joke.

"Now, Mr President," she said with a hint of coquetry. "How do you know you can't create miracles until you've tried? You are too modest."

"It's not a case of modesty, signora. And it's not even fear for my life because what you are asking will certainly be seen as weakness. At such a moment, you see, my enemies will strike. Which poses the following question — what's the point of being this benevolent ruler if, the moment he aspires to a kind of saintliness, he gets a bullet in the head?"

It was Signora Modeste's turn to listen as he proceeded to explain what he called the realities of the situation. History had been cruel to Angladesh because it had nearly always been occupied by conquerors. Geography had been cruel because the land was inundated nearly every year. And also cruel by race. This might not be seen as a misfortune but his people refused to be disciplined and were unable to adapt to modern ways. The President, however, went on to congratulate Signora Modeste on her concern for his people, to admit that he often missed the stimulating conversation they were now having and that, as an absolute ruler, he was a very lonely man. Which gave him the most awful moods of depression; did she ever get depressed herself?

She confessed that she did and for the next few minutes the conversation became warm and personal, a kindly woman comforting a man permitting himself a short respite from being a tyrant.

But then she said, when she felt the exchanges permitted such a suggestion: "It's true your country suffers a lot of natural disadvantages but there are two areas where you could make changes which would have an instant effect on your people . . ."

"For example?" interrupted General Chowdhury.

"First you could be less severe on non-violent opposition. If they're not the ones who would murder you, as you've already said, what difference would it make to show more tolerance towards them?"

"What difference would it make!" exclaimed the President. "Why, as I've already indicated, it would be seen as weakness. My army leaders would arrange my murder the instant they saw that weakness . . ."

"But do you like having your prisons full to overflowing?"

"They're not full. There's plenty of space for more."

"Well, torture. Even your government admits it takes place."

"It's the quickest way to reform people. Experience shows they never forget what they've been through." The President gave a private nod of his head, of satisfaction, as if that had disposed of lenience towards political enemies, and said: "And what's the second area of benevolence — where I could do so much good?"

At this point, Signora Modeste was both encouraged and discouraged. True, the tyrant was adamant on the point of not tolerating non-violent opposition, probably because he lived in fear of his life, but at least he had not shouted her into silence or called for his guards to throw her on to the street. Not even the status of deputy-director of COM could protect her from the fearsome rage of a madman. And after a moment of hesitation, she decided to proceed. The dream was not yet blighted.

"Well, Mr President, my next appeal to you is to do all you can to raise the living standards of your people. You see . . ."

"I see clearly, signora," the President interrupted sharply, the first time he could be described as being rude to his visitor. "Every rupee I can spare goes to helping the people. I am dedicated to that. But, as I've said, we're a poor country. We borrow and borrow and borrow — but it's never enough."

"That depends," said Signora Modeste, bravely responding to his rudeness with a show of her own firmness. "It depends on your priorities. I can think of one area where a country like Angladesh could economize immediately — within twenty-four hours."

The statement had an unusual effect on the absolute dictator. Instead of being angered by such direct suggestions, the mood of enjoying a discussion between equals extended to an even greater tolerance.

"And where would you suggest I economize?" he asked with interest.

"Well, in the most obvious place."

"And which is?"

"An area of extravagance which the country can't afford." But Signora Modeste realized that the President had still not grasped the oblique reference. "I am referring to the military."

"The military!" The general sounded genuinely shocked. "You mean defence?"

A long silence followed. She waited for her host to speak angrily but the frown was never projected into words. When she decided it was safe to continue, she said:

"I can never understand why poor countries do not recognize the real enemy. Is it really their neighbouring countries or could it be poverty? Misery? Even starvation?"

General Chowdhury sipped at his orange juice before replying. He seemed to need an interval to adjust to new and outrageous ideas.

"You are talking like a pacifist, signora. But even your Western countries put the defence of the nation first. It's the same whether it's America or England or Angladesh . . ."

But he suffered the rare experience of being impatiently interrupted.

"Come along, Mr President," said Signora Modeste, briskly. "Who is going to invade you? Your neighbours are either so powerful you couldn't hold out for a day, or they're so weak they couldn't defeat a troop of boy scouts." Then, a show of further impatience, she rapped the polished table. "Besides, Angladesh is so poor, what would be the point of invading it? For the prize of fifty million starving peasants and a stretch of flooded land!"

As she finished her provocative outburst, Signora Modeste waited for a reciprocal explosion of anger. She felt she might have deserved it; but there was none. The expression of the President suggested that he was neither in a manic phase nor a depressed one. Simply thoughtful. Serious. And subdued. Then his motherly guest smiled, a reward of tenderness. For the male. For his behaviour. Well, at least for listening to her. And she thanked him, not having anything more to say, and politely suggested that they might continue their meal.

"It's been very interesting, signora," said the President, as the servants came in again, like a whole platoon of soldiers ordered to advance. "I can't take your remarks seriously, of course, but I've enjoyed our discussion. At least you didn't suggest that I should dress in a business suit like a Western president." He laughed at the private picture of himself. "A leader must look the part, a soldier serving his people, wearing the uniform of commander-in-chief." There was an interval of watching the stewards serve the honey delicacies of the country and, with them, came a sweetening of the atmosphere. As if not a contentious word had been said all evening. "If you would like to go on a tiger shoot, signora, I would be happy to arrange it," offered the obliging President. "I know how you Western women enjoy riding on elephants — which reminds me how once . . ."

Signora Modeste listened politely to one hunting story after another, of the fury of wounded tigers, of the surprising strength of wounded buffalo, of snakes, of crocodiles and of the rare white rhinoceros. When, later, the President escorted her to the limousine which was to return her to the Grand Hotel, he again repeated how grateful he was for such a stimulating evening.

What that good daughter of one of the poorer areas of Palermo was never to know was how General Chowdhury passed the rest of the night. On her departure, he immediately went to his secret cupboard of best French cognac and spent the next hour in solitary meditation; and Signora Modeste was never to be informed of the result of that meditation. Although it was well after midnight and the ten ministers and generals he wished to consult were fast asleep, he got them out of their beds and had them brought to his presence within the next half-hour. And Signora Modeste would hardly have recognized her host from the fierce expression on his face. At two in the morning, it was not that of a man who would tolerate dissent.

At about the time Signora Modeste was consuming the delicacy of tiger meat cooked in its own blood and her son at the International Hotel was considering how best to assassinate Klaus Krenk, the tough old arms dealer was sitting up in bed and dictating another chapter of his memoirs. The scene was more homely than previously because Grace appeared resigned to her fate and, following a number of nights together, had established with her employer a relationship that could not be described as one of closeness but which was certainly one of friendly informality.

Krenk still followed his habit of propping himself in bed and having his notes on the counterpane in front. And, before speaking, sipping at his mineral water and ensuring that the recording machine had been switched on. It had; and Grace, in an exotic negligée, was similarly ready for a further chapter of his memoirs.

"I come now to the subject of bribery and I set down these notes from the experience of thirty years of this very necessary practice. Before I describe, therefore, how the use of bribery by responsible parties has contributed to the present prosperity of the world, I want to define the many variations of the practice." This he proceeded to do, Grace scribbling quickly because the subject seemed to encourage his eloquence, soon coming to the important contribution caused by what he called INERTIA. "Within every society, there is inertia of effort, of ambition and of purpose. Once that inertia is transformed into motivation, into a strong drive to achieve something, to seek the most profitable results, not only is the purpose achieved but all of society is the gainer."

Klaus Krenk was happy. It was a rare emotion but less rare

now that Grace had submitted to becoming his mistress, a mistress, at least, in his own mind. Because, he reasoned, people frequently became the willing and unknowing prisoners of what they had previously resisted. And also adding to his happiness was the fact that her presence gave a stimulus to dictating his memoirs as though he needed to impress a witness; preferably that of an attractive woman.

From his analysis of inertia, and the need to conquer it, which was one of the great social services achieved by bribery, Krenk moved on to the moral aspect of the practice. In many instances, the overcoming of the inherent inertia in a society could also mean a victory for goodness and decency. But how? Where? And Krenk proceeded to give examples of his theme.

"Let us for the moment call these two countries Nari and Qari," he said, having checked his notebook for his secret code. "They went to war, two countries with governments and leaders that can only be described as mad, people sacrificed as if it were the old World War One all over again. From the first day of the Nari-Qari war, I knew it was only a matter of time before one side or the other turned to Klaus Krenk for help. But I must admit I never dreamt it would be in the form that it took."

In his deep voice he went on to describe how that terrible war gradually became one of attrition and stalemate until Qari, desperate for victory and having had to expand its forces with thirteen-year-olds, resorted to chemical warfare and dropped bombs spreading plague that infected hundreds of thousands of Narians.

"The government of Nari, which still had a good revenue as an oil-producing country, contacted me in Zurich and said I was the only man in the world who could find the urgently needed supplies of vaccines and antidotes for this kind of plague. It was an honour to think that so many hundreds of thousands of lives depended on myself but there was still an unresolved matter. What would be my commission?"

With that question satisfactorily settled, he had set out to trace the manufacturers of the vaccine and the antidote. A little was available in Europe but the only worthwhile quantities ready for immediate purchase were in America, and that country had placed an embargo on all trade with Nari, even medical supplies.

"I then began a moral crusade for the lives of hundreds of thousands of innocent victims." As he made this claim, Krenk was being totally sincere. He had not, in that instance, been an arms dealer, he had been a . . . "The correct word, Grace, is Saviour. I repeat, Saviour!" And he described how, with the dual persuasiveness of his pleas and the sweetening effect of bribes, he had achieved the impossible. "It was one man against the United States — and I won."

"With the help of a couple of archbishops who needed money for restoring their churches, of a rabbi who ran a Zionist fund and a Red Cross director whose requests for medical supplies were never questioned, I began my campaign. I then had to bribe the usual lot, American senators and officials near the President, who of course are never a problem, heads of Customs and Excise officials at two airports and, lastly, once that support was lined up, those most directly involved. They were the directors of the pharmaceutical companies and a number of the smaller airlines who, once assured of government permits and that the embargo had been lifted, were prepared to give priority to such a humanitarian mission." Klaus Krenk smiled with satisfaction at his choice of phrase. "The word bribe was never mentioned because these good people were not being bribed. They were receiving rewards in recognition for helping to relieve suffering."

And he went on to describe what he called one of the greatest airlifts in history, comparable with the relief of Berlin in the late nineteen-forties, missions of mercy to the starving millions of Africa and bringing the last of the Americans out of Vietnam. The airlift had meant the saving of millions of Narian lives, a temporary defeat for the wicked Qarians, a useful profit for the pharmaceutical companies and well-earned gifts for a couple of hundred intermediaries. And although Krenk omitted to mention in his memoirs the five per cent of his commission on hundreds of millions of dollars, he recorded for future readers of his work that he had received Nari's highest honour, the gold medal of the *Order of the Trusted and the Most Noble*.

Soon after, tiring suddenly, Krenk ordered Grace to switch off the machine and come to bed. He told her how pleased he was with her but on this night found himself too fatigued to do more than sleep with her in his arms. But it was not a long sleep. It still seemed the middle of the night when the telephone woke Krenk. He allowed Grace to sleep and answered it himself. When the secretary to General Chowdhury stated his identity, the surprised Krenk dragged himself further from sleep. The President wished to see him immediately and would he get dressed and drive to the palace in the car that was already on its way to bring him.

"That's the worst of dealing with lunatics, Grace," he exclaimed to the young woman still soundly asleep. "They get bright ideas in the middle of the night, curse them. And as well as being manic-depressives, they're all insomniacs."

Commonsense told him that Grace would not be needed and when he emerged from the government bungalow, the limousine was waiting for him. There were hints of daylight in the far sky and a fragrant coolness and sweetness that came with dawn in very hot countries. It was six in the morning.

"Sit down," said the President, a brief greeting from behind the desk of his vast office. "I want to talk to you."

"It's always a pleasure, Mr President," said Krenk politely, privately cursing the man and having already decided that his strategy must be one of pacifying the lunatic and putting off decisions for a more sensible hour of the day. "What do you wish to discuss?"

"First, we'll have a drink. A bit of the strong stuff, eh?"

To Krenk's surprise, the devout Muslim president produced from his desk a bottle of cognac and two glasses.

"Too early for me, Mr President."

"Really?" But it was not too early for the President, though possibly because, not having been to bed, it was still the previous evening. A glass quickly drunk, he now announced: "There's been a change of policy, Mr Krenk. After detailed discussions with my staff, we've reconsidered our plans to turn Angladesh into the strongest military power in the area."

The President paused, as if to assess the visitor's reaction. There was none. Except a polite question.

"That's all right," said Krenk, years of experience having

taught him that this was a common stratagem for seeking a better deal, even reopening negotiations altogether. "What are the details you wish to discuss? I would guess it's the problem of the cost of maintaining nuclear submarines?"

"It's hardly a matter of maintenance costs, Mr Krenk," said the President, his face haggard and bleary-eyed after what his visitor deduced had been a sleepless night. "It's the cost of maintaining the whole of an expanded military force."

One of the Kings of the World tried to interpret the rather cryptic statement of the Light of Angladesh. He failed. And resorted to saying, defensively:

"Everything is negotiable, Mr President. In a deal as large and as complex as ours, I accept there may be a need for adjustment."

But saying the obvious did not assuage Krenk's sudden uneasiness. It was not the absurd hour of the day, the fanatical intensity of an unbalanced president or even the evidence of the man uncharacteristically being on strong drink that was disturbing; Krenk's instincts were too acute to miss the sense of a real crisis. And it came.

"The need for adjustment is greater than you think" said the President. "The deal's off."

Among the lessons learnt by Klaus Krenk in his dealings with high statesmen and military leaders, with crooks and lunatics and zealots and tyrants, was that one never lost one's temper or admitted to being shocked; but in this instance, disturbed from his night's sleep, it was difficult to maintain his usual self-control.

"What do you mean, Mr President?" he said sharply, clearly irritated. "You mean the whole deal — everything?"

"That's right. The lot."

"The lot!"

"The lot."

Outside the three long windows of the presidential office, the sun was rising into a pink sky and the early stirrings of the population were becoming audible. Other sounds to intrude into Krenk's brief sense of paralysis were the ticking of a clock, the slight whirring of the air conditioning and the President's breathing.

Very calmly, Krenk said: "With respect, you have

announced a major decision. Isn't it a little unreal to discuss it at this hour when we have a meeting later this morning?"

"It is not unreal for the Light of Angladesh to change his decisions at any time of the day or night," the President replied tersely; and perhaps contemptuously. "As head of the nation, I am free to have second thoughts any time I care, to give any orders I please and, in your case, to consider or dismiss your pleadings."

Pleadings? The word wounded. Was the lunatic suggesting that he, Klaus Krenk, was pleading? But there was no other possible interpretation.

"I must remind you that your minister has signed certain binding undertakings, Mr President," he said, not attempting to hide the anger. "In our agreement, there are all kinds of penalty clauses. You don't think I would have involved myself in all this preparatory work, all the deals that are waiting to be completed, without adequate guarantees?" He paused. The President was listening. A minor triumph. "So none of this unilateral nonsense about cancelling the whole deal."

To Krenk's astonishment, the President attempted a smile. It was a benign smile that blended with an expression of fanatical intensity. And the reasoned tone of his reply added to its frightening effect.

"I will go this far. I will give you a brief explanation even though, as the country's absolute ruler, I don't have to," said the President. "As the father of the nation, I see my people as my children. This latest catastrophe, and I am referring to the floods, has made me aware of what my people most urgently need. Does that make sense to you?" A pause. The President was clearly not reassured by his visitor's incredulity. "Well, let me go on. Before my people are defended against a foreign invader, they have to be defended against the day-to-day ravages of poverty, of nature, of misery, all of which can be just as deadly . . ."

Krenk did not hear the rest of the President's speech. Enough had been said to prove the man not only to be deranged but to be dangerously deranged. He thought of reminding General Chowdhury, who occupied the same uniform as the President, of his pride in the military traditions of the country, of how the proof of any ruler's power was to be able periodically to parade in front of the people and himself the might of their armed forces, but a deeper frustration dictated what he should do next. He stood up, turned his back on the President and walked to the door.

He heard a shouted: "Where are you going!"

"I'll talk to you when you've sobered up," Krenk retorted, with comparable anger.

"If you don't return to your seat, you won't leave this palace alive."

Not fear but contempt, honestly felt, caused Krenk to turn. A sequence of thoughts that correctly put the man in his place went through his mind. I'm being threatened by a tin-pot dictator. I'm being insulted by a bloody nigger. I've had to listen to a raving lunatic . . .

"Let me remind you, Chowdhury," Krenk said, in measured tones of superiority, "of whom you're dealing with. My influence extends throughout the world, not just over a nation of the poorest and the most ignorant people in Asia." And, emboldened by being heard without interruption, Krenk continued with even more conviction. "My friends and contacts are placed in all the centres of power; they are all so deeply involved in my affairs that they do as I say. When they are told to obstruct your overseas trading, banking and other arrangements, they'll do just that. Secondly, your government will suffer the international publicity of being sued for compensation in half a dozen countries, not by me but by our contractors and suppliers . . ." What else could he add? Krenk asked himself. Then said, imperiously, "And, to give you some idea of my personal substance, you might like to know that my private fortune is probably greater than all the wealth of your national treasury."

As Krenk was concluding his haughty riposte, the President's hand went under the desk. In a moment, two guards had stepped into the office. They were in khaki drill uniform and held automatic weapons. The President spoke to them in a language that Krenk could not understand, and they moved forward to stand just behind him.

"Well, Mr Krenk," said the President, still speaking with menacing moderation, "there is an obvious way of avoiding having our overseas affairs obstructed, of not being sued for

compensation and of protecting the good name of Angladesh." But before he pronounced this obvious way, he made
Krenk suffer a long pause. "As well as being president and
commander-in-chief, Chowdhury is the Chief Justice,
supreme head of the Court of Appeal and Chief Public
Executioner. With all this authority, who can question my
rights? I have therefore decided that you will never leave the
country."

As Krenk was dragged, struggling, from the magnificent
room that served as the President's office, a series of threats
and abuse that quickly became incoherent shattered the early
morning silence of the palace. His friends would not only
rescue him from a mad tyrant — he would be toppled from
power, the whole of Angladesh would suffer, rebellions would
be encouraged, hostile neighbours would receive the most
modern weapons . . .

In the corridor outside, other soldiers joined their two
colleagues in forcibly carrying Klaus Krenk into captivity, a
wild confusion of swinging arms and kicking legs until, out of
sight of any possible witness, he received a blow on the head
from the butt of a gun. The single blow was enough. Without
dignity, a limp and helpless body, the Angali peasants in
uniform carried him away. And with the powerful arms dealer
there also disappeared the merchant statesman and the author
of the unfinished *King of the World*.

In other parts of the world, colleagues and associates were
later to ask questions. Was he tortured or shot or hanged? But
no one lamented. Was he still rotting in prison? No one was
moved to find out. Had he, with his considerable wealth,
bought his freedom and then slipped into anonymity? Again,
no one cared. The man had vanished and although he left
behind a certain confusion in his business affairs, that was
where it ended. As Krenk, in his more cynical mood, might
have said: The cemeteries of the world are filled with indispensable men.

CHAPTER TEN

When John-Paul reached New York, he went in pursuit of his fiancée, Grace, who had already returned. To describe his efforts as a pursuit, was not an exaggeration. Why was she avoiding him? But it was soon apparent to that normally optimistic young man, that she was. Day after day, then, he was forced to go through a furious programme of trying to reach her by telephone, ringing the bell of the family home, waiting in his car with a view of the entrance and making enquiries through their friends.

His calls, whether on the telephone or at the front door, were received by members of her family suddenly behaving like strangers, by the oriental maid employed by the rich Greek banker or by a woman whose dress suggested she was the cook and who seemed annoyed at having been brought from her kitchen. Then John-Paul, accepting that a high wall of hostility had been erected between his fiancée and himself, and deciding in his present state of paranoia that the family was conspiring to keep them apart, took to writing letters. The address on the envelope was always in a disguised handwriting or in a variety of styles but his declarations of love remained constant.

Why was she avoiding him! Not quite a question — more an exclamation. If she no longer loved him, he would accept the fact — but surely she should tell him! If Grace's experience with Krenk, for whatever reason, had changed her feelings towards himself, well, why not state the fact? Had he ever been unreasonable, or anything less than kind and loving! But Grace remained hidden and incommunicado.

John-Paul considered the irony of the situation. He had travelled round the whole world, well, almost, and had managed to remain on the trail of Krenk and his party, and yet here, in New York, a developed city with the most advanced forms of communications and transport, he was unable to reach his elusive fiancée. Because, until she made a declaration to the contrary, nothing between them had changed!

In the days since his return from foreign parts, preoccupied with his purpose, he had seen his mother only twice. And that good woman, on the first occasion, as if she knew what her role must be, acted as a patient listener, serving to let him unburden himself, recount what he had been through for the sake of saving Grace, confess his hopes and his follies. But she made a significant contribution of her own. She had received from her local COM representative news that Krenk had been arrested on a charge of insulting the President of Angladesh. She was not able to add, however, what the likely result would be except to say that if Krenk did not quickly gain his liberty, he would probably rot in jail for years or face the maximum penalty, which was to receive a thousand lashes before being hanged.

On John-Paul's second visit to his mother, more subdued because of a further period of unsuccessfully trying to reach Grace, he was more ready to ask advice, a son not too grown-up to admit to problems he could not resolve. What, Mamma, should he do? This time, however, that good lady was neither so patient nor so sympathetic. He received what she should have delivered at their meeting months before, as sharp and tough a rebuke as that professional woman had ever directed at the nastiest representative of the most reprehensible delegation at COM.

"You've brought this on yourself. When you embarked on your purpose of murder, when you persuaded me to get you a COM passport, when a mother's natural fears for a son under arrest caused me to fly out to the East to help you, you were taking advantage of my vulnerability. But now you're back in New York, my boy, where you're unlikely to start killing people and where you're not a fugitive carrying false papers, I'm happy to think that the worst fate you'll suffer is to lose your fiancée."

"But I'm shattered, desperate," cried her son. "Doesn't that concern you?"

Apparently it did not and the good Signora Modeste, almost as if she had been anticipating this moment with pleasure, having told him that a young man's love was a reality within an illusion, rather as the comforting idea of life after death was convincing only to those who wanted to believe in the fantasy, repeated her advice that he shouldn't waste another thought on a girl who was apparently avoiding him; and to accept the obvious. Besides, his reward for his suffering had been to come safely through experiences that had strengthened his character and given him a better understanding of the lives of others.

It had been, said the deputy-director of COM, still adopting her severe professional manner, the best years of his education. He would profit from the painful lessons for the rest of his days. Then she chased him from her presence, saying that young people should live in the future and not in the past.

John-Paul, however, remained in the past. The obsession with finding and confronting Grace was as great as ever. Neglecting his studies at the university, his friends and other interests, he continued his crazed search of New York as he had travelled in pursuit of Krenk, rushing from one place to another though this time not to save her from the tyrant but from herself, from whatever was affecting her mind. After all, he reasoned, how could he free himself from the memory of the unlikely meeting in Acca when, spontaneously, they had greeted each with tears and kisses! Could that have changed so quickly!

No longer the phantom Hitchbottom or the make-believe Bonuomo, John-Paul reverted to his name Modeste. With it, curiously, it seemed to change his personality, introducing doubt and fear where, during his pursuit of Krenk, there had only been an obsessive courage. Could he really have lost Grace? Was he doing all he could to find her? But New York, like the planet itself, could be a surprisingly small place. People who had not met each other for years could find themselves face to face at street corners, in department stores, at adjoining tables in restaurants and even in elevators forbidden to carry more than six. Or on brief journeys, such as happened on one of the ferries that made the short passage across the bays and shipping channels of New York, when John-Paul had reason to cross from Manhattan to Staten Island, perhaps five miles away.

In the company of two hundred other passengers, he had taken his place along the rail of the ferry, Manhattan's assembly of skyscrapers, as though America were a small enclave like Hong Kong or Macau and needed to crowd its citizens into a cramped area, falling astern and sombre Staten Island rising in front of them. Across the water, as John-Paul leaned on the ferry rail, stood France's gift to the country, the goddess-like figure of the Statue of Liberty on its tiny island, still significant enough to the descendants of one-time immigrants to claim their attention, or at least a glance from many of them. And there, goddess-like, too, was Grace.

Or was it? Beyond some heads leaning forward and figures standing upright, others seeming to be in constant motion and others choosing that moment to walk away, was the unmistakable profile of his fiancée. But, again, was it? As calmly as the sudden excitement permitted, John-Paul passed behind the backs of a dozen passengers. There was a space on the rail next to her and, as casually as he could, he rested his elbows on it. He wanted to avoid surprising her, to materialize as gently and as naturally as consciousness from a dream . . .

But Grace seemed to become aware of his presence without really turning.

"You . . . No, no!"

The exclamation was accompanied by an expression of such terror that, knowing she would flee, John-Paul seized her arm.

"Don't struggle, Grace," he pleaded, as she tried to pull away. "Yes, it's me. It really is. Please . . ." And he waited for a softening of her familiar yet unfamiliar face, for her to recover from the shock, to overcome whatever delusions, sickness and folly had possessed her. "Tell me, why — why?"

His presence seemed at last to be accepted by a mind that was fighting to deny his existence. He noticed her paleness, the eyes troubled yet dull at the same time, as though she might be on a tranquillizing — or deadening — drug, a disturbing conclusion, as was the impression — uncharacteristically — of a neglected appearance. But suddenly a more recognizable Grace sprang out of hiding, that of a bright and determined young woman.

"Well, I'll be honest," she exclaimed. "It wouldn't be the same."

His reply to such an outrageous remark was immediate —
but in the form of a protest.

"What do you mean — it wouldn't be the same!"

"Well, it wouldn't, would it? How can it be!"

Liberty joined Manhattan in falling behind the ferry, Staten
Island came closer, the crowd began to press against them.
And a first doubt to press on John-Paul's resolution.

"But it can be!" cried the young man, the doubt develop-
ing. "What do you mean!" Yes, what did she mean? "We go
back to how it was, Grace." Couldn't the obviously troubled
Grace see that! "Why do you think I pursued Krenk round the
world? My only motive was to bring you back to safety, so we
could be as we were."

Her pale eyes, restored to their penetrating beauty, studied
his frowning face for a few moments, then appeared to come
to a private conclusion. To be honest.

"Well," she said calmly. "I'm not as I was."

"What rubbish — of course you are!" he cried. "You're the
same as you were. No one can change in such a short time."

"They can. And I have. Now don't ask me more."

Understanding came to John-Paul in a series of slow and
reluctant admissions. He touched her cheek, the other hand
still restraining her by the arm, his silence as meaningful as
anything he could say. We won't talk about it. Ever. I
promise. That's something that didn't happen, your time with
Krenk.

He said: "I love you, Grace. That's all that matters." His
declaration, audible to the passengers pressing against them,
brought curious glances. "Don't you still love me?"

"Don't ask that! I'm not answering — I don't want to
answer!"

But he did not hear the rest of her sobbing protest because
with a wrenching movement of desperate strength, she had
escaped from his grip and plunged into the barrier of bodies. It
took John-Paul a moment to recover but by then she was
beyond reach, pushing easily between passengers who, as if in
complicity with her, seemed to resist his efforts to follow her.

"Excuse me, excuse me, excuse me . . ."

But politeness brought no miraculous parting of shoulders,
of passengers beginning to form into a solid mass for disem-

barkation. A mass between Grace and himself. As he pushed through successive barriers, every passenger now an enemy, John-Paul held to a single conviction: She can't have disappeared. She's on the ferry. I must make use of every moment before we tie up, before the passengers disperse, vanish, Grace with them . . .

Or had she chosen to hide in a normally inaccessible part of the ferry — an area forbidden to the passengers? The possibility became a certainty. Steps led down from the deck, then more steps. With the crowds now above him, it was easier, easier to move and easier to search . . . I'm going to find you, my darling. You won't escape. You and I are going to have a sensible meeting, a private meeting, without the mob, without those inquisitive faces almost pressing against our cheeks.

There was a wide gangway deep in the ferry, close to where the engine was pounding away like the beat of a giant heart, and a notice which read: *Crew's Quarters.* The certainty that Grace had chosen to hide rather than disembark now possessed the young man. Recklessly, he opened door after door, searching for her, in cupboards, in cabins, in recesses, nothing forbidden to him . . . Until, emerging from searching a cabin that formed part of the crew's sleeping quarters, he was confronted by two heavy and menacing men.

"Grab him!" they shouted simultaneously and, together, seized John-Paul by the arms and the collar of his jacket. "We've been looking for you!"

And, apparently, they had, because before being turned over to the precinct police on disembarkation, John-Paul learned that there had been a number of thefts, and a special watch — unfortunately for him — had been set on the cabins. His protestations were ignored, his attempt at an explanation ridiculed, his wild outburst of indignation an excuse to thump him in the ribs, and a plea to call his influential mother ignored. First by the ferry captain, then by the officer in charge of the police station. They, apparently, 'had their man'.

The cell into which John-Paul was thrown, exactly an hour and a half after his frenzied search for Grace, contained two drunkards returning to relative soberness, a man with his face covered in blood and a couple of black drug pedlars. It was a relief that not one of them chose to speak to him and he was allowed to settle himself to contemplate fate. His own fate. His own fate because a single question preoccupied him. Since Grace, for whatever reason, had chosen to end their relationship, had rejected him, should he take her decision seriously? Should he really regard it as the end?

In the grim cell of the precinct police station, John-Paul tried to make sense of a bewildering situation. Her transformation, he reasoned, might have been guilt at what she must inevitably regard as her shameful intimacy with Krenk. And that her fiancé, once discovering the truth, would forever after regard it as a betrayal. Or it might be that she had discovered a taste for a life of luxury and style, something a student of modest means could hardly provide for her. Or, a third possibility, decided John-Paul, her family, on learning all that had happened, had convinced her that she would be marrying a man capable of murder, who could kill her in her sleep, hurl their children from the top floor of a building, take it into his mad head to poison them all simultaneously.

But, gradually, as the hours in the precinct prison passed, and he waited for justice to take its laggardly course, and before, as it turned out, he was released without charge on the following day — thanks to a mother once again coming to the rescue of her son — his recent maturity came to a number of conclusions. One began with the facts. One continued with the facts; and one ended with the facts. Grace's travels with Krenk, no matter what had taken place, had obviously affected her deeply. Just as he, John-Paul, was no longer the same simple innocent who had started on his adventures months before, so Grace, too, had changed. So why argue? Why attempt the impossibility of trying to reverse what had already happened? Grace had made a decision. She had chosen to flee from him.

To continue to pursue her, to hope that the separation was no more than a passing problem to be healed by time, was to ignore the reality of change. It was an unhappy, devastating conclusion. For them to start again, as if change had not occurred, would be to pretend that the past could be disregarded. Which it could not. Was the conclusion, therefore, that the ultimate condition of man was helplessness?

The iron bars of the precinct cell went from floor to ceiling, the same as those common to the lives of all those imprisoned round the world. But for John-Paul they no longer created alarm or anger. In pursuing Krenk from country to country for the sake of his darling Grace it seemed he had too often stumbled into and out of a hidden side to society. For the unjustly sentenced and the justly, for the innocent and the guilty, for the partly innocent and the partly guilty . . . But it was a dividing line that defeated the reflections of the young man.

One of the drunkards burped. One of the drug pedlars cursed. The man with the bloodied face groaned. And as he stared at them, John-Paul saw them as a triptych illustrating the eternal enigma of that dividing line. Where were the absolutes by which men's actions were judged?

John-Paul sighed. He was beginning to glimpse a number of vague truths, not clearly, more in his consciousness. But one truth was clear, one that he could put into words and which summarized how it was between Grace and himself.

"Well, that's that," he said aloud. "that's that."

Not one of his cell-mates replied or even looked up. They had clearly, in their own harsh and unfortunate lives, come to that same conclusion. It had simply taken a young man protected by a life of some comfort and security a little longer to discover it for himself. And that, surely, was that.

And the good Signora Modeste? What became of her?

Although she never again surrendered to the self-indulgence of THE DREAM, she persisted with her habitual dedication to her convictions. Day after day, on the thirtieth floor of the New York skyscraper, she attended to her duties in her own unique way. Which meant that not only did she work for the Community of Mankind; she also served the community of mankind.

An unceasing sequence of international problems and disputes held her to the obligation of resolving them, passing across her desk, sending her into committee rooms, meeting the leaders of member-states and requiring quiet diplomacy. And if they were all issues of such magnitude that no single person could have resolved them, the good deputy-director nevertheless influenced them by her modest participation. With patience and sympathy, she continued to display those virtues which had brought her the title of La Mamma.

There was one matter, however, which briefly troubled her conscience following her return from Angladesh and her remarkable meeting with General Chowdhury. Although John-Paul appeared to have recovered from the blighted romance with the beautiful Grace, Signora Modeste remained disquieted by the single foolish, dishonest and uncharacteristic episode that had stained her otherwise honourable career. It was the way in which she had colluded with her son in what might have turned out to be murder, and in making criminal use of her privileged position in COM to assist his dark purpose.

Quite casually, in conversation with the Director, she happened to mention her guilt. At the time, Count von Baum had replied with a shrug, as if implying that it was all in the past, a matter no longer of any importance. But, soon after, the signora was intrigued to learn that the Director had apparently discovered misdemeanours of such seriousness that his displays of anger exceeded any he had shown before. He was furious. He was outraged. And the cause? From certain records which he had been examining, an individual by the name of John-Paul Bonuomo was entered as having served as a representative of the Community of Mankind. Second grade, junior status, overseas posting.

There began a search for this phantom employee of the international organization. Who was this Bonuomo? Where was he? The Director, in his determination to solve the matter, was at his most ruthless. Trembling assistants and clerks were accused of inefficiency, stupidity and, if such an imposter had duped COM, of criminal gullibility. And who was the culprit who had forged his, the Director's signature? And that of Signora Modeste? Then, having inflicted terror and confusion on all who might have been even remotely concerned with the outrageous event, the Director appeared to relent. The fault, it was decided, must have been with the computers. Some mischievous hand, or perhaps the hand of God, had either fed spurious information into the unquestioning and gullible machines or they had been infected with a virus or a bug or whatever term was used to describe such a technological disease.

With a single command, Count von Baum had the name of John-Paul Bonuomo expunged from the records. No one by that name had ever represented COM. And most approving of all was Signora Modeste. She, too, like the computers, could claim that the dreadful episode had never really happened.

But there was another area of pretending, a fantasy continued for some time, which she had no intention of changing. It was the few moments of nearly every day when all the peoples of all the countries represented by their delegates on all the floors below her seemed to congregate in her presence. First she would contemplate the crowds on the busy avenue under her window and wonder at the miracle that had brought people of every kind and race and creed to settle in the same place, to form a community. Then, having seen the evidence of it below, she would cross to the wall of her office where the same diversity was displayed on an enormous, framed chart.

It had to be enormous. It listed all the countries of COM and the names of the heads of delegations. She knew them all but, collecting them in the same frame, they appeared to have a visual dimension. And on each country she could impose, in her mind, the face of its chief delegate. She could almost, from memory, repeat their names. And La Mamma, on this particular morning, made a determined effort to do just that.

Ratsiraka, Kim, Bongo, Bishop, Santini, Fujimoto, Abdoulaye, Zainuddin, Haq, Van der Post, Dubois, Bom, Nguyen, Chikweche, Mapalala, Frobisher, Lee, Nan-cheng, Bermudez, Hansen, Spyropoulos, al-Bashir, Klein, Levallois, Kozlowski, Nassir, Huber, Gbagbo, Samba, Dos Santos, Verwoerd, Sopardjo, Webster, Lisboa, Al Khalifah, O'Reilly, Moses, Nagy, Jumbe, Carnogursky, Jayawickrema, Moon, Perez, Stamatis, Jancic, Patel, MacDougall, Bergstrom, Yacoub . . .

At the end of her soundless recital, Signora Modeste was very pleased with herself. She had remembered them all.